Simon Petherick
originally trained
scripting governm
The Last Good Man
in London and C

The Last Good Man

'The novel speaks eloquently for itself...love, certainty, longing, regret, survival. The story features all that and more.' *Daily Mail*

'A searing story of love, loneliness and tragedy... powerful plotline and stark imagery...descriptions are deeply evocative of the beautiful yet often savage coastal landscapes.' *Cornwall Today*

'Clearly has an intimate knowledge and love of the Cornish coastline and its unique type of village community...a keen eye for descriptive detail and a talent for emotional understatement, building to a heartwrenching climax.' *Western Morning News*

'Powerful images of the Cornish coastline and the village community.' *Eastern Daily Press*

English Arcadia

Simon Petherick

First published 2018
www.thewordmachine.org

The Word Machine

ISBN 9780957629462

9 8 7 6 5 4 3 2 1

Typesetting and jacket design by T. Griffiths.

Printed and bound by CPI Group (UK) Ltd,
Croydon, CR0 4YY.

Earth to earth! That was the frank note, the joyous summons of the day; and they could not but jar and seem artificial, these human discussions and pretences, when boon Nature, reticent no more, was singing that full-throated song of hers that thrills and claims control of every fibre. The air was wine; the moist earth-smell, wine; the lark's song, the wafts from the cow-shed at top of the field, the pant and smoke of a distant train – all were wine – or song, was it? Or odour, this unity they all blended into? I had no words then to describe it, that earth-effluence of which I was so conscious; nor, indeed, have I found words since. I ran sideways, shouting; I dug glad heels into the squelching soil; I splashed diamond showers from puddles with a stick; I hurled clods skywards at random, and presently I somehow found myself singing. The words were mere nonsense – irresponsible babble; the tune was an improvisation, a weary, unrhythmic thing of rise and fall: and yet it seemed to me a genuine utterance, and just at that moment the one thing fitting and right and perfect. Humanity would have rejected it with scorn; Nature, everywhere singing in the same key, recognised and accepted it without a flicker of dissent.

Kenneth Grahame,

A Holiday

Chapter One

There is something particular about the English landscape: claustrophobic, damp, silent. A contained savagery,
a cramped stage where for centuries man and nature have
grappled for ascendancy. The willow whispering her secrets
down into the silent river, the red-tongued brambles creeping over unfrequented bridleways to render them impassible,
the endless trickles of water which tell tales of escape from
farms, canals, reservoirs. Ancient oaks bear mute witness to
the devastation of rape fields, gnarled fingers of ivy strangle
furious statues. Dark-eyed kites soar over bleached motor-
ways, settling now and then on blue roadsigns advertising
fried chicken. The dead give up their bodies to devouring
worms in cemeteries filled with crooked gravestones stained
with lichen.

In this clearing, surrounded by thorned hedges and
despairing willows, a young woman lies awkwardly on the
grass. She is wearing jeans, and one leg is bent behind her
in an unnatural pose. She has a white cotton top and her
blonde hair is spread out upon the neat, short grass. Her
long fingers lie calmly upon the ground, palms facing up
to the canopy of branches overhead. The scene is so still,
so quiet and the only movement, barely perceptible, is the
steady flow of blood from her eye down her cheek, nestling
stickily into the stark white of her collar.

And then, from the other side of the clearing, a scream.

Chapter Two

Darius Frome approached the heavy iron gates that stood just back from the narrow road. The light was beginning to fade on this early summer evening and the tranquillity of the late June air was for him filled with anxiety. He had felt it uncomfortably in his stomach as they had walked the two miles from the station at Marlow. The closer they had come to this entrance, the further they had climbed up the long Quarry Hill road through the darkening woods, the more he had smelled the disturbance in the air. He hadn't expected it. Perhaps it wasn't a smell; it was a deeper sense than that, which communicated itself to him directly.

Now as they stood in front of the tall gates held on both sides by heavy stone pillars, he felt it sharply. All his senses were alive to it and it seemed for a moment that there were sounds in the air too, sounds of agitation. He heard the breeze whisper in the trees. A blackbird began to call.

He lifted up the rusty gate lock. He pushed at the wrought iron which shrieked from corroded hinges in the still evening air.

– Is this really it? The woman's voice was light, curious.

– This is it, Tink, said Darius.

– It's funny, she said, and her laugh created an island in the dense summer evening.

Darius looked down at her and smiled.

– That's good, he said.

He took her hand and they walked through the gateway. He pushed the metal behind him as they passed, and the gate clanged loudly, echoing down ahead of them into the gloom.

– You really lived here? she said.

They began to walk slowly, hand in hand, down the driveway away from the gates. He was taller than her, and carried a bulky rucksack on his shoulders. The straps dug into the T-shirt he wore over his broad shoulders, and his long dark hair reached the top of the canvas. One of his bare arms was covered in tattoos. His eyes glowed wide in the evening light, which was just strong enough still to see the tanned brown skin of his face. She wore a purple dress which brushed the cracked tarmac of the drive and green sneakers which made no noise as she walked. In the twilight her dyed silver hair was ruffled gently by the summer breeze.

He looked at her. She was searching ahead into the disappearing light and he could see the delicate line of her cheekbones. Her body arched, seeking to find what might be ahead and she seemed somehow both to reassure him and by her very presence to emphasise the disjunct of this return.

– Yes, I did. A long time ago.

On either side of the driveway, elms reared up out of the earth, their branches reaching out to entwine with one another above them, a canopy of twisting limbs and leaves which blocked out the last of the fading light. In between the tree trunks, grey lawns stretched out into the far distance on both sides. A monochrome movement caught his eye, a flicker of black on the grass.

He raised his arm and pointed.

– Rabbits, he said.

He looked back at the entrance gates as they continued their slow progress, and could still see the cold grey stone of the single-storey coachhouse they had passed. The shutters were all closed and a bird, heavy enough for an owl maybe, spread its wings and lifted itself from the roof. Fly away, he thought. Fly away from here.

– Are you OK, Darius?

– I'm OK. He squeezed her hand. You must be tired. I'm sorry I made us walk from the station. It used to be my walk home from school.

– I liked it. It's not Cornwall though, is it?

4

– It's another world.

He thought of the valley in Cornwall they had left that morning. The buildings scattered around, the old barn, the vegetable allotments where they all grew communal food, the brightly painted walls of the cottages. He missed the smell of salt water in the air. Couldn't he have brought that with him to overcome this sensation, this tangle of worry that sat in the pit of his stomach? Or had he just brought his concerns with him? Was that what he was feeling?

– Maybe Cornwall is over, Tink.

He could see her shake her head in the gloom and then she looked up at him.

– No, Darius, it's not. Not if you don't want it to be.

The others would be there now: someone would be making supper, the chickens would be being shut in for the night. He thought of the big skies that soared above their valley and out to the sea.

– I'm not sure what I want, he said.

She took his arm.

– Stop thinking. Just for once. Were you a little boy here?

– I guess.

– I can see you, she said, straining her eyes to look past the elm trees bordering the drive. You're running on the grass. You're laughing. You look happy, Darius.

He frowned.

– I don't think so.

She tugged at his sleeve.

– Oh but you are. I can see you!

She let go of his hand and stepped in front of him briefly, her eyes shining up at him, then she swept her arms around her, encompassing the darkening parklands.

– You are a happy little boy! she laughed, her voice ringing out in this still summer silence.

His deep, strong voice sounded tired:

– I was, Tink. Once. When I was a kid, before it all happened. I've never really told you about it. I've never really told anyone about it. I will. Now we're here, I will have to,

5

I know.

He frowned again.

– On top of everything else, he said.

She touched his cheek and her smile looked sad to him now.

– Sorry, he said and they carried on walking down the driveway as it curved past the outline of a broken statue on a plinth. He reached down and picked up an arm with a jagged edge where it had broken off.

– I remember this, he said. Why is it broken?

– You'll have to remember lots of things, Darius.

He would, he knew. He would need to remember.

It was just four days ago, the previous Sunday, that he had found the envelope on the doormat in the little cottage in the valley where he had lived on and off for the last ten years. He had found the valley first. It had lain uninhabited for years, and the scattered farm buildings were falling apart. It was no more than about four or five acres in all, with one untarmaced road going in and out. Ten years ago it was a wilderness of gorse and fallen trees and broken glass. He and two friends had bought it cheaply at an auction and had begun the slow process of rescuing the land and buildings, gradually making the broken down cottages habitable, the land fit for growing.

Darius's grandfather, Sir Zachary Frome, had been the leader of a political party in the 1940s called Level Ground which had fought for common ownership and the end of private property, and in honour of him Darius had proposed that they named the valley Level Ground too. He and his friends had wanted to create a new way of living, a communal place where people would share and grow together. It was more a vision of living with nature than it was a political endeavour but now, with what had happened over the last two months, it looked like that vision was dying and he felt despondent about its future.

He'd taken the white envelope into the kitchen and laid it on the table while he began making coffee. Once he'd sat down, he ripped the envelope open. Inside was a card, stiff and cream-coloured, with these words printed in one line:

Down There. 4pm, 25ᵗʰ June 2017. You are invited.

He'd known the significance of the date immediately. It was a week away, but the date itself had its own particular meaning: Sunday the 25th June would be exactly twenty-five years since it happened.

Now, four days' later, as he and Tink walked slowly and patiently down the long driveway, he went over it again in his head.

Only four people in the world knew about Down There. Him, his brother Francis, Francis's wife Belinda, and his father, Sir Richard Frome. Any one of them could have sent him that card – or all of them. He hadn't spoken to any of them for years. Occasionally Belinda would write with news, carefully written letters which kept him informed of family matters – the birth of her two children, his father's dementia, her work and the work of his brother Francis – without imposing any demands on him. Occasionally he would send a postcard in reply, but the last time he'd done that must have been a couple of years ago.

– Tell me again, Tink: what did my brother say to you when you phoned him the other day?

Tink was silent for a moment, then:

– Well, I wasn't really sure why I was phoning him, she said.

– Because I didn't want to, he said. And I didn't have his phone number. You were being nice to me.

– Tink is always nice to Darius, she said, and he felt her squeeze his arm again. What I most liked, she said, was getting the number from Directory Enquiries. When they said there was a number for Francis Frome at The Range near Cookham Dene, I said, it's not pronounced Frome as in Rome, but Frome as in Room.

Darius smiled.

– It's important, I said to the girl. These things are important. Anyway, she gave me the number, and I phoned, and your brother answered, saying, Francis Frome – and he pronounced it like room, so I knew it was your brother.

– And then what?

– I said, my name is Tink and I am making a telephone call on behalf of one Darius Frome.

– What did he say?

– He said, I've been expecting this.

– Of course he was expecting it. He sent me the card.

– He didn't say that. He was quite rude. He just said, when is he coming, and I said we would probably turn up at some point on Thursday 22nd. And then he said fine, and then he put the phone down.

– And that was it?

She crossed her arms and stopped.

– What do you mean, that was it? I think Tink performed her task quite admirably.

Darius laughed, and was aware of the feeling of release which Tink's humour gave him.

– Tink is always admirable! I just meant, my brother didn't say anything else?

– Nothing at all. He doesn't have your aura, Darius. It is missing from him.

– Well, I couldn't say. I haven't spoken to him for fifteen years. Maybe it was a mistake coming early. We should have just come on the 25th, just come and gone on the same day. I don't know why I thought we should come earlier.

– You said you had a feeling, she said.

– I know.

– You always trust your feelings, Darius. They're the only things we can trust.

He knew that was true. But once again he sensed the lack of harmony about him, this persistent discordancy. He was starting to feel overwhelmed.

They continued to walk, Tink back beside him. Ever since he'd received the note on the 18th, she hadn't asked him what Down There represented. That was her way, not to probe or ask questions. Darius admired her natural

8

opposition to attachment, had admired it since they had met a few months before. It contrasted with his own determination to control, to manage, to overcome.

What did Down There represent to him? Everything and nothing. Everything that was primitive and essential and savage and beautiful about nature, about the world, about life itself. But nothing too. Because since it happened twenty-five years ago, he had never been back, and he had banished it from his mind. He had escaped Down There. Until now.

– By the way, Down There is a place, he said. It's on this estate. I'll show you before Sunday.

Tink didn't answer, because at that moment, the crowding elms ended their hold over the driveway, and the two of them emerged into open space. Ahead, a huge house stood quietly about a hundred yards away. As they stood, the moon broke free of some clouds overhead and a silver light suddenly played down over the lawns in front of them and illuminated the building.

The house was white and presented a long low facade to them, about a hundred and fifty feet from one end to the other. Bold lines of white stone ran horizontally between three floors, each with twelve sets of latticed windows separated by a dark render. The window frames were all painted white, and they glowed all along the front of the building in the moonlight. The overall effect was extraordinary, as though this were not a static building but a moment caught in time, an architectural capture of the fluidity of a powerful river. In the sudden moonlight, thick streams of ivy could be seen clinging to the walls, tentacles creeping out onto window ledges and up onto the tiled roof. The walls looked stained here and there where pieces of render had come away, as though the house itself were bruised. On either side of the low, wide building, huge rhododendrons, fat with green leaves and pink flowerheads, hemmed the structure in. Four tall sets of chimney pots along the ridge of the dark roof thrust up into the night air, seeking escape.

– Blimey, said Tink.

Darius suddenly felt unprepared for this return, his first visit back to the Range, his family home, for twenty-five years. He stared at it, horrified.

– You're serious? Tink continued. You lived here?

He nodded, not able to say anything. As though drifting towards a whirlpool, he felt his senses accelerating madly: he could smell new scents in the night air, he could feel the movement of the rhododendron leaves up ahead as they marked his arrival, he could sense beneath him the workings of the earth: the moles, the worms, the ancient chemistry of plants. His face now was caught in the moonlight: his brown eyes wide beneath a creased brow, his olive skin taut at the cheekbones. He swept a hand through his tangled dark hair.

Tink put a hand on his arm.

– It's all right, Darius, she said quietly.

He realised his muscles were tight; a bead of sweat ran down his strong bicep, down towards a clenched fist.

– Breathe, she said.

He nodded, and began to take deep breaths, filling out his stomach and lifting up his chest, breathing out slowly into the still night air. He closed his eyes, and he let the noise in his head rage for a little until it began to quieten and he was able to imagine a familiar landscape in his head, the green of the Level Ground valley. He kept his focus on that for a few seconds, seeing the line of trees that stood on one ridge of the valley and then following the slope down to the familiar cottages and the barns and allotments. Then in his mind he saw a small boy standing still and looking back at him and he realised it was him, thirty or more years ago, playing here on the lawns at the Range. To the left, an old woman watched him: his beautiful grandmother, who first told him about his grandfather's vision and how it all began, back then. Down There.

He opened his eyes again and stared at the silent house. Then he looked at Tink.

– It's OK, he said.

10

Chapter Three

Sir Zachary Frome was that rare beast which the English aristocracy produces every so often: a member of the landed gentry with passionately revolutionary views. Taking on the Baronetcy and possession of the Range on the death of his father in 1931, he was determined, at the age of just twenty five, to devote his life to the cause of social justice.

His father had commissioned the house from Sir Edwin Lutyens in 1903 as a gift to his wife, who had given birth to their son, Zachary, in the first floor bedroom suite three years later. The Fromes, given their Baronetcy by Queen Victoria at the start of her reign in recognition of services in India, had always embraced modernity, whether that meant building the Indian railways or taking membership of the Liberal party and supporting the suffragettes.

Yet Sir Zachary's victory speech on winning the Parliamentary seat of Plymouth Devonport in 1936 gave little indication of the road he was subsequently to take. Standing up on a windy hill overlooking the naval dockyards running alongside the Tamar, with his new wife Felicity at his side, he cut a curious figure: tall, angular, his oiled black hair already beginning to recede from a prominent forehead, his eyes darting behind the thick lenses of round metal glasses.

– As a proud member of the Liberal party, I am humbled by your faith in choosing me as your Member of Parliament. I promise to serve the people of this city to the very best of my ability, with every ounce of passion and devotion I can muster. I will support you in your endeavours to support your families through your hard work and your dedication to your great city. I will take the side of the working man in his reasonable quest for fair wages for fair work. I will offer a helping hand to the hard-pressed mother who has to feed her young ones and maintain a home. I will work tirelessly to improve the services and facilities of the city to ensure that sanitation and proper health services are available to all, not just the few. I hope you will come to feel vindicated in the faith you have placed in me and will see me as your true voice in Parliament.

His clipped, patrician tones received some scattered applause from the motley crowd in front of him: dockyard workers in thick suits with ties and caps, a group of schoolchildren fidgeting under the eye of their teacher, weary female cleaners on their way back from shifts. The diarist in the local paper referred sardonically to the Troublemaking Toff, in reference to the disquiet amongst some local business people at Frome's advocacy of workers' rights during his election campaign.

Later that day, on the train back to London in order to take up his seat in the Commons the following day, Zachary talked excitedly to his wife over dinner in the Pullman car.

– We've done it, Felicity! We're on the way. I think they received me as one of their own, don't you? My new constituents. How grand that sounds!

– You were tremendous, my love. You were towering.

– I'm going to make a difference, my dear. I respect our friend Orwell in going out to Spain to fight, but there is a bigger fight to be had here, in my opinion. There is great work to be done.

As he talked enthusiastically about his plans for alleviating the overcrowding in Plymouth's slum districts, Felicity gazed at him with a deep well of love and affection. Lady Felicity Frome – her title bestowed upon her six months before on their wedding day in Westminster – was two years older than her husband. At the age of thirty two, she had already achieved success and some fame as a novelist, in particular for her novel *Antonia's War* about the tragic story of a World War One nurse in Flanders.

She looked at Zachary now, sipping her glass of wine

and nodding as he spoke almost breathlessly about sewage improvements and antenatal care, and she felt filled with pride. Her blonde good looks, her bold crimson lipstick and amused smile had deterred many a potential suitor in the past, particularly once she began to appear in the newspaper diary columns as celebrated author Felicity Drummond. But Sir Zachary Frome had had an otherworldly quality to him when they were introduced at a cocktail party in Belgravia a year ago, as though he didn't really notice quite how high up the desirability scale Felicity lay. He had been delightfully open from the start, not hiding the fact that he had never heard of her or of *Antonia's War*.

– I shall visit Hatchards in the morning and purchase a copy, he had said at the party, on learning of her work. I don't have much time for leisure, but I shall make a point of reading your novel, which I am sure is excellent.

There was almost a childlike innocence about him which was hugely attractive to Felicity: a complete lack of guile, and a straightforward sincerity about his sense of purpose.

– I intend to stand for Parliament, he had told her at that first meeting. My father always planned to do so, but he left it too late. He would have made a fine Liberal Member of Parliament. I intend to make it my life's work, to further his own political views but to take them further, to redress the inequalities and the suffering which our country's obsession with class – an obsession held by some of my own family, I regret to say – has brought about.

This was all new to Felicity Drummond. The daughter of a Midlands industrialist, her family had never mixed in aristocratic circles, and certainly never discussed workers' rights over dinner. Intelligent, forceful, creative, she had had the confidence to joust in the London literary world of the 1920s and had swiftly built a reputation. Before meeting Zachary for the first time, she had just returned from a summer holiday in the south of France, staying at a villa with a rather cynical literary set – Cyril Connolly had stood on the table at a restaurant in Antibes and sung his own lascivious version of the Marseillaise to the annoyance of the patron. It was 1935, the clouds of war were gathering over Europe, and the mean barbs of the artists and writers of her own set suddenly seemed feeble in comparison with the challenges faced by the world. She was enthralled by this serious young man who seemed determined to face them.

Zachary came up to her two weeks later at a rally close to Parliament Square where he was due to speak from the platform on the subject of Combating Fascism at Home. He had touched her arm as she was talking to someone, and held out a copy of her novel.

– I would be honoured if you would sign my copy, Miss Drummond, he had said, his eyes blinking behind those thick lenses. I have been carrying it with me all week in the hope I might spot you. I congratulate you on the verisimilitude you have achieved in the depiction of life in the trenches. It is most impressive.

They were engaged a month later and now, married on the train back to London after his own great success, she recalled her first visit to his house outside of London. She had stayed in plenty of grand houses over the years, so it did not strike her as odd that this curiously charismatic young man should own such an enormous building as the Range. He told her he had inherited it together with the Baronetcy on the death of his father five years before.

– You live here alone? she asked, as they wandered through the echoing corridors of the three floors, looking into dark rooms where furniture lay draped in sheets, the shutters of the windows clamped shut.

– I live in a few rooms on the ground floor, he said. I have a housekeeper who lives in Cookham. I have no need of butlers or maids – I am perfectly capable of boiling an egg. And my work gives me little time to spend on the administration of a house like this, so for the time being, I keep the majority of it as you see, slumbering.

– Show me the rooms where you live, she commanded. She was bold, but inside, hidden from his view in the dark empty spaces of this mansion, she felt an overwhelming attachment to the place. She sensed how it energised him, and she was aware herself of the power it contained. There was something – what was it? – something very alive, very visceral about the house, despite its current draped and shuttered-up condition. She could almost hear the house talking to her as their footsteps echoed down the long corridors. No that wasn't quite it: it was as though the house were talking to itself, carrying on its own conversation in total disregard of their presence. Each of the figures portrayed in the paintings hung on the walls seemed not to look at her, but at each other. She was not remotely intimidated by this; rather, she felt she understood.

They descended one of the staircases back down to the ground floor and he opened a door.

– This is my study, he said, a little sheepishly. I don't keep it in much of a state for visiting authors.

The room was square, with a huge desk at one end, covered in piles of paper. Two walls were lined with books, with more of them stacked on the floor beside the two sofas. A silk paisley dressing gown was draped over a chair, and there were ashtrays filled with stubs on the floor. Another bold Lutyens flourish, an overtall fireplace with parallel lines of crystal shooting up from a mantlepiece dotted with invitation cards, dominated the main wall opposite the door.

Felicity walked over to the bookcase and inspected the titles. Biographies of nineteenth century political figures, hefty economics tomes, a battered copy of Marx's *Das Kapital*, bound series of left wing magazines.

– All very serious, she said. Not a novel in sight.

– I warned you, he said. I don't really have much time for entertainment. I teach three days a week at the school in Marlow, but now that I plan to challenge for the seat in Plymouth, I have even less time. It's difficult enough keeping up with the new thinking as it is, now I have to immerse myself in the inequalities of the city I hope will adopt me.

– But you must read fiction sometimes, she cried, settling

down on one of the sofas and taking out a cigarette. You must have a favourite novel, everyone does.

He reached down and lit her cigarette, then his own. He looked a little awkward, then strode over to one of the corner bookcases and pulled out a slim volume. He came over and handed it to her.

Felicity looked at the title and laughed.

– *Wind in the Willows*? A children's book?

As soon as she saw the look of pained embarrassment on his face, she regretted her frivolity.

– Tell me what you like about it. I have to confess, I have not read it, so you have the advantage over me.

He sat on the arm of the sofa opposite her, still looking uncomfortable. Then he seemed to take a decision, as though suddenly, she could be trusted.

– As you can tell from my very poor analysis of your own excellent novel, *Antonia's War*, I am no literary critic.

She smiled.

– I for my part am very grateful for that, otherwise you might with all justification point out the many injudicious phrases and awful cliches with which it is littered, she said.

– I doubt that, he said, with all seriousness. However, I have been taking an interest in some of our country's writers, mainly with my own political views in mind. What I have discovered is that writers such as Mr Grahame – he held up the book to show her the cover again – and others such as Thomas Hardy and William Morris and Lewis Carroll have all been fascinated by the same speculation which dominates my mind with ever increasing force.

– And that is? she asked.

He leaned forwards.

– The transformative power of landscape over the national psyche. All countries, all civilisations, have their poets. One thinks of Don Quixote in Spain, Goethe in Germany, Mark Twain in America. But what binds this collection of English writers of the last fifty years is what I have identified as their common aspiration to create a spiritual vision of

Englishness. A country of byways and hills and woods and rivers where the inhabitants were gifted by Nature herself with an understanding of Oneness, of the equality of all things under the sun.

He stood up and marched back over to the bookcase, returning with another book. He showed her the cover: *Jude the Obscure*, by Hardy.

– You will know this book, he said, his eyes now shining. You will have read it and understood it far better than I. But what I admire most about it is the author's depiction of our landscape, and his sympathy for young Jude Fawley who walks all the way to Christminster only to find the company of man a bitter disappointment. A disappointment made all the more difficult for him after his own sense of wholeness and contentment in his county of Wessex.

He paused for a moment, staring at the two books in his hand.

– It is all a part of what I think I am on the verge of discovering, he said at last. A new politics for our country, but one not based upon just logic or economics or even justice itself. Of course those must be at the heart of any truly democratic and revolutionary movement. But what I am working on is a politics of belief. A politics which can give a man a spiritual world in which he feels at one both with his fellow man and with everything around him.

He stubbed his cigarette out forcefully.

– At heart, I wish to create a movement in this country which takes as its guiding principle the natural equality of all people, of all living creatures, of the natural world itself. A movement where no man has rights over another, just as no salmon in the river Thames down below this house may stake a claim over his neighbour for ownership of the water through which they both glide.

Now he was silent, and Felicity looked at him. He was extraordinary.

– Read me something, she said gently. From *The Wind in the Willows*. Read me your favourite passage.

Zachary looked up and seemed embarrassed.

– You must forgive me, he said. I sounded deranged, no doubt.

– You sounded no such thing, she said fiercely. Read to me.

He opened the volume, looked through the pages, and then with a satisfied Ah!, he said:

– There are so many passages in this book which I admire. I used to have it with me often when I rowed my little boat here on holidays back from Eton. But let me read you from the most remarkable chapter in the book, Chapter Eight, *The Piper At The Gates of Dawn*. Then tell me if you think it is a children's book!

He cleared his throat.

– It is the chapter where Mole and Rat set out to find the lost baby otter, and after searching all night in their rowing boat, they come across an island they had never found before.

He began to read.

Then suddenly the Mole felt a great Awe fall upon him, an awe that turned his muscles to water, bowed his head, and rooted his feet to the ground. It was no panic terror – indeed he felt wonderfully at peace and happy – but it was an awe that smote and held him and, without seeing, he knew it could only mean that some august Presence was very, very near. With difficulty he turned to look for his friend, and saw him at his side, cowed, stricken, and trembling violently. And still there was utter silence in the populous bird-haunted branches around them; and still the light grew and grew.

Perhaps he would never have dared to raise his eyes, but that, though the piping was now hushed, the call and the summons seemed still dominant and imperious. He might not refuse, were Death himself waiting to strike him instantly, once he had looked with mortal eye on things rightly kept hidden. Trembling he obeyed, and raised his humble head; and then, in that utter clearness of the imminent dawn, while Nature, flushed with fulness of incredible colour, seemed to hold her breath for the event, he looked in the very eyes of the Friend and Helper; saw the backward sweep of the curved horns, gleaming in the growing daylight;

saw the stern, hooked nose between the kindly eyes that were looking down on them humorously, while the bearded mouth broke into a half-smile at the corners; saw the rippling muscles on the arm that lay across the broad chest, the long supple hand still holding the pan-pipes only just fallen away from the parted lips; saw the splendid curves of the shaggy limbs disposed in majestic ease on the sward; saw, last of all, nestling between his very hooves, sleeping soundly in entire peace and contentment, the little, round, podgy, childish form of the baby otter. All this he saw, for one moment breathless and intense, vivid on the morning sky; and still, as he looked, he lived; and still, as he lived, he wondered.

"Rat!" he found breath to whisper, shaking. "Are you afraid?"

"Afraid?" murmured the Rat, his eyes shining with unutterable love. "Afraid! Of Him? O, never, never! And yet – and yet – O, Mole, I am afraid!"

Then the two animals, crouching to the earth, bowed their heads and did worship.

As she looked at her husband now, still talking about his plans for Plymouth on the train back to London following his election, Felicity remembered the sense of wonder she had felt in that room in the Range nine months before as he had read from *Wind in the Willows*.

– I have never heard that, she had said quietly, when he had finished. It is remarkable. Pan himself. I had no idea.

He had looked up at her from the pages of the book.

– You see it, don't you? he had said.

And now, with his election, with their marriage, with their future together at the Range, she felt too as though they were blessed, as though they were on the verge of something great, something which could change the world in which they lived forever.

Chapter Four

Darius paused in front of the wide, white wooden door. A weak yellow lamp set above it combined with the moonlight to identify them: he, tall and well-built, the rucksack still on his back, the fading green T-shirt showing strong tanned arms, the one with tattoos raised in readiness to knock; she, petite and standing on her toes, her back turned to the door, playing something invisible with her hands out towards the trees across the lawns.

Twenty-five years. Nothing would have brought him back but for the wording on that card a few days ago. **Down There. 4pm, 25th June 2017. You are invited.** You are invited. Of all the things, that had been the last he might have expected. He hadn't even been aware of any kind of anniversary: he just didn't think about it. He hadn't thought about the Range, about Down There, about all of it, for such a long time now. After all the years of travelling around the world and then the last ten years in Cornwall, he still kept his mind turned away from what had happened back then. It was his way: maybe not the best way, but it was the way he'd developed. He had buried it, and no-one had the right to tell him that was wrong. But perhaps all the problems in Cornwall recently, perhaps they had contributed to his acquiescence to the invitation. Once more, he felt the uncertainty in the air. If he'd just needed a change, why had he come here?

He turned around and looked out at the view Tink was surveying. The pale line of trees under which they'd walked over to the left. The grey lawns, with an indistinct shape over to the right: that must be one of the formal gardens. It was true, he had been happy for a time here. His Nana teaching him about the plants; sleeping out here at night in the summer and learning the calls of the owls; later, getting stoned in the orchard with his friends. He'd put it all from his mind, after what happened.

He swung back and grabbed the brass lion knocker and hammered it back into its plate. The sound was like a rifle shot echoing in the dark from one side of the huge facade to the other, and his muscles tensed once more across his shoulders. He felt Tink's hand settle gently on his arm as the sound of footsteps came from inside.

Twenty-five years. His stomach tightened as the footsteps got louder, and the words reverberated in his head. Down There. Down There. He could have ignored the card, thrown it on the fire. No-one made him come. What did he think he was trying to achieve by coming back here?

A bolt was pulled inside, and the door swung open. There stood his brother, Francis Frome. A bright chandelier behind him in the hall cast a glow around him and put his face temporarily in shade, so that Darius couldn't quite make it out, just seeing the casual clothes – jeans, a crumpled white shirt – and the outline of his round glasses below a bald head.

– Darius.

For a moment, nobody moved. The two brothers faced each other, the elder, Francis, more obviously echoing the tall, thin physique of their late grandfather, Sir Zachary. Darius, in comparison, seemed to represent some other strain, some other possibility, in his build, his tanned outdoor skin, his thick dark hair.

Francis moved back a little to make way and as he did so the light from the chandelier illuminated his face. The last time Darius had seen him, he had been sixteen years' old. He stared at his brother, who looked back at him, unblinking, unsmiling.

The silence was broken by Tink:

– Hello, she smiled, extending her hand. I spoke to you on the telephone a few days ago. My name is Tink.

Francis looked discomposed, and moved his stare away from his brother.

– I'm sorry, he said. Francis Frome. He took her hand briefly. What did you say your name was?

– Tink.

– I see. He turned back to his brother, putting his hand out.

– Darius, he said.

They shook hands briefly. Darius remained silent, and Francis stepped back to allow them to enter.

The hall was another Lutyens embellishment: a wide, octagonal shape formed of bare white limestone, with four doors leading off it and symmetrical patterns carved into each of the other four panels. Instinctively, Darius looked up – it was still there, although more faded now. The improbable scene painted on the ceiling, taken after Manet's Dejeuner sur l'Herbe, showing three people – two men in suits, a naked woman staring at the viewer – all three seated on the grass in positions familiar from the original. They were sitting in a grass clearing, surrounded mostly by tangled bushes and writhing branches. Behind them, in a trompe l'oeil effect, a second naked woman lounged against a stone plinth, looking away from the group towards a gap in the foliage, painted with some skill to achieve the correct effect when viewed from below, where a river was clearly identifiable. Over the years, when he had thought of the house, he had thought of this painting, commissioned by his grandfather during the Second World War.

– It's still there, Francis said, his voice flat.

Darius turned to look at his brother.

– Why wouldn't it be? he asked.

Francis shrugged.

– I have no idea, he said.

At that point, one of the four doorways leading off the hall crashed open and two children ran in, followed quickly by a woman trying to catch hold of them. The two children stopped in front of the three adults. Boy and a girl, both looked under ten. The girl stared at Darius.

– Are you Uncle Darius? she demanded.

The sound of Tink's laughter played around the hall, and the woman moved forward to take a hand each of the children.

– Sorry Darius, she said. They've been so excited about meeting you.

Belinda Frome was handsome, deep brown eyes and well-kept skin over prominent cheekbones. Her dark hair was edging here and there with touches of grey over her shoulders, the overall effect one of confidence, security. Darius recognised her immediately, even after so long an absence. But still, he was startled. She smiled, then turned to Tink.

– Hello, I'm Belinda. You must be tired. I can't believe he made you walk from Marlow station. That bloody hill. You should have let us come and pick you up.

– There was no need, Darius said.

A silence, then Belinda said:

– Children, be polite and introduce yourselves.

The little boy pushed past his sister and stood in front of Tink.

– I'm James and I'm seven years' old.

Tink made an excessive curtsey and replied:

– Good evening James, and thank you very much. My name is Tink and I'm twenty-eight years' old. And who are you?

The girl stepped forward.

– Alice Frome of The Range, near Cookham in Berkshire. I am older than James.

Tink bowed her head.

– I can see that, Alice Frome. Thank you very much for inviting us.

– Come along, said Belinda, brightly. Let's all go down to the kitchen and have something to eat. The children have already eaten but they can stay up for a bit. You must both be starving.

She led the way back to the door they had come in through. Darius paused, then shrugged the rucksack off his shoulders, laid it down on the floor against the wall. Meanwhile, James grabbed Tink's hand and ran ahead with her, followed by Alice and Belinda, Tink laughing in mock protest. They were already through the door before the two men had moved.

– Well, you're here, said Francis. It's been a long time, Darius.

Darius looked at his brother.

– I came because I was invited. Or was it instructed?

– You mean the card? Francis frowned. Well, we might as well have it out now. What's it about? Why did you send it?

– Don't muck about, Francis. I know it was you. There's only one other person who knows about Down There, and that's Dad. From what I hear from Belinda's letters, the old man's not been capable of sending correspondence for a while now.

A flash of anger crossed his brother's face.

– Of course Dad didn't bloody send it. He can't even get himself dressed in the morning. You have no idea about anything, do you Darius? We look after him. Belinda...I don't know how she does it. You don't have to think about him though, do you? We live with him. Of course he didn't send the card. So why did you?

– I didn't, said Darius, calmly. You did.

– Jesus Christ, Darius, snapped Francis, glaring at his brother. Nothing's changed, has it? Still playing games. You're over forty years' old, Darius. Are you never going to grow up? Why the hell are you bringing Down There up again?

Momentarily, Darius looked confused. He thought back to the moment four days before when he had pulled the cream card out of the envelope.

– You both got a card? he asked.

Francis just snorted, and moved towards the door the

others had gone through.

    – OK Darius, we'll play pretend, just like we always did.

Darius grabbed his brother's shirt to stop him.

    – Answer me: did you both get a card?

Francis twisted his arm out of Darius's grip and shouted:

    – Yes we both got the fucking card, Darius. Down There. The 25th of fucking June. Two days' time. We both got it.

Darius stepped towards Francis, calm now. He brought his face close up to his brother's.

    – I didn't send it, Francis.

Chapter Five

It was a surprise to Felicity quite how much she enjoyed her new life as, in the words of one of her more waspish London friends, the lady of the manor.

– It's not a manor, she had replied with mock seriousness. It's a Baronetcy. Entirely different thing, you know.

But gradually, her trips up to town on the train from Marlow station to attend a reading or a cocktail party in Mayfair became more and more infrequent, and she herself was surprised to notice that days could go by while Zachary was away in Plymouth or in Parliament when she was quite on her own at the Range. She corresponded with her publisher about plans for a new novel, was occasionally visited by her parents, cringing on the first visit when her father spent dinner trying to advise Zachary on stock investments. Her husband took it in good grace.

– I do not underestimate Sir, the importance of capital in the national infrastructure, I beg to differ, however, in both its use and ownership.

– Lovely man, your husband, her father said to her the following day as they left. Mad as a hatter, but a lovely man.

Felicity was an only child and the bond between she and her father had always been fiercely held. Bill Drummond had carved out a small empire from the iron smelting factories located in and around Corby towards the end of the last century. A combination of physical strength and native intelligence had enabled him to climb out of the poverty into which he had been born, and as a boy he'd learned the mechanics of an industry on which the growing rail network depended through an often dangerous daily exposure to the fires and cauldrons of the ironworks. By the time he was twenty three, he opened his own furnace and employed his own men, winning their respect through a mixture of rough physical justice and financial acumen.

She had grown up in a fine house outside of Corby, surrounded by fields and homesteads, and was adored by her father who delighted in her wit and intelligence. He instructed a governess to give her additional lessons to those administered by the local school, and by the age of fourteen she had her own library of the classics, all of which she'd read. He swept aside the doubts of his timid wife when it came to consider further education, and insisted she sit for exams at London University. She won a scholarship – the financial proceeds of which he returned to her college, Bedford, as part of his endowment of a new library within the grand Regent's Park cluster of buildings – and he roared with laughter at her tales of London literary life once she had graduated and had begun her own assault on her own industry, that of London's community of writers of the late 1920s.

Now in his sixties, and less physically strong owing to an endemic chest infection brought on by the years inhaling the red hot fumes of the smelting furnaces, he was thrilled by the unconventional politics of her entitled young husband.

– That lad of yours, he'd say, as they strolled around the lawns of the Range, he has something about him that I very much like. It would not be possible for me to disagree more with the bloody poppycock he tells me about abolishing private ownership, but I like the shine in his eyes. You've got a good one, Felicity, mark my words.

The summer of 1937 was glorious, and Felicity sought her father's advice as she realised how much of the running of the estate would be down to her. She had her own funds from *Antonia's War* at her disposal and did not wish to impose on her father's wealth as she set about the task of landscaping the gardens. Like many aristocratic families, the Frome family's wealth lay primarily in the stone of the building and the green of the land rather than the cash in the bank. She was delighted to notice that Zachary had no idea how much money he earned as a Member of Parliament and they agreed that the management of household finances might best be allocated to herself. Discreetly, she corresponded with her father on how best to maximise their joint incomes, and he gave her sensible advice on increasing the yield on some of the nearby land which was let out to tenants.

Over that summer, she made sketches of the grounds as they stood and how she intended them to look. She made a visit to Sir Edwin Lutyens to ask him about his intentions when designing the Range at the turn of the century. He received her very formally in a gloomy house in Belgravia, sitting opposite her in his formidable library with a rug over his lap. He no longer worked, and his health was declining.

– I was struck, my dear lady, he said quietly, by its position. If I remember correctly, the house stands on a hill above the Thames facing south with the main grounds before it. The ground at the top of the hill gave on to a level plain, enabling me to set out the lawns facing away from the river with the back of the building turned away from the steep slope down to the water below. Most houses on the Thames, from Richmond to the Cotswolds, look towards the river from whatever height they sit, but your husband's father was very particular about wishing the house to look southwards. His family had spent time in India, and we talked at considerable length about the light there, which we both so much enjoyed. The solution, therefore, was clear: we would build his house with its back to the Thames. We ignored it. I relished your late father-in-law's strength of mind in agreeing with my solution.

The main task that summer, therefore, was to employ gardeners to develop the south-facing grounds, all the way from the stone gatehouse at the end of the long curving drive. The elders which had been planted in 1903 all along the drive were becoming more mature, but there was little else of formal structure to break up the wide expanses of lawn. Zachary's father had never had the time to think much beyond the house itself, and the acres in front of the house were little more than fields. Zachary himself, while his devotion to the Range and to the land around it was absolute, had little conception of design.

Felicity surprised herself by the intense pleasure which she found in her new vocation. With typical intellectual vivacity, she learned about botanical species, about the different constituents of soil, the hardiness of certain plants over others. She studied the history of garden design, and expounded to her father by letter on the merits of Pliny the Younger's formal structures at Tifernum Tiberium in Tuscany, or le Nôtre at Versailles. At the same time, she read the weekly magazines and turned the topic of telephone conversations with her London friends from the latest literary sex scandal to enquiring about the colour of the almond blossom in the garden of the disgraced couple in question.

She set the gardeners to work on creating a formal structure for the lawns. At one end, she directed Box-hedged collections of white verbascum in the manner of Vita Sackville-West at Sissinghurst, whose emerging gardens were all the talk of Country Life. At the other, she laid out paths stretching out across the lawns to create linear visual patterns in the style of the Kensington Gardens.

While they were busy with the south-facing front, she began to explore the rear of the house. Here, Lutyens's comment was quite accurate: the Thames was ignored. Standing on a hill about three hundred feet above the river, the view down to the water as one emerged from one of the rear entrances was obscured by a jungle of trees, shrubs and foliage. From higher up, say from the window of one of the nurseries on the top floor of the building, one could catch glimpses of the water down below, but on leaving the building through the kitchen doors, it would have been impossible to know the great river was there at all.

The Range's estate included the section of hill – perhaps a hundred yards in width – which linked the river with the house. Leaning one day out of one of the top floor rooms,

Felicity could see how on either side of their section of the hill, the land had been cleared and tamed. Boathouses sat placidly upon the water, backed by green slopes of grass, on either side of the thick vegetation and woodland which made up the Frome land. It was as though the house were deliberately turning its back on the river, refusing to participate in the gentle camaraderie of river life with its waterside villas, its sculling crews, its tied-up dinghies. The Range was haughty indeed.

– The main path down to the river is taken from the gatehouse, her husband had said when she first moved in as his new bride. Instead of following the drive to the house, there is a little footpath which bears off right and eventually you end up down by the river where I keep my dinghy in our old boathouse. The access to the water is a matter of a few yards – the rest of our river frontage is wild and inaccessible.

In her curiosity to come to a complete understanding of her new environment, Felicity decided, one hot afternoon that summer while the gardeners were busy out the front attending to a new sequence in the formal gardens, to explore the densely packed greenery beyond the building at the back. The rear of the house was bordered by a narrow stone veranda which ran the entire length of the huge house, edged by a set of imposing modernist stone columns which provided an effective barrier – there was literally no access beyond. She clambered over the stone columns at one end of the house and began to investigate what lay beyond. She was shielded from the heat of the sun by the house itself, whose roof was just high enough to create shade.

Pushing into the greenery with her gloved hands, she could see immediately that the interior was much too dense for entry: tangled barbed brambles wrapped themselves around tree trunks, clouds of stinging nettles sat alongside thick shrubs entwined with bindweed. She walked slowly along the length of the veranda, pausing every now and then in the quiet stillness to poke her hand into the undergrowth to try to explore further, but each time the silent woods resisted her approach.

After about half an hour, she had travelled from one end of the house almost to the other and was about to clamber back up onto the veranda when she noticed a slight gap in the green barrier, no wider than a couple of feet. She ducked under a low branch and found herself at the head of a narrow path which led into the dark wood. As she edged further in, feeling to the right and left with her hands, she realised that this was a deliberately cleared path – she could see in the gloom the clipped edges of branches where a secateur or a saw had been used recently. She continued on, noticing the enveloping sweet smell of the vegetation all around her, the snap of a breaking twig under her feet causing her to start.

The path took a couple of twisting turns and then began to incline, so that Felicity could sense she was beginning to head downhill. She carried on, still feeling her way in the sunless surroundings with her arms extended to either side of her and her gloved hands brushing the edges of the forest. There was just enough light for her to see a few feet ahead of her at a time, and she carefully picked her way down the ever-increasing slope. There was absolute silence all around her, and the summer heat of the lawns was now a distant sensation in the cool of the woods.

She felt a thrill of discovery. This was a secret path, clearly maintained quite recently, but obviously kept so obscure that no-one would be likely to come across it, were they not deliberately exploring as she had been. Down and down she stepped, stumbling occasionally on raised roots, her face touched every now and then by a leafy branch. After some time, she sensed an alteration in the atmosphere, the sweet cloying fragrance of the interior now seeming to give way to a cleaner, more refined air. She kept on, the low-ering path twisting one more time before, without warning, it emerged into a bare circular lawn, no more than thirty feet across.

She felt her heart beating as she stood in silence on this

lawn, the sense of liberation after the claustrophobia of the secret path briefly overwhelming her. Then she noticed in the centre a stone plinth, about three feet high and wide, with moss staining its sides. She walked up to it across the neat grass of the lawn. On closer examination she could not make out any markings, but there were several cut branches on its surface which looked as though they had been deliberately placed there. She walked all around it, tracing her ungloved hand on the rough surface of the stone, but could see nothing which might identify its origin or purpose. It just stood there.

Without thinking any further, she scrambled onto the plinth and got to her feet, turning slowly all around. She gasped. There it was, explaining of course the change in the feeling of the air a few minutes back. There, in front of her at the edge of the grass lawn, through a slim break in the trees, was the Thames, just yards away from her, flowing silently and heavily in apparent disregard of this new visitor. She was transfixed, staring at the water as though seeing it for the first time. For several minutes she didn't move and she felt a peculiar sense of being thrown into a play or performance without warning. It was not as though she was interrupting the performance, however, it was more as if the drama was waiting for her arrival to begin.

Felicity remained standing on the plinth for some time until the spell was broken by her own sudden realisation of her exhaustion. The exploration, the climb down the path, the heightened emotions she felt, all combined to make her want to curl up on the stone of the plinth and go to sleep. She knelt down, then lay in a huddle, tucking her cardigan about her, and fell instantly asleep.

When she awoke, the light had changed, and the clearing beside the river was no longer quite so vivid. How long had she been asleep? With a start, she looked around her to find the gap in the woods from which she had emerged and, spying it, she jumped from the plinth and headed towards it. Any further delay and the light would be going and she would have no way of finding her way back up the path. Just before she ducked back into the woods, she turned for a final look across the clearing to where she could still just see the glint of moving water. Then she turned to begin the climb back up to the house.

Later that evening, after she and Zachary had finished dinner on his return to the Range from Parliament, and the housemaid had cleared the plates from their table, she looked at him and said:

– Darling, I found a secret path today at the back of the house which took me all the way down to the river. Why didn't you tell me about it?

Her husband smiled.

– Ah, he said. I wondered when you might come upon it, my dear. I knew you would. I thought I might let you find it in your own way. You discovered Down There, didn't you?

Chapter Six

– You're up early.

Darius turned around and saw Belinda standing in the kitchen doorway.

– Early riser, Belinda.

She walked over to the Aga and took the kettle, filling it with water at the enamel sink. The kitchen was long and low-ceilinged, with trellissed windows looking out onto the veranda at the back of the house. Darius was sitting at the wooden table drinking a cup of tea.

– Not as early as your brother. He's already left for the day.

– I heard his car. Does he leave that time every day?

– Usually. Sometimes he works from home.

Darius watched his sister-in-law put out cups and plates onto a tray. She was wearing white cotton pyjamas, and her dark brown hair, thick and luxurious, played casually over her collar. Her feet were bare, and she moved delicately around the kitchen as she gathered things.

– I don't even know what he does.

Belinda turned around and leaned against the kitchen worktop. She crossed her arms and looked at him. Darius noticed for the first time the delicate thin lines on her forehead. Then she smiled and with a shock he remembered the dimples that appeared either side of her lips.

– Yes you do, Darius. You know very well what he does. He runs the Magenta Hedge Fund. He makes enormous amounts of money.

Darius smiled back.

– Yes, but what is it he actually does to make all that money in his hedge fund?

– Ah, said Belinda. That's the thing. He describes it as a modern alchemy. Base metals into gold, you know. Only with your brother, he seems to have found the knack of turning anything into gold. Even people.

Darius raised an eyebrow.

Belinda shrugged.

– He does what he does, Darius. You ask him.

– I will. Although I can't pretend that I'm that interested, Belinda. I imagine he still lives in that strange world of his where people like Tony Blair swan around?

– Oh God yes, they're all still around, she smiled. Pigs and troughs, you know.

– And he's still a big player in the party?

She sighed.

– Yes, Francis is still crucial to them. But you ask him, Darius. Your brother's career is no longer my specialist subject.

She walked across the kitchen and opened a cupboard, pulling out a packet of biscuits. Darius watched her. Over the last few days, since receiving the card, he had wondered about seeing Belinda again for the first time since it all happened. He had wondered how he would feel. Now here she she was. There was something instantly recognisable about the way she moved across the stone flags of the kitchen floor, a light sway in her walk and a delicate treading of her bare feet. She looked at him as she walked back towards the tray beside the Aga.

– You've aged better than us, she said, smiling. She put the biscuits on the tray then came back and sat down opposite him. All that hair, she said. There's not even a smidgeon of grey in it. How unfair is that?

He smiled.

– And the tattoos, she said, reaching over and touching his left arm. I suppose you got them in some impossibly glamorous Pacific island?

– Actually in a tattoo parlour in Bodmin, he said, and they both laughed.

They were quiet for a moment. Belinda looked over towards the window which looked out onto a kitchen garden. Darius watched her face, remembered clearly now the line of her nose, her smiling lips.

She turned back.

– Seriously though, she said. It's been a long time, Darius.

– I know.

– Didn't you feel strange about coming back here? After all this time?

– Of course. It wasn't something I'd been planning. But that invitation – it was very strange, Belinda. How could I ignore it?

She nodded.

– We both got it, she said. In separate envelopes. Francis went apeshit. He thinks this is all your doing, by the way.

– I know. He told me last night. What do you think?

– I don't know, Darius. I really don't know. I made Francis go along with it. He was all for ignoring the invitations, carrying on as though they'd never arrived, but I told him we couldn't ignore something as strange as that.

– Well, I guess we're going to find out, one way or the other. You're right, it did feel strange last night, being back here. The walk up from Marlow, that was when I started feeling it. Got much stronger when we came through the gates. I don't know how to describe it. Not what I was expecting, and also not very comforting. I felt uneasy.

– Well, it's been twenty-five years. You were bound to feel something.

– Yes, but...I can't put my finger on it. I'll have to think about it.

She looked at him carefully.

– I was wondering too, about what you'd be like. You're so hopeless at returning my letters, I hardly know anything about you.

– That's not true. I sent you a postcard a while ago.

– That was two years ago, Darius. You told me that you'd built your own charcoal burner in the woods somewhere

37

and were making charcoal. That was pretty much it I think. You've kept your distance.

– Have I? Sorry, he said. He looked at her. It's never been that deliberate, he said. It's just what I did. After prison. I just kept away. It wasn't anything to do with you.

– I know, she said. We all coped with it in our ways, Darius. I'm not criticising you. I'm really happy to see you.

The kettle began to whistle from the hob, and she got up to turn it off. He watched her pour a little water into the teapot, swill it around and then pour it out. Then she set the pot back on the tray, added tea leaves from a tin box on the window ledge, and poured the water in. She set the kettle back and covered the teapot with an old woollen cosy. All the time, he watched her movements closely, struck by her calm confidence, her fluidity.

– I'm happy to see you too, Belinda. I'm sorry to have been such a stranger.

– I don't want you to be, she said, her back to him still as she arranged the cups and saucers. I want you to feel at home. This is your home as much as mine.

– I can't say I ever felt much at home here, when I was a kid, he said, looking around the kitchen. If I'm honest, I can't even remember this kitchen really, although I know it's pretty much how it was. The table's the same, isn't it?

She turned around, leant back against the sink and looked around the room. She sighed.

– Yes, the table is the one your mother put in I think. Richard said she didn't like the one your grandmother had here. I haven't done much to the kitchen. I haven't done much to anything here, really. It's got a bit of a life of its own, this house. It sort of seems to look after itself. I've never quite felt at home here either, if you want to know. It always slightly feels like I've wandered onto the stage of a play that's already started.

– Do your kids enjoy it?

– Oh God, Alice and James adore it. They were tiny when we moved here from London. James was just one I think, and Alice was three. They're entirely at home here, they think everyone lives in a house like this. I spend all my time trying to explain to them how everyone else in the world lives. But yes, they are happy here.

– I'm glad. I suppose I was happy in my own way here. I liked the place more than the people. Apart from Nana, of course.

– I remember your grandmother. What a woman. You were her favourite, weren't you?

– I don't know about that. But she understood me. She was the only one. The rest of them thought I was a moron.

– Maybe, she said. Maybe they were a bit scared of you too. Everyone's probably a bit scared of you, Darius.

He frowned.

– Sorry, she said quickly. I didn't mean...

He shook his head.

– It's OK. I know.

There was another silence. Darius looked away, across towards the other window in the far corner where he could see a squirrel running down the trunk of a tree. What had he expected from this visit? He hadn't really thought. Tink had told him that was the best way to approach it, not to plan or prepare. Just let it happen, she'd said.

– It's going to be a strange weekend, Darius, Belinda said, her voice softer. We need to all be careful with each other.

He looked up. Her face was worried, he thought.

– I know, he said. Tell me about you. How's the charity?

Once he'd settled back in Cornwall ten years ago, after his years of travelling, Darius had begun to receive occasional letters from Belinda and she had told him about her work as a director of the international charity set up by his grandfather, Zachary. He had formed World Action alongside others in the 1950s to combat poverty around the world. Belinda had joined it as a junior office worker twenty years ago, had served as a board director for the last fifteen.

– It's my twentieth year this year, she said. They're going

to give me a carriage clock or something.

– I shouldn't think they'd dare, he said, smiling. Is it all going OK?

– It's pretty good actually, she said, coming back over to sit opposite him again. We went through all those problems a few years ago with a bit of rogue Chief Executive and then all the criticism in the press had a terrible impact on fundraising. We were probably set back twenty years by it, in terms of the funds available to us. But we got through it, we're still here and we're doing good work again.

– I met one of your people when I was out in South Africa in the '90s, said Darius.

Belinda raised her eyebrows.

– You got involved in World Action? she asked.

– Well, he said, laughing. Actually I met this girl at a party in Capetown and she worked for your lot, but I don't think we discussed world poverty very much.

Belinda laughed, shaking her head.

– Darius, she said. How nice to have you back.

At that moment, the kitchen door opened and Alice appeared, holding a teddy bear.

– Mummy, Grandpa is making shouty noises, she said, walking over to Belinda and glancing shyly at Darius.

– All right darling, her mother said. He wants his tea, I got behind talking to Uncle Darius.

She ruffled her daughter's hair, then walked with her back over to the kitchen worktop to pour the tea.

– What were you talking to Uncle Darius about? asked Alice.

Belinda poured tea into a cup, smiling.

– Uncle Darius was just telling me about his charity work, she said. Helping young ladies, is that right Darius?

– I was telling your mother about my travels, Darius said from the table. Are you going to be a traveller, Alice?

The little girl held onto her mother's white pyjama top and looked at him over the top of her teddy bear.

– I might be, she said.

– I'll tell you and James some stories today. I'll tell you about the fishermen who catch the dreams of fishes.

– You can't catch dreams, the little girl said, looking at her teddy bear but sneaking glances at him.

– Oh but you can, he said. I'll tell you about it today.

Belinda looked at him.

– Do you want to come up and see your father? I've made his tea. You haven't seen him yet, have you?

– No, I haven't, he said. Is that OK?

– Of course it's OK, you silly man. He's your father. Darling, I won't be long, she said to her daughter. I'll just take Uncle Darius up to see Grandpa then I'll come down and make you some hot chocolate. OK? You start getting the things out and I'll come back down and help you.

She kissed Alice on the head and picked up the tray.

Darius followed Belinda out of the kitchen and down a long low corridor. He hadn't even walked around the house yet, he realised. Their steps echoed against the white stone walls, and he suddenly recognised this as the long corridor at the rear of the house where he used to race Francis on their bicycles. He could hear their shouts and the clatter of metal as they crashed into each other.

They came to some stairs and Belinda started to climb.

– He's seventy nine next week, she said ahead of him. I think he misses your mother. You didn't come to her funeral.

– I know, he said.

– You should have done, really.

– That's probably what she'd have said, he replied.

Darius followed Belinda up the stairs. A faded red carpet laid down the centre of the stone stairs muffled their steps. He pictured his mother and father, standing in front of him all those years ago, his father's domed forehead creased in irritation, the glasses, the receding hair, his mother glaring at him. Waving poor school reports at him, police cautions, bills for damages. Always complaining. Always disappoint-ed. What's the matter with you, Darius? Why can't you think before you act, Darius? Why can't you be more like your brother, Darius?

– Maybe I should have come, he said. I don't know. It didn't feel like it had much to do with me, when I heard.

– It doesn't matter, she said. Do you know much about dementia, by the way? It's not a lot of fun.

Belinda had stopped outside a door. She turned to look at him.

– He usually thinks I'm his old secretary, Betty. The one who used to work for him when he was an MP.

He nodded, and she opened the door.

His father was sitting in an armchair by the window. He was talking to himself in a low voice, looking out at the grounds which were bright in the early morning summer sun.

– Got to meet the bloody Minister today. Stupid oaf. Takes all my time just correcting the idiotic mistakes he makes.

He looked up.

– Oh, Betty. I was wondering when...

He noticed Darius standing beside her.

– Who's this? New Parliamentary Clerk?

– Morning Richard, said Belinda. She set the tray down on the table in front of him. She leant over and kissed him on the cheek.

– It's Darius, Richard, she said softly. Your son, Darius.

– Someone's got to get to grips with this committee time-table, the old man said, making a grab for the tea. There's not a chance in hell we'll be completed before the recess if we don't get a move on.

He slurped noisily at the tea, then picked up a biscuit with his other hand.

– Hello Dad, said Darius. He came forward and laid his hand on his father's shoulder. He was shocked how tiny the old man felt – underneath the dressing gown it felt like a fragile bone he was touching.

Richard Frome stared glassily ahead as he munched on his biscuit and drank his tea. His eyes were bloodshot, the skin of his face dry like paper. The cup shook slightly in his hand, and his long fingers were veined with blue.

– It's a lovely day today, Richard, Belinda said brightly. She picked up a pair of white underpants which were lying on the floor and put them in a wicker basket in the corner of the room.

Darius knelt down on the floor so that his head was level with his father's.

– How are you Dad? he asked, gently.

The old man slurped the last of the tea and set the cup unsteadily back on the saucer.

– Nice tea, he said. He looked at Darius. They won't be long, young man. Plenty of cars, you know. It won't take long.

Darius looked into his father's face. There was nothing, no sign of recognition. The dry skin on his cheek twitched irregularly, and his drooping eyes were sunk in wet red flesh. Somewhere in that frail, shaking face was his father, but Darius struggled to put the two together: the father he remembered, and this unexpected apparition, this stick insect.

Belinda came back over to the window.

– The nurse is coming to see you today, Richard, she said. She wants to check your INR.

He nodded, then closed his eyes. After a few seconds, his head dropped down to his chest, and a spittle of saliva appeared at the side of his mouth.

– He falls asleep a lot now, said Belinda quietly.

Darius reached forward and wiped the spittle from his father's face. Then he very gently laid his hand on his forehead, and closed his own eyes. He searched for the energy in the old man, but he could feel inside of him that the flame inside his father was weak and flickering. He stayed there, eyes closed, focussing on the embers of a weak fire, which glowed unsteadily in a desert landscape in his mind: a wide, bare landscape of dunes, and just this last hint of a fire in the ground, a few dry burned twigs scattered around the edge, and in the centre just a few glowing red embers.

Belinda interrupted him.

– Annie will be here soon, she said quietly to him. She's our daycare assistant. She'll come and get him dressed. Let's leave him, let him sleep.

Darius opened his eyes, looked once more at his father whose head was slumped down in sleep, and then stood up.

– He's dying, Belinda, he said.

Chapter Seven

– I was an unusual child, I suppose, Zachary said eventually.

Felicity looked at him across the dinner table with great warmth, not wishing to hurry him or press him. He would tell her the story in his own, inimitable way.

– I saw little of my parents from the age of ten or so, he said, taking off his metal-rimmed spectacles and rubbing the glass with a napkin. My father was out in India for much of the war, serving in the diplomatic service, and he and my mother stayed out there for several years following the Armistice. I meanwhile had become accustomed to spending school holidays here at the Range with various governesses and aunts. There was no shortage of money – the gambling scandals which took over my father towards the end of his life hadn't set in by then, so the Range in my memory was filled with people each time I came back from Eton: housemaids, cooks, butlers, gardeners, drivers.

– I'm doing my best to reinstate that atmosphere here, my darling.

He smiled, putting his glasses back on and looking at her with adoration.

– It is a wonderful thing, your appreciation of the Range, he said. The gardens are magnificent. I don't know how you do it all.

He got up, and walked over to the fireplace, which had one huge single log gently charring in the grate.

– So you see, I had a lot of time on my hands as a young man, he continued. I read of course, and followed my own natural curiosity which led me to much of the works of political economy which you found on the bookshelves the first time you visited me here. But I also wandered about, and I had a little rowing boat just like Ratty and Moley's which was moored down on the river at the bottom of the path which leads down from the gatehouse. I pottered about in that thing for hours on end, looking out for otters and recording details of the plants I found in endless notebooks.

– It must have been 1922, I would think. I would have been 16. It was a long hot summer here, and Mother and Father were away in India the entire season. I had the occasional chum from Eton come to stay, and I made the odd visit, but mostly I was here, and it was that summer that I discovered Down There. I was poking about in the boat on the edge of the river, and I lifted up the skirt of a willow tree which was dangling in the water. I think I was searching for nests.

– There it was. Just a few yards from the water's edge, a majestic stone plinth, standing on its own in a clearing of grass, surrounded by the woodland which leads back up the hill. I moored my little boat and explored. The grass was short, but not as though it had been cut by a human hand – rabbits, I concluded, were tending this bower. But who had created the scene? Who had set this stone in its place? I couldn't tell. And oddly, even on that first day of discovery, I did not feel so great an urge to discover its history. Normally, as you know, I can become quite pedantic in my research.

She smiled.

– Not pedantic, darling, she said. Just very thorough. It is one of your many attributes.

He grinned, schoolboyishly pleased.

– But on this occasion, my dear, I felt as though research might – how can I put it? – might somehow tarnish the place. It was just so entirely perfect that I had no wish to disturb its secrecy, to uncover its origins. I just distinctly remember an overwhelming sense of homecoming: I had come home. This place was where I was supposed to be. I did not need to know who or what had commissioned the stone, or whether it was in fact the last remaining evidence of a much older building. I just knew that this was my very own secret place, that it belonged to me. Does that sound odd?

He was leaning against the fireplace now and looking at her with such sincerity that she felt impelled to get up and go to him.

– It doesn't sound remotely odd, she said, resting her head on his chest. I too felt something extraordinary there today.

– I'm so glad, he said fervently. So glad. You are the only other person whom I know to have been there, and it pleases my heart so greatly that you, who I love and admire so very much, should recognise its distinction.

He paused for a moment, and she lifted her head, smiling.

– Go on, she said, sitting down at one of the chairs beside the fire. He began to pace.

– Well, it has become a place of significance for me, he said finally. I don't know how else to describe it. Dr Jung, whose work you know I greatly admire, has his own secret place, his own Down There. He calls it his Bollingen Tower, and it is a place beside the lake at Zürich where he retreats regularly to contemplate and work. I read a piece about him recently in one of your friend Connolly's papers. Apparently he treats Bollingen as the place where he allows his mind to relax and wander – giving sway to his unconscious, as he puts it. He says it puts him in mind of a reversion to child-hood, and he even plays childish games there on his own.

A slight raise of her eyebrows made him smile.

– No my dear Felicity, I shall not reveal to you my habits Down There. But I came to feel as a young man very similar intuitions as I hazard the great philosopher himself felt, as though somehow I were accessing a much deeper realm. Without wishing to sound even more ludicrous than I'm sure I already do, I felt a sense even then, as a 16-year-old boy, of what Dr Jung calls the Collective Unconscious. I felt taken out of my usual world, the world of Eton and the Range and books and days fishing on the river, and I felt instead as though I were plunged into a new mystical landscape, a place where I existed not as the son of a Baronet but as a mere component of a huge, universal truth. I spent hours there that summer in 1922, and many more hours since, learning to unravel my own more material preconceptions and concerns and allowing myself to reach into far greater potentials of thought and feeling.

He strode back towards her and placed his hands on the arms of her chair, his eyes shining.

– It is the source, dear Felicity, of the ideas I have been developing these recent months and years of our new political future. You know how frustrated I get with the limitations of my fellow Liberals. Decent men, every single one of them, and yet they cannot see beyond the constraints of the system which enslaves them. Even Lloyd George, God bless his name, even he in his advanced years has little more to offer. When I was with him last week at Bron-y-de, he was trying to persuade me of his New Deal and his faith in Beveridge and his plans for a social contract for our country. Oh, I applaud the decency of the notion of course, but it is mere managerialism. It offers nothing to the ordinary man who burns for a new way of life. I sense the same timidity, the same unwillingness to strive for fundamental change, in the Labour Party, so much so that I still feel unable to contemplate crossing the floor to join them.

– The structural changes in the shape of society which I wish to propose, though they are of course important in themselves, are much more important than this tinkering with the engine of society, in that they will lead to the emergence of a new kind of man, with a new kind of mind, new values, a new outlook on life, and, perhaps most important of all, new motives. Without Down There, I am convinced I would not have been able to develop these ideas recently. But it is only now, with the passage of time and experience and this wonderful new opportunity in Parliament, that I feel able to incorporate what I experienced as a schoolboy Down There.

He pushed off from her chair and began to stride about the room.

– What I discovered Down There as a young man was the absolute equality of everything. The river flows past the trees and each sustains and respects the other. The rabbits eat the grass, the stone of the plinth sits happily and easily in its location. There is nothing Down There which is either out of place or unwelcome. And when I first discovered it, I realised that I, too, was able to place myself alongside the grass, the trees, the stone, the water, neither as their sovereign nor their servant, but as their equal. I realised, in short, that nothing on this earth of ours has the right to place itself above anything or anybody else. And what that means for us, for our English tribe, is that we must embrace a new political philosophy of absolute equality, in which no man has supremacy over another.

– Man simply must live for something bigger than himself, he continued, not even looking at Felicity now. He has a positive longing to live for something bigger than himself. As long as society bids him live for himself alone there is a part of his nature, a part of his power, which is bound down. But it is not easy to release this power. There is buried deep in the heart of man some terrific power other than the economic motive which, if it could be released and harnessed to a totality which was good instead of to a totality which is evil, would yield to mankind a future as undreamed of today as our present society was undreamed in the days of Henry VII.

He paused, almost breathless, and his eyes shone with feeling. She walked over to him, stroked his head tenderly.

– I admire your passion so much, my darling, she said. And I understand you.

– I know you do, he said, more quietly this time. And I know you have found now the source of my crusade. Down There, all these years I have been returning to that spot for solitary contemplation, has taught me that there is a greater world where the concerns of materialism and wealth are as nothing in face of the wonder that is the natural universe. A world where man stands alongside his fellow creatures and his environment as one, as part of a Collective Whole. A world of harmony, where the river meets the land.

– There is so much more I need to do, now that I am fortunate to have found my place in Parliament, to meld these ideas into a coherent political philosophy which I can promote. There are kindred souls around. Priestley will come down to the Range soon for discussions, we may even persuade our friend Orwell to put down his Spanish guns one day. It is growing, this movement which began down there beside Ratty and Moley's boat – it is growing, and it will become unstoppable. I know that.

– I know that too, she said. I know that with all of my heart.

Chapter Eight

– You can't just say that.

They were back in the kitchen and Darius was leaning against the dresser at the far wall. Tink had woken up and was standing sleepily by the Aga waiting for the kettle to boil. Belinda was moving swiftly about the kitchen, preparing the children's packed lunches which were set out on the table.

– I'm sorry, Darius, she continued, concentrating on the Tupperware boxes in front of her, but you can't. I've spent pretty much every day with Richard for the last few years. His dementia is very advanced now but apart from that, his health is stable. His blood pressure is good, his INR jumps about a little bit but that's OK, it's nothing unusual. His appetite has decreased a bit I suppose, but then he's almost eighty. He should be allowed to eat less if he wants.

– I'm not really talking about the symptoms of his physical health, said Darius.

Belinda looked up at the clock on the wall.

– Shit, she said. I've got to get the kids out of here in five minutes.

She grabbed what looked like a walkie talkie.

– Alice! James! Five minutes, downstairs!

She looked over at Tink and smiled.

– Sorry Tink, she said. Bit of a rushed welcome this morning. Did you find green tea?

Tink held up a teabag from her mug and smiled back.

– Got it. What's with the radio?

– Oh that! Belinda laughed. The bloody house is so big I put a speaker in upstairs so I can chivvy the children without having to walk a mile. They take forever getting their school uniforms on.

– That's so cool, said Tink.

– It's ridiculous, I know, but you learn different coping mechanisms, living in this house.

She looked up at Darius.

– Your mum must have had her methods too, Darius.

– Oh, she had methods all right. I suspect you're still an amateur compared with her. She ran this place like a military academy.

Belinda smiled again.

– I'm going to pick up some shopping in Marlow after I've dropped the kids at school, she said. I'll be back in a couple of hours. I need to do a couple of World Action hours today, but it doesn't matter when. Just make yourselves at home. I mean...oh, you know. Just do what you want. Annie is upstairs with Richard.

– I'm not being weird about Dad, Belinda, said Darius.

She looked across at him.

– I know, she said. I did warn you, dementia is a bit of a scary thing when you encounter it. And that was the first time you've seen your dad in twenty-five years. It's bound to be unsettling, Darius.

He shook his head.

– No, it's not that.

He looked over at Tink, then back at Belinda.

– Look, we've got plenty of time, and you've got to get the kids to school. Let's talk later. But I know about this stuff, Belinda. I've been around it for a long time.

– What, dementia? Really? Belinda was stuffing Tupperware boxes into brightly coloured backpacks.

– No. Working with people's souls. Reaching into them. I spent years in Mexico learning it. Dad just made it very clear to me upstairs. He's preparing to move on. He's begun the journey.

Belinda stopped what she was doing.

– Oh, she said.

The kettle whistled and Tink took it off the hob and

began to pour water into her mug.

– Darius can see things we don't, she said. He sees in spirit.

Darius could tell that Belinda wasn't sure what to say. He walked over towards the table, saw a set of car keys at the end and picked them up.

– Go on, you'll be late for school, he smiled. These your keys?

– Yes, she said. Sorry, always rushing in the morning. Let's talk more when I'm back.

Chapter Nine

– My husband believes in the equality of man, Felicity said.

Her companion on this autumn stroll through the gardens at the Range was her publisher, Nigel Jenkins, down from London for the day to discuss her new novel. Her two-year-old son, Richard, was asleep in the pram which she pushed ahead of her as they visited each of the planted gardens she had created out on the front lawns.

– So I hear, said Jenkins.

– But real equality, Nigel, said Felicity, emphasising her point by pressing his arm. Real equality, not some token idea to win votes. His starting point is nature itself: the balance of nature is achieved through the equality of all living things having access to it.

– I'm not so sure I'd feel quite as sanguine about natural equality if I were a rabbit being chased by a fox, said her publisher amiably.

– Don't be flippant, Nigel, she said. Zachary's arguments are gaining ground. I am so terribly proud of him. He has almost finished his manifesto, and you must publish it.

– Well, his name is rising all right, said Jenkins. We could do well with it. There is an atmosphere for that sort of thing at the moment. Something to do with these damn bombing raids, I suspect.

– It's not just the war, Nigel, she continued. It's more than that. Zachary has tapped into something very profound, I am sure of it. It is so simple, don't you see? Your rabbit and your fox, they share the same space, the same land. Although nature is cruel too, as you point out, it is the obvious model for us: the shared ownership of land, the equal distribution of profit, the common stewardship of industry.

– And he thinks people will follow him? Everybody earning the same, everyone sharing everything out? I'm not so sure, Felicity. After all, and I don't wish to give offence, but with this beautiful estate which you've created, it might look as though he were wanting to have his cake and eat it too. The benevolent patriarch, that sort of thing.

– Zachary is already making plans to leave the Range to the nation. It is a complicated thing but he is working on it. And I support him in that. But that's not what's important, Nigel: it is the right and duty of the progressive not merely to give the people what they do desire, but to teach them what they should desire.

Jenkins laughed.

– My word, you are a believer, aren't you?

She grabbed his sleeve more urgently this time.

– Yes I am, Nigel. I believe in him absolutely, passionately. This terrible war, don't you see, it must never happen again. This must be the last time. And how can we stop it happening again if not by ending the struggle of man over his fellow man? Let us all submit to the natural law of equality, and there will be no space for conflict.

– I admire your passion, Felicity. And yes, I'll publish his book. Tell him to send it to me when it's finished. We'll do a good job of it, you know that. Just don't have me down as a convert, that's all.

She smiled.

– Oh, I know you, Nigel. I was a cynic myself too, I don't forget that. But we must all become converts before this war is out.

She leaned forward to tuck the blanket into her baby's pram.

– How can we build a world for Richard, for your children, unless we say, once and for all, never again? And how can we be sure this will never happen again, unless we change? Don't you feel how this war has infected everything? It's like a horrid, grey fog, it creeps into every room of every house, it casts its pall on every human relationship, it dampens down every single human yearning so that we are all just in its thrall, all going about day by day in our normal lives but as though we're in an endless play, a play on a horrible broken down stage that just won't end, that goes on and on. On and on and on.

There were tears in her eyes now, and he let her rest her head against his chest. After a while, she sniffed and turned back to take the handle of the pram.

– Is it very bad down in Plymouth? he asked gently. I hear the bombing has been awful.

She lowered her head and was silent for a moment. Then she spoke, much more quietly this time.

– Awful. Absolutely awful. He insists on being there, he says he must and I understand. There was another raid last night. He telephoned me this morning. He said the whole city seemed on fire. I heard the same from Nancy Astor – she's promised me she makes Zachary join them in the basement bar of a hotel called the Grand, close to her house, whenever there's an air raid. They all gather there, apparently, and drink cocktails and sing songs to keep their spirits up. But he's so determined to help people, I'm terrified he'll go out during one of the raids and…

– Damnable thing, he said. But look here, Felicity, you won't go rushing off down to him, to Plymouth, promise me that. It's far too dangerous. Promise me you'll stay here at the Range until he's back.

– I see the bombers flying overhead at night here, on the way into London, she said. I can't bear it.

– You promise? he repeated.

– I will see, she said quietly, looking down once more at the pram with the sleeping child.

– It will end, he said, more softly this time. It won't go on for ever. One day, we'll get it all back. Zachary will be back here soon. Tell him he needs to come and see his publisher, that'll bring him back.

She smiled slightly.

– That's the spirit, he said. Who knows, he may be right,

your husband. Maybe we will want something different after all this.

He looked around at the finely sculpted lawns and bold plantings as they continued to walk slowly.

– You've made your mark here, all right, he said. Never had you down as green-fingered, I must say. Have you shown Orwell? He's always banging on about gardens in the Statesman these days.

– Eric is down next week. Zachary will be back for that. There's a conference here on the formation of the new party. It's going to be called Level Ground. Will you come?

– I suppose I will be obliged to attend as the new Leader's publisher, won't I?

She laughed again.

– Nigel, you are incorrigible.

But it was good, she realised, to have a dose of the familiar old London cynicism. Nigel represented, still inhabited, the world she had left, the world of gossip and parties and betrayals and ambition. It was not a world she missed in any way, but just for a moment, with the thought of her husband facing another night of bombing two hundred miles away and the prospect of hearing those thundering engines overhead again tonight, she clung to it as though to a liferaft in a stormy sea.

– Tell me about London, she said. Do you all behave terribly in the blackout?

– Atrociously, he said. You wouldn't believe how badly. One just never knows if one is drinking one's last cocktail.

She smiled.

– And you, Felicity? Are you bearing up all right, here on your own?

– I'm not on my own. We still have people working here, those who can and haven't been sent off. Zachary is here as much as he is able to be. And Richard keeps me busy – he doesn't sleep well, we can hear the bombs fall from here, and we can see the glow of the fires.

They had reached the front door of the house, and he

went forwards to open it onto the octagonal white stone hallway. He looked up at the painting on the ceiling.

– This looks new, he said. I can still smell the paint.

She joined him, looking up at the freshly painted interpretation of the Manet.

– It was Zachary's idea, she said. We got a very nice young man down from the Royal College. Zachary wanted something which would represent the Range. He says the two seated gentlemen in suits are he and I.

– I see. And who are the nudes?

– According to Zachary, they represent the two trees in the garden of Eden: the tree of knowledge and the tree of life. Most people think there was just one tree in Eden with the apple and the snake, but apparently there were two. Anyway, our glamorous ladies are representations of the natural world.

– Very profound, I'm sure. Rather fun, too. Talking of industry…

– Almost done, Richard. Don't worry. You have been most scrupulous in not mentioning it so far. Give me another month and I will send it to you.

– Revolutionary France, you said?

– Yes. I wanted to get away from the present, and there was a lot of hope in Paris in those days, alongside the terror. It's a novel about hope, I think. Paris must have been so terrifying then, as London is now. So it's a way of thinking about what we're all in now without having to think about it too directly, if you know what I mean. I have the title already.

Jenkins waited.

– Don't you want to know what it is? she asked.

– I'm waiting patiently, he smiled.

– *Marianne*. I'm going to call it *Marianne*. She is the beacon of light in the darkness of the Terror.

He nodded.

– It's perfect. It will be timely, I feel it. We all need that hope. People need a big story, something to hold on to. This could do very well, Felicity. I'm going to try and corner some extra paper for this one.

— You haven't even read it yet, you silly man.

— I don't need to. That's why I'm your publisher. Just finish it soon. Leave the rest to me.

Chapter Ten

The sun was climbing in the sky as Darius and Tink wandered slowly across the lawns at the front of the Range. As they walked away from the house, there was silence again, interrupted by birds singing in the summer sunshine. They came up to a ragged hedge and Darius indicated they should squeeze through a small gap. On the other side was an overgrown garden, a square-shaped enclosure which was bordered on all sides by the hedge. There were gravel paths around the edge and across, but they were interrupted and strangled everywhere by weeds and ivy. Clumps of thick grasses sprouted out of stone bowers.

– I can't believe it's like this, said Darius, shielding his eyes from the strong sunlight. He looked all around. That oppressive sense of conflict closed in on him again, the feeling of warring natures. He felt it everywhere here. It was all so disconcerting; when he'd impulsively decided a few days ago to come up the Range early, a couple of days before the 25th, it was partly because, he knew, that he wanted to get away from Cornwall but also he did feel a sense of nostalgic curiosity. The arrival of the card had prompted him to speculate on his old home. He had imagined it lying here, a vision of natural perfection as his grandmother had always insisted upon. Instead, he had found this bewildering neglect.

– It's a bit unloved, said Tink.

– Yes, that's it. It's unloved.

He walked slowly down one of the paths, pushing brambles away from his face.

– My grandmother, Felicity Frome, planted this back in the 1930s, he called out. When she married my grandfather, Sir Zachary, she employed loads of gardeners to landscape the grounds. She loved making these boxed gardens, and they were all different: some had colour in them, some had just white flowers, some just had herbs.

– Do you remember her? Tink asked, taking her own route around the enclosure.

– Yes, very well. She was here throughout my childhood. My grandfather died when I was quite young, but she lived to ninety. She lived in her own set of rooms in the house, but she spent most of the time out here looking after the gardens. They were beautiful, Tink, he called out. They were really beautiful, these gardens.

They continued to make their own ways through the weeds and the brambles, and then reconnected at one end of the enclosed garden. He swept some leaves and twigs from the surface of a stone bench, and they sat down. He closed his eyes, and for a moment he could see his grandmother bending over with a pair of secateurs, dead-heading rose bushes. He smiled as he imagined her straightening up and, seeing him, giving a wave. They sat in silence for a while.

– She sounds more like you, your grandmother, said Tink. I can't find much else of you in this strange house.

– I loved Nana, Darius said simply. She was the only one I could talk to. My mum and dad didn't get me, and Francis and I were quite competitive I suppose, in our different ways. Nana made me feel like I might belong here, have some connection with it, when most of the time I just felt like a stranger.

– Tell me about her.

– I still miss her, Tink. She was very clever, very clever with words and with ideas, not like me. She wrote books, she had lots of novels published. You can still buy them. She had really striking cheekbones, and she wore red lipstick every day, and she smoked cigarettes. She was always trying to get me to read books, but I never did.

– That was naughty of you, Darius.

– Oh I tried. I didn't have any interest then, but I tried, just to please Nana. She said I reminded her of her husband, although I can't imagine why. He was really clever too, he was the one who started that political party I told you about, Level Ground. It's why I named the valley after him. I tried to read his books but, you know, I was a kid and I never got round to it. I just liked being outside. I liked nature, even back then.

He opened his eyes and looked once more on the desolate scene. It wasn't possible to picture his grandmother here now. He shut his eyes once more and he felt the sun on his face. He tried to banish these insistent feelings of conflict, these sensations of violence which had enveloped him since their arrival the previous evening. He summoned up in his mind the still, sun-bleached landscape that had appeared in his mind earlier that morning in his father's room. There was no fire now, just the dry yellow sands of dunes stretching out in front of him, and it quietened him to see the rolling shapes of the dunes in his head.

– She died the first year I was in prison, he said finally. I think it was too much for her. The whole thing.

– She was an old lady, Darius, said Tink quietly. Perhaps it was just her time.

He shook his head.

– I haven't told you about it. You never ask, because you're good like that. You're not like me, always blundering in and insisting on things.

She smiled.

– Big blunderer.

Her eyes were closed in the sunshine and he stroked her silver hair.

She opened her eyes.

– I think it was fine you telling Belinda about your dad, she said.

– She thought I was nuts.

Tink shrugged.

– Doesn't matter. She won't think that after a while. It's just not what she knows about. But she's nice, I like her.

They were quiet again, sitting in the summer heat.

Then Darius said:

– I made Nana unhappy, Tink. I destroyed every-thing. Everything. I ruined Nana, I ruined her. She died of unhappiness.

She put her hand on his.

– No you didn't. Tell me more about little Darius. The one who played out here with his Nana.

He opened his eyes to look at her.

– I was a tearaway. I was like the opposite of Francis. He was always studying and discussing politics with Dad and winning prizes. I just liked being outside. I used to track animals in the woods at Quarry Hill, not to kill them, just to try and follow them, see where they went. I used to sleep out there sometimes, climb out of my bedroom window and shimmy down the drainpipe when my parents thought I'd gone to bed. And I used to help Nana with the gardens, she taught me everything about planting. When I was little, I could tell you all the Latin names for all the plants.

– What's that one, she said, pointing at an overgrown bush with yellow flowers in front of them.

He laughed.

– Well, it's actually called Senecio Jacobaea, but most people think it's just a weed. Ragwort is its other name.

– You do know! Tink clapped her hands with delight. Clever Darius!

– But I don't understand it, he said, frowning again. Why is it like this? Why are these gardens all overgrown? It doesn't take that much time to keep them up. Nana and I used to do most of it on our own. Why does the whole place feel like nobody loves it? Even the front of the house has render falling off it. Our cottages in Cornwall are in better nick than the Range. He earns a fortune, Francis – he's got millions. Why would he want to leave it like this?

Tink hummed and swung her legs off the stone bench. Darius looked out over the writhing tangle of green and felt the tranquillity of the landscape that had been in his head fade away once more. To be at war with nature, that went against everything he understood, everything which he had spent his life on. What was it about the Range? Looking out over this particular garden, he struggled to identify the original pattern of planting which he had watched his Nana tend thirty or so years ago.

– She was so in love with this place, Tink. When I was growing up, she made sure the gardens stayed like they were when she and Grandpa were here together. She said it was glorious then, always cars coming and going down the drive with new visitors from London. When Grandpa got famous, during the Second World War, she said the Range was always alive, there were always people walking out here in the gardens, making plans, preparing speeches.

– I can see it, she said. It must have been cool. Why did he call it Level Ground?

– I don't really know that much about it. It was revolutionary for its time. He advocated the common ownership of land, equal pay, equal rights. He was a radical, all right. He had a lot of followers during the war, he was trying to get enough support and win enough seats in Parliament that he could form a government. Even Churchill was worried by him, apparently. People were fed up after all the years of war, they wanted a new world. He was very passionate, Nana said. She loved him, she really loved him.

– I like him. Did he look like you? She brushed his thick, dark hair, smiling at him.

Darius frowned.

– No. He looked much more like Francis. Big dome head, receding hair, glasses. Skinny. I never looked like him or Dad. I never looked like anyone.

– You look like Darius. Darius the King.

Now he laughed.

– That's not how Mum and Dad saw it, he said. I was just always the troublemaker. Nana understood. She said I was an explorer.

– What happened to his party, to Level Ground?

– It failed. The Labour party got in after the war and

I think they took all the votes he thought he might get. He joined them eventually, the Labour party, became an MP for them. But Nana said he never really liked them, never believed in what they believed. He called them Second Hand Tories.

– I think your Nana could tell that you understood him, even if you didn't read his books.

– Maybe. I don't know. I thought about him a lot when I bought the valley. Now it feels like I've let him down too.

– Why? Just because of a few arguments? You get too fixed in your head, Darius. You really do. You haven't let anyone down. That stuff will just blow over.

Was she right? He felt despondent about his valley in Cornwall. The invitation to Down There had come just at the moment when he had felt most unhappy about it all, which was partly why he'd decided to come up to the Range early, just to get away. His two other co-founders had been arrested three months ago after a police raid discovered they were growing cannabis in a neighbouring valley. He had felt furious with them, they had had endless arguments late into the night. The other two defended their actions, said that the principles behind their foundation of Level Ground included absolute freedom and that that should include their freedom to do what they liked with the land. They accused him of hypocrisy, of cosying up to the forces of the State. He accused them of threatening their ability to demonstrate a sustainable way of living, of ruining the project just so they could get high.

– It's not a project, Darius. This is where we live. We're not all part of your plans, man. Just because you don't like grass doesn't mean we don't have our own right to enjoy it.

It was a bitter argument which raged for weeks, over kitchen tables, out in the fields. It was as though ten years of resentment had been building up, of which he had been unaware. His doctrinaire attitude, they said. His bullying. He couldn't see it; all he could see was the stupidity of what they'd done.

– You know it's not as simple as that, Tink, he said. You know that the whole thing might just come to an end. If they get convicted when the trial comes up, that'll be it. It'll all be over. No-one will trade with us, they'll all just think we're a bunch of stoned hippies.

Tink for the first time looked irritated.

– You don't know that. You don't know if it will all be over. Things happen all the time to people and life carries on. Level Ground will be fine. Half the people you trade with down there probably even buy the grass, without you knowing. You're just very strung up about it.

– I just want it to work. I don't want it to look like this place – he waved his arm in front of him – all unloved and broken. I want more people to come and live in the valley. I don't want it all to collapse.

– It's not going to collapse, she said calmly. But even so, what if it did? What if you had to leave Cornwall? You've spent your life travelling, you could go anywhere. Nothing stops you being Darius, the Darius everyone loves.

He looked at her. Was she right? What if you stopped holding on to things, what happened then?

– It felt like I was building something, creating something. That we were all doing it, together. I've never done that, don't you see? I've never stayed put and built something which had real value.

She lay her hand on his.

– You just don't know how much you create, she said quietly.

They were quiet again for a while. Then Tink said:

– Tell me more about when you were young here, with your Nana.

He sighed.

– I don't know. The thing is, when I was growing up here, I became a bit of a yob. I just couldn't see the point of school – I liked wandering around on my own, spending nights in the wood. Then one day I found an old motorbike when I was about fourteen, it had been abandoned off one of the lanes near here, and I fixed it up myself and kept it hidden in Quarry Hill. Instead of going to school, I'd sneak off and get the bike, go and nick some petrol out of someone's car and just drive around. I used to go everywhere on it. It used to make Nana laugh.

Tink smiled.

– Of course it made her laugh, she said. Did she tell on you? I bet she didn't.

– No, Nana never told on me. She promised me she wouldn't, as long as I promised her I would try and do as well as I could when I did go into school. I sort of kept my side of it. I did try. I got my geography O level.

– I bet you did much better than you're saying, said Tink.

– No, I really didn't.

He shut his eyes again, and he thought about the bike and where he used to hide it underneath the low branches of an old oak in the woods.

– Soon after I found the bike, he continued, I discovered drugs too, and that was pretty much it with me and school. After that, there just didn't seem any point in pretending that I was taking any of it seriously. I realised I could get up to London quite easily on the bike so by the time I was fifteen I was hanging out in Soho. I was quite big for a fifteen-year-old so I could get into the clubs without much fuss.

– You were doing drugs at fifteen? I was a good girl when I was fifteen, I was still doing cookery classes.

– I used to nick stuff in those days as well. I sold a few bits and pieces from the house, then I'd nick stuff from my friends' houses. I got caught occasionally but I just used to get told off, shouted at. Nothing much happened – my dad was an MP by then, they probably made allowances. Then after a while I realised I could sell the drugs on, so I dealt for a while at school. I was dealing by the time I was sixteen, Tink.

He frowned again.

– That's what Nana didn't like. She hated that. She didn't know about the dealing, but she knew I was smoking and

68

taking acid and all that. She got really upset. She couldn't understand it. That's what really disappointed her. I really disappointed her.

– I don't think she was disappointed, said Tink quietly. She loved you, Darius. She was a wise woman. She was just worried about you.

They sat in silence again.

– Did you get caught dealing? Is that why you went to prison?

He was still, his eyes closed. He didn't answer.

– Your Nana wouldn't have been that mortified by you going to prison Darius, not like you think. It was in your nature, she could see that. She was an old lady by then. You didn't cause her death. She just died because it was her time.

Darius's face hardened again. Ever since that card had appeared on the doormat a few days ago, he had known he would need to explain everything to Tink. In the three months they'd known each other, he'd found it was never her way to probe, to make claims or judgements. He admired that about her and contrasted it with his own obsessional nature. He was always imposing himself, making himself a part of every situation. Tink never did that. She had a lightness about her, an ethereal disconnection which was attractive because it was instinctive. But he'd known at some point, he'd have to tell her about it. About Down There, about everything that happened. It's just that he hadn't realised he would have to confront it all so soon.

– No, it wasn't that. I wasn't caught dealing.

He hesitated for a moment, then he carried on.

– It was manslaughter, he said. I went to prison for manslaughter, Tink. I killed someone.

Chapter Eleven

Felicity was driving the car at walking pace. She had applied her own blackout paint onto the headlamps the previous day after instructions from one of the Air Raid Wardens in Marlow, and the two thin pencils of light were scarcely visible in front of her on the road. Occasionally she glimpsed another set of weak lights coming the other way as a car passed her, but her attention was fixed on the road, as she did her best to avoid the rubble and the craters. Even with the windows tightly shut, the acrid smell of burning was almost unbearable.

– Can I stop for a minute? she said, turning to the uniformed policeman beside her. I need to...

– No ma'am, you must keep going. The next raid could start at any time. We need to get you to safety.

The policeman had stopped her as she had entered Plymouth an hour before. As soon as he found out she was the wife of one of the city's MPs, Sir Zachary Frome, he insisted on travelling with her to direct her to the hotel where her husband was staying.

She had only decided yesterday on the spur of the moment to drive down. Zachary had cabled the day before, saying he would not be able to come back to the Range for a second week running.

– MUST REMAIN. DUTY INSISTS. PEOPLE SUFFERING UNBEARABLY. LOOK AFTER RICHARD.

It was that request which had prompted her to act. It had sounded so final and somehow, after all the weeks and months of living on the edge, of holding everything together back at the Range, it had felt like too much. She needed to be with her husband. She couldn't bear the thought of him being hit by a bomb, of losing him forever. It was impossible. Her mother and father were staying with her and did their best to persuade her not to go.

– What about the child? her mother had wailed the day before. What if...

But her father had interrupted his wife.

– Leave her be, Mother, he had said firmly. We've said our piece, but Felicity must do what she thinks is right. We'll look after Richard and she will be back in no time. You bring that husband back with you, he's running himself into the ground down there in Plymouth.

Now, as she carefully turned a corner in the dark, she wondered whether she had made a terrible mistake in coming. She hadn't realised how far west Plymouth was – the journey from the Range had taken her over five hours. They were in the centre now and the devastation was appalling. Peering out through the window, she could see that they were driving down whole streets whose houses had been flattened by the bombing. Piles of rubble lay either side of them, cleared to keep the road open. Everywhere, the smell of ash and cordite and sometimes the strong smell of rotting, so powerful it made her gag.

– Not a welcome sight, ma'am, said the policeman, who must have sensed her horror.

– I had no idea, she said softly. I had no idea it was like this.

– We've taken an awful punishing.

As he said that, the relative quiet was suddenly broken by the rising tone of an air raid siren, quickly assuming a deafening wail which was so loud she couldn't hear the words that were coming out of his mouth. Then he grabbed the wheel and leaned close to her.

– Stop the car! he shouted. We must take cover.

Felicity was so frightened she let the car stall with a jerk. The policeman was already out of his side, and he quickly appeared at her open door.

– Now! he shouted, and pulled at her arm.

She let him lead her in the dark. She could hear foot-steps ahead and the sound of a child crying, then shouts from across the street. He dragged her past a building whose windows were all blown out and she caught sight of a scared face.

– There's someone in there, she cried.

He paused.

– Where?

– In that house. She pointed back to the house they had just passed. The deafening siren still rose up and down but then she also heard something else: the awful familiar engine drone of bombers.

He ran to the window.

– How many of you in there? he shouted. You need to get to the shelter.

– Waitin' for my mum, she said she'd be back. It was the voice of a child.

– Come out with us, we'll take you.

– Can't. Door is jammed. Bomb hit us last night.

Felicity looked at the front door which was twisted and blackened.

– Come to the window, I'll get you, the policeman yelled.

Suddenly a terrific explosion burst behind them and everything was lit up in a flash. The noise seemed to fill her head, her entire body. Immediately too, the crashing sound of masonry and then as she looked behind her, a sheet of flame leaped across the street about fifty yards away where the bomb had hit.

– Now! screamed the policeman.

Felicity turned back to the window and saw a little girl's terrified face. She shouted in the policeman's ear:

– Lift me up and I can reach her.

Without answering, he grabbed her by the waist and hoisted her up. Felicity reached out her arms and caught the little girl's fingers. She pulled and the girl came closer, then she managed to grab hold of her by the armpits and dragged her through the open window. As she set her down on the

73

pavement, which was illuminated orange and yellow now, another blast further down the street almost knocked her off her feet. The policeman lifted the child onto his shoulder and took hold of Felicity's hand, dragging her away from the roar behind them.

As she stumbled after him, she turned and was horrified by the sight: writhing sheets of orange flame and black smoke pouring out of a shattered house. She could see her car already with a fire burning inside it, yellow tongues licking the front window.

She felt the pull of the policeman's hand as they rounded a corner. Above the cacophony of siren, bomber engines, screams and shouts, the roar of flames and the crash of buildings collapsing, he yelled in her ear:

– There is a church down here, St Saviour's. We can go there. They won't touch a church, surely.

Now as the night was lit up by flame, Felicity could see occasional figures running down the street. She looked at the girl he was carrying and did her best to smile at her – the girl stared at her in silent fear. Overhead, she glimpsed a flash of metal and she realised a plane was flying quite low. Then suddenly there was a crackle of machine gun fire and bullets began to ricochet off the road's surface. She looked up again and just for a moment, she saw the face of a German fighter pilot behind his glass screen. He seemed so close she could almost reach out and touch him.

– He's firing at us! she screamed.

The policeman called out something and stumbled. He fell to the floor, the little girl landing on top of him. Felicity bent down and lifted her off him.

– Are you hurt? she shouted.

He shook his head, but reached down to his leg.

– Just my leg, he yelled. Caught one in my leg.

There was a terrific roar as the fighter plane swept over their heads.

– He'll come back. We must keep moving, the policeman shouted.

Felicity held the little girl tightly, pressed her face against the girl's ear.

– Don't be frightened, she said. I'll look after you.

Then she held out a hand:

– Pull yourself up on my hand, she called. Quickly.

He grabbed hold of her, cried in pain as he stood up, then they continued on their way, Felicity clutching his arm as he limped beside her.

– The church, he said, a little more weakly now. It's round this corner.

But as they turned the corner, another sheet of flame was ahead of them, this time pouring out of the windows of the church. Smoke was beginning to billow out too and the wind blew the black stinging vapours into their faces. The girl began to cry.

– Not the church! Not the bloody church! the policeman cried despairingly.

– Won't they bring fire engines? she said.

He shook his head.

– Not while the raid is on. Not while the sirens are sounding. No-one is allowed out.

He stared at the flames coming out of the church window across the street.

– Damn them, he said. Damn them to hell.

Then a voice called out from further down the street.

– You there! Get out of here. Get to the shelter.

– He's been shot in the leg, Felicity cried out. And we have a child. Can you help?

She heard running footsteps then two figures emerged from the smoke. One was in uniform, the other had a belted raincoat and Felicity saw the glint of a bald head.

– Are you badly hurt? the uniformed man barked at the policeman.

– No sir. Just my right leg above the knee sir.

The other came to reach for the child. As he came close, Felicity saw it was Zachary. When he saw her, he stopped.

– Felicity? What in God's name are you doing here?

75

His face was suddenly illuminated by the glare of flames from across the street and she could see a mixture of shock and anger on his face. His cheeks were smeared with black and a cut above his eye was bleeding.

– No time for that, sir, shouted the uniformed man. Can you take the child, ma'am?

Felicity nodded, and squeezed the girl slightly

– She's fine with me. Help him, she said.

Both men got either side of the policeman and, half-lifting him off the ground, they began to run down the street away from the burning church. Felicity followed immediately behind.

– The shelter is at the bottom of this street, Zachary called out. Can you keep up Felicity?

– Yes, we're right behind you, she shouted. Keep going.

There was another sudden roar of engines as the fighter plane flew back over their heads but the pilot must not have seen them as the machine guns remained quiet. Instinctively Felicity ducked, clutching the child's head to her chest. Ahead of her, the three men had reached a set of railings and were beginning to ease the policeman down the steps. As they reached the door, Zachary turned round and held his arms out for Felicity to pass the little girl to him.

Inside, the shelter was illuminated by candles flickering on several tables. The curved roof glistened with condensation and every space seemed filled with people. There was a low murmur of conversation, the sound of a baby crying somewhere. It was hot and humid with so many people in there, and Felicity couldn't help herself from swallowing hard as the smell hit her.

– Get that door shut! a man's gruff voice shouted from the back.

She nodded apologetically and pulled the door tight behind her. Zachary was standing in the middle of the room.

– We have an injured man here, he called out. Do we have a doctor here?

– I'm no doctor but I'll take a look at him, an old man said.

– He's taken a bullet in his leg, Zachary said as the old man came over.

– I've seen worse than that on the trawlers, the man said. Lay him down, let's get a tourniquet on him. He'll be all right.

– Does anyone know this little girl? Zachary called out again, holding the child aloft.

– That's Phyllis Porter's girl, a woman said.

– Where is she? Zachary demanded.

– Pass the girl to me, Mr Frome, the woman said. I'll care for her.

She came over and as she took the child, who was still-speechless with fear, she whispered something in Zachary's ear. He looked back at her, his face expressionless, then he laid a hand on her shoulder.

– God bless her, he said quietly.

– What about the church, Mr Frome? another voice called out. Can't you do something?

He shook his head.

– Not yet, I'm afraid. One of those swine is up there firing his gun, it's too dangerous. The fire engines will be here when the All Clear is called. We'll have to wait.

– It's not right, Mr Frome, the voice continued. Our lads don't bomb their churches, do they? They took St Andrew's last week, and now it's St Saviour's. I reckon as they're proper devils, them Nazis.

Felicity watched her husband as he continued to speak to various people in the shelter. They all knew him, and she was touched by the way they all called him Mr Frome. That would have been his doing, she thought. He had told her he didn't want to lay attention on his title in his dealings with his constituents.

Then she felt a flash of anger. What had he been doing out there during the air raid? She had made him promise that he would always seek shelter during the raids, that he wouldn't put himself at risk. And there he had been, out with a soldier in the street with bombs falling around them and a Messerschmitt strafing the ground. Was this what he was doing every night?

She saw him stand up across the other side and look towards her. For a second they stared at each other, then he strode over and took her arm, guiding her back towards the closed door where there was a little space free of other people.

– The girl, Felicity said. Have they found her mother?

Zachary shook his head.

– The girl is now an orphan, he said bitterly. He looked at her. Where did you find her?

– She was trapped in her house round the corner. We got her out through a broken window. What happened to her mother?

– She was down the road at a neighbour's, borrowing some milk. Direct hit.

He bit his lip, and she could see suddenly the depth of exhaustion in his face. The cut above his eye was dry now but she could see it had bled. She put her arms around his neck and pulled him to her. They held each other close for a few seconds and she could feel him shaking slightly. She held on to him until he was calm, then they looked at each other again.

– Why are you here? he asked, simply. Is there trouble?

She shook her head.

– I just couldn't bear not being with you, she said.

He too shook his head.

– It was not right, Felicity, he said quietly. You can see what it's like. You must promise me you will return tomorrow and stay at the Range until all this is over. You must promise me that.

– Only if you promise me to take more care, she said. Why were you out there? You said you wouldn't.

He shrugged, as though at the end of his strength.

– It is so hard for them, he said. They need all the help they can get. They are down on numbers and there are not enough people to patrol and make sure everyone gets off the streets. They get scared, he continued. They get scared and make mistakes, forget where the shelter is. I have to help them.

– Then I won't leave you, she said fiercely. I won't go back. If you won't promise me, then I will stay with you. I cannot live without you, Zachary. Don't you understand that?

– What about Richard? he said. Where is he?

– He's fine, he's with my mother and father at the Range.

– You must go to him tomorrow, he repeated. Your place is with him.

– I won't. He is safe. If we die, Zachary, he will survive. My parents will care for him. But I will leave you to this awful fate. I would rather die with you.

He took her hands.

– We are not going to die, he said. There is too much that must be done. Look at these people, he said, turning to look back into the cramped shelter. They deserve a better world. It is our duty to bring them that world.

– Then promise me, she insisted. Promise me. You cannot save everyone, Zachary. You can do so much more for these people if you keep yourself safe. Then you can build them that better world. Who will do that if a bomb takes you? Who will look after them then?

He stared at her in silence for a moment, then he nodded.

– If I promise, will you go back tomorrow? I will be back at the weekend.

– I will.

He touched her cheek gently.

– I promise I will not leave you, he said softly. I love you too much for that, my dear Felicity.

Part Two

Chapter Twelve

– Darius, how many times must I tell you, please take your filthy shoes off the breakfast table. It's disgusting.

Francis sniggered.

– Yes, Mother, Darius replied sarcastically. Taking what seemed like an age, the boy eased his legs off the edge of the long wooden table in the kitchen. They were clad in faded jeans with what looked like oil stains on them, his feet shod in heavy black leather boots.

– Farguckarging bargitch, Darius muttered at his older brother, who grinned.

– And stop using that ridiculous language, it's extremely childish. You're sixteen years old, Darius, you're not a baby any more.

– No, Mother.

Violet pursed her lips and shook her head in an irritated way as she bustled about the kitchen.

– I have a lot to do today, Darius, and I would appreciate it if you would consider getting yourself to school. Your grandmother will be down soon and she won't be impressed if you are late again.

– Nana doesn't care, said Darius. She's all right.

– Of course she's all right, she's your grandmother. And she does care. And so do I, and so does your father. How are you going to get to university like Francis if you keep being late for school?

– No idea, yawned Darius.

His mother sighed.

– Francis darling, please do something about your brother.

Francis laughed.

– He's a force of nature, Mum. You know that.

Darius bit into another piece of toast, and raised his middle finger at his brother. His long dark hair curled on the shoulders of a white T-shirt, his tanned brown arms muscly. By now, this morning altercation with his mother, Lady Violet Frome, had become such a routine that he scarcely noticed it. He had long realised that his nature, his very being, somehow offended the sensibilities of the very organised, the very determined, Violet Frome. Her role as lady of the house, of wife to ex Labour MP and now editor of the prestigious Sunday Chronicle Sir Richard Frome, gave her a complete sense of purpose. The Range was run with precision, and his refusal to follow compliantly in the footsteps of his academically excelling brother was a source of continued irritation to her.

He watched her as she put on spectacles and began writing a list on a thick white kitchen notepad, no doubt organising another remarkable evening for the good and the great of the Left. His mother was celebrated within the Party as a great hostess; future Labour ministers were identified and encouraged at her dinner table, others not so fortunate in their reception given a chilly dismissal. Darius was permanently expelled from these gatherings, for fear of spoiling her stage. He couldn't care less. He turned to look at his brother.

– So is the girlfriend coming today, then? he asked him.

– I think so, said Francis. She was going to phone the house before she gets the train. She's bringing a friend.

– What? said Violet from the other side of the room. You didn't tell me Belinda was bringing a friend, Francis.

– Didn't I, Mum? Sorry. She's called Annabel. She's nice. She's reading English at Kings.

– I'm sure she's very nice, if she's a friend of Belinda's. You just might have warned me. I'll have to get another bedroom ready. She eats meat, I hope. I've ordered the food for the weekend now.

– You've never even met Belinda, Mum, said Darius. How do you know her friend's nice? They might both be complete cows.

Francis threw a crust at his brother.

– Wargankarger, he said.

– Oh for God's sake, don't encourage him, Francis, said Violet. Darius, for the last time, please go to school.

– How come you get such stupidly long summer holidays? Darius asked his brother. Do they run out of things to teach you at Cambridge?

– We're expected to read, you little oik. Books. You've probably never seen one.

– Does Belinda read books? Darius replied. I bet she does. Dirty ones, probably.

– Shut up Darius, said Violet.

The kitchen door opened, and Felicity shuffled into the room. Violet rushed over and took the old lady's arm.

– Felicity, you should have waited for me to help you down. You know those stairs are getting harder for you.

– Morning Nana, Darius called out. I'm just off to school. The family genius here is preparing for another day of leisure.

He stood up and came over to the two women, gently kissed the old lady's lined cheek. She smiled at him, the bright red lipstick glinting.

– Good boy, she said softly.

– Later, Darius called out to the room, as he slipped past his grandmother and out of the door.

He walked down the long, white-walled corridor, pushed open a door at the end and gathered up an old leather bag that was lying on the floor of the octagonal hallway. He pulled out a Walkman, pressed headphones into his ears, and Oasis hammered into his head as he pulled the massive front door open.

Darius cut straight across the clipped lawns heading up towards the main gates. He had no particular plans for the day, certainly no intention of getting the bus into school in Marlow. Fuck that. Once he was out of sight of the house, he set his bag down again beside one of the elms bordering the driveway and rummaged for tobacco and papers.

As he licked the adhesive side of one of the Rizzlas and began to lay out the origami of a new joint, he wondered what his brother Francis's Cambridge women would be like. He tipped tobacco onto the white paper, then dug into his jeans pocket for a small ball of tin foil. He undid the package and lit a lighter beneath the brown resin, sprinkling crumbs of grass on top of the tobacco.

Stuck up, inevitably. Patronising, probably. Francis had just finished his first year at Cambridge, and was of course doing well. Darius twisted the paper at the end of the joint, put the other end into his mouth and lit it. He pulled the sweet-smelling smoke deep into his lungs, closed his eyes and felt the fumes swirl inside of him. After a few seconds, he exhaled, the stream of smoke hovering in front of him before it dissipated into the summer morning air.

Secretly, Darius was proud of his older brother's academic success. It pleased him. Francis was a dork, a swot. He excelled in a world which held no interest for Darius, so he supposed this girlfriend, Belinda, and her chum she was apparently bringing – they'd be prim, plain, frumpy girls, all swooning about his brother's intelligence.

He smiled as he took another toke from the joint. Oh Francis, you're so clever, they'd say. Why can't you be more like your brother, Darius, his mother would say, beaming at her favourite older boy. Jesus. It was going to be sick-making. He'd need to keep out of the way as much as he could. There was a party in Marlow this weekend, he could stay over there. There was that new girl who'd started in school, the redhead. She was cool. Maybe she'd be there. He'd spotted her giving him the eye earlier in the week.

He needed more gear, particularly if he was going to escape to the party. He felt in the top pocket of his denim jacket, and pulled out some notes. Seventy quid. Not bad.

But he'd sold most of his Mary Jane in school this week, so he'd need to get up to London today to get more.

You're My Wonderwall, Liam wailed into his headphones. He pulled again on the joint. The guy in Denmark Street last week had offered him acid as well as dope, but he hadn't had enough money last week. He had more today. Acid might be fun. See what that redhead made of that.

School was finishing for the summer soon. Two months of freedom. He was planning to head to Biarritz with some of his mates, two months of surf freedom, two months away from this ridiculous stately home. Maybe this time he wouldn't come back. Maybe he could find some work when he was out there and stay on beyond the season. Something outside, be a gardener or something. And go surfing. Why not? What was to keep him here? They'd probably be relieved, his father would send him the odd bit of pocket money just to make sure he stayed away. There was nothing to keep him here.

He was sixteen years' old. It wasn't his fault he'd been born into a family he didn't recognise. A dynasty, more like. Francis was well placed to continue the Frome dynasty. He could take the baton, go into politics after Cambridge, continue the family name. It wasn't anything to do with him. His friend Dave at school said to him once that he reckoned he'd been swapped by accident in the hospital where he'd been born.

– Somewhere in Marlow right now, mate, there's a fucking confused kid with not much hair and thick glasses who's grown up wondering what he's doing with a bodybuilder dad and bar lush mum. You'll be reunited one day.

The image of Felicity came into this head as he stubbed out the remains of the joint on the grass. Smiling sadly at him, her red lipstick and her watery eyes, her white hair pulled back from her forehead.

– I know, Nana, he said out loud, standing up. I know. I can't help it. You know that. I just don't fit in here, Nana.

One day, he'd get away. There was a world out there, a

world filled with pleasure and pain, a world to explore.

He picked up his bag and carried on walking up the grass parklands until he reached the stone gatehouse. He pulled open the iron gate, closed it behind him as he left. He walked down the road a while, then turned left into a narrow lane. After a few minutes, he struck up into some woods and soon found the clearing where he kept his motorbike.

Felicity sat at the breakfast table. She had bought the table as a surprise for Zachary one year, was it 1938? She couldn't remember. It was all such a long time ago. Everything was such a long time ago.

She looked at her hands holding the mug of tea. Blue veins stood out over her dry, white skin. Her crimson nail varnish was chipped. She smiled. She would never have allowed that to happen before.

I really don't give a shit, she thought, and the idea of the word made her smile again. I sound like Darius, she thought.

– Visitors today Felicity, Violet called out brightly and slightly too loudly as she bustled around the kitchen. Francis's new girlfriend Belinda is arriving. Apparently she's bringing a nice friend called Annabel. Reading English at Kings. You'll have to tell her about your books.

Why did Violet always shout?

– That's nice, my dear, said Felicity, looking up at her daughter-in-law. Her voice was soft and a little quavering. Are they staying long?

– I hadn't really asked, Violet called back, crashing a saucepan down onto the Aga. At least a week, I'd have thought. Francis says they've all got huge reading lists to get through. He's doing so well at Magdalen, isn't he? Got a First in his end of year exams, did he tell you? Zachary would have been so proud of him, don't you think?

– Of course he would, Felicity answered, yet more softly.

Next week, it would be twelve years since Zachary died. Oh my darling, she thought. I miss you so. I just keep on plodding on here, I don't seem to get any closer to joining you. Why did I have to be so damned healthy? Forty five years together, we had. She had read in the Sunday newspaper about a couple who had just celebrated their 75th wedding anniversary and she had instantly felt cheated, as though some malevolent being had torn thirty years from her, thirty years she should have had with her husband.

The kitchen door opened, and Richard Frome entered, the ceiling lights making his bald domed head sparkle as he walked over towards Felicity.

– Morning Mum, he said, leaning down to kiss her cheek. What is it? Why are you crying?

– I'm not, don't be silly, Felicity said, wiping her eyes with the sleeve of her dressing gown. It's this lovely hot tea that Violet has made me, it always makes my foolish old eyes water at first.

– Oh, said Richard, and sat down at the head of the table. Well, it looks like it's going to be John Smith, he said, spreading out the newspapers in front of him.

– I know, I just wish he wasn't so bloody Scottish, said Violet, as she poured more tea from the pot.

– He's the best we've got, Richard said. Kinnock blew it, even he knows that. Better a dour Scot than a Welsh windbag, eh Mum?

– It all passes me by these days dear, said Felicity.

– We need someone with the broad appeal to take down Major, her son continued, taking the mug of tea set down by his wife. Smith has the merit of being steady, the public might warm to that after all those Kinnock mishaps.

– John Major won last time because women fancy him, said Felicity. He's got a very saucy look in his eyes, you know. Not safe in taxis, we used to say.

Richard looked up at his mother, the lights glinting on the lenses of his glasses.

– Sometimes I just don't know when you're joking, Mum, he said, then turned back to his newspapers.

All the time, she thought. I'm joking all the time these days. Roll up, roll up. Come and and see the circus freak, come and watch Felicity Drummond pretend to be an old lady. Laughs in it for everyone. Oh dear, she thought. Pull yourself together, Felicity. Can't start the day like this.

– Will he make a good PM, dear, this Smith?

Violet interjected from the other side of the room.

– He's solid, Felicity, that's what Richard thinks. It's the only way for us to get back into power, convince the public we're a serious alternative to that John Major that you find so attractive. You've met him anyway, he's been here for dinner at least twice. Nice man. Likes hill climbing, I think. Probably all Scottish people do.

– It's all rather a long way from Level Ground, though, isn't it? Felicity continued, looking at her son. All this focus on power, I mean. Not so much talk about what's going to be done with that power. What does he believe in, this Smith?

Richard looked up at his mother.

– Come on Mum, he said. Even you can't take Dad's career as a lesson in how to introduce change. Level Ground lost the 1945 election, remember? Lost every seat they challenged, apart from Dad of course.

– I know, dear, but we lost it talking about ideals, about the need for change, passionate ideas about the common ownership of land and the end of unemployment. Not about who would make the voters feel the most comfortable.

– Level Ground got wiped out in 1945 because people didn't want what it offered, Mum, her son objected, taking off his glasses and rubbing them. We're trying to create a new politics here, a real alternative to the Thatcher years. Smith's a good man, he's a lawyer and he's Scottish, but apart from that he's a man of principle I think. He's fair and he's decent. He can win an election. That's what counts. It's got to be about the race for power.

The race for power. Felicity sipped her tea while her son went back to reading the newspapers. How Zachary would have shuddered at that phrase. It wasn't that she didn't admire her son's determination. In a way, it was even more admirable that he had devoted so much of his career to rebuilding the Labour party after the 1979 election. Callaghan's loss had been Richard's too, losing his own seat after just five years as an MP. She knew it was the bitterest blow he had suffered. He was a good man, he had been so proud the night of his election, looking out into the hall at Zachary and her as the Returning Officer announced his victory. Then just five short years as an MP before Margaret Thatcher's victory swept away so many Labour seats, including her son's. Poor Zachary had passed away the year after. Richard never had much of a chance to prove to his father what he might do, what he was capable of. She knew how that sat with him. He had been editor of the *Chronicle* for seven years now, and she knew that the Labour party thought very highly of him. She wasn't blind to all the dinners and drinks that he and Violet held here. Her son had forged a role for himself as kingmaker in the party, it seemed to please him.

She reached over and laid her thin, feathery hand on her son's.

– Daddy would have understood it all much better than me, dear, she said. I'm sure you're right.

– It's time for new people anyway, Violet called out loudly. There'll be another general election in five years, and Francis will be three years out of Cambridge by then. It's his generation who will move things forward. We've got to get behind them, encourage them to be ambitious, to make plans. There's really no time to lose.

– Does Francis want to become an MP too? Felicity asked.

– Of course he does, Felicity, Violet said. He's running for President of the Union next year. He told you about it all the other night. Don't you remember? And he's already Chair of the Cambridge Students Labour party. He's an excellent speaker. He's a real Frome.

– Sorry dear, I forget so many things these days. That's wonderful. He's such a clever boy.

Politics ran through the Frome family like a river. Now

Francis, thought Felicity. Another generation at Westminster. She supposed it was all for the good. Francis was a good boy. So different to his brother, of course. Darius, she worried so much about Darius. He had such a good heart, but so impetuous. So headstrong. She didn't want him to be like Francis, as Violet kept nagging him in her unrelenting way. She loved the very essence of Darius, she could see the romantic side of Zachary so clearly in him, in his love of nature particularly. No, let Francis be Francis and let Darius find his own path. She must be supportive of his brother's ambition.

It was just that... Her mind wandered back to those wartime summer days in the garden, all those exciting meetings, the pamphlets, the radio broadcasts. The Range had been a powerhouse of change, a meeting point for so many idealists, so many wonderful people who all came to hear Zachary, her darling Zachary, talk about the future, about how Level Ground was winning more and more support across the country for his vision of a new postwar world of equality. She couldn't imagine Francis speaking like that. He seemed to her – what was it? – he seemed to have no fire in his belly. That was how she saw it. He seemed cold.

Oh Zachary, she whispered to herself. That was our time. It's all gone, and you're gone and I'm still here. Foolish old Felicity.

She lowered her head and sipped her tea.

Satisfied with the fresh supply now at the bottom of his leather bag, Darius steered the Honda out of Soho and down Piccadilly heading west. It was three o'clock, it would be four by the time he got back home. They would think he'd been at school, and anyway they'd all be fussing about Francis's girl and her friend. He planned to call in and show his face, then sneak Down There, roll some joints.

There was rugby training tonight at the Marlow rugby club down by the river. He might make it. Darius was strong and big for his age, and he had played in the first XV for the school team for the last year. It gave him additional cachet at school, both with the girls and with the teachers when he failed to turn up for yet another lesson. He liked the cama-raderie of the rugby field, and the brutality of the game was an excellent antidote to the thin intellectualism of the Frome homelife.

As he got on to the dual carriageway at Chiswick round-about and speeded up, he thought again about the summer. It was the 20th of June today, school would be done in a fortnight. Only two more weeks before he could escape. It would be his first proper trip. He'd done summers down in Cornwall before, originally with his parents around, then just with friends staying in tents at Newquay. This trip to Biarritz though, it felt to him as though this was going to be the start of his new life, his life away from the Range, from all the nonsense.

He didn't articulate what it was he wanted, he just knew that he was suffocating at home. He didn't resent Francis's popularity – he didn't want the life that Francis wanted. Francis would be successful, he would become an MP like his dad and grandpa. He would take over the Range even-tually, he'd install some ideal wife and when their dad died he would become Sir Francis Frome. He laughed into the wind as he swerved the bike to overtake a van. Sir Francis fucking Frome.

All Darius knew was that he didn't want any of it. He wanted to be like those knights that his Nana had read stories to him about when he was a kid, the ones who had wandered the world in search of the Holy Grail. He wanted to be challenged, but he also knew that he had an affinity with the natural world which was stronger than the lure of any kind of academic or business life. He was at one with himself outside, in the woods, on the rugby field, in the water.

By the time he'd hidden the bike in the woods and walked back home, it was four thirty. He could hear voices coming from the sitting room, so first he crept upstairs to his bedroom to hide the stash. He kept some papers and tobacco and a ball of the resin in the pocket of his jeans, then came back downstairs. He walked quietly past the closed door of the sitting room and headed down another corridor towards the back of the house.

– Darius! his mother called out. Is that you out there? Come and be sociable.

The sitting room door opened and his mother appeared at the far end of the corridor.

– Where are you going, Darius? Come and say hello to Belinda and Annabel.

– For fuck's sake, he muttered to himself. OK Mum, he said, turning back. But I've got to get over to the club soon, rugby training is earlier today.

– Just come and show yourself for a minute, Violet insisted. She ushered him into the room. The sitting room at the front of the house was huge, with a grouping of sofas and chairs in the middle around the enormous stone fireplace with its outlandish bursts of crystal glass spreading out above the mantlepiece. This was the room his Nana had told him once was the first she ever saw in the Range – it had been used by his grandfather as his study when he lived in the house alone. Darius walked over and kissed his grandmother's cheek.

– Hello Nana, he said.

– Hello dear, good day at school? Felicity touched his cheek, smiling at him.

– Dull as fuck Nana, he whispered, grinning.

– Stop whispering, Darius and come and say hello to Francis's friends, his mother called out.

He stood up and looked across at the sofa the other side of the low table.

– This is Annabel, said his mother, pointing at a blonde, pretty girl wearing jeans. She looked up and smiled at him, but his father was in the middle of a conversation with her.

– And this is Belinda, his mother continued.

He looked at the other sofa. Belinda was talking to his brother. She looked up as Darius walked over.

– Hi, he said.

– Hello, said Belinda. Your brother was just talking about you.

He looked into her dark brown eyes. She was smiling, and he noticed how her cheeks created a tiny dimple on either side of her lips. Her dark hair was thick and glossy. She held his gaze.

– I wouldn't believe any of it, Darius said. Francis is an idiot.

Belinda laughed, her tongue touching the top of her white teeth. Darius looked at his brother.

– Nargeot bargead, he said.

– Moron, said Francis.

Darius stayed for a few minutes more, hovering on the edge of the animated conversations, before he repeated his need to head over to Marlow rugby club.

– Back later, he said over his shoulder as he walked back out into the octagonal hallway. He shut the heavy front door behind him, then turned immediately right to walk along the long front of the Range, turning the corner at the end to walk to the back of the house. Soon he was edging into the narrow gap in the thick hedgerow at the back, and then he slowly picked his way down the path.

After a while, he emerged into that familiar patch of grass, bounded on all sides by the untamed undergrowth. It was still only late afternoon, there were several hours of sunlight left in the day and as he walked over to the stone plinth in the middle, he could see the glint of the moving Thames through the trees. The rowing boat was tied up to the bank underneath the drooping branches of one of the willows and he could use that to cross the river in a little while to the rugby club which was over on the other side on the edge of Marlow.

He scrambled up onto the top of the plinth and pulled out the tobacco and papers and resin. Sitting cross-legged, he patiently rolled a joint.

It was years ago that Nana had told him about Down

There. Maybe when he was ten. It turned out that Francis, being three years older than him, already knew about it – their father had told him. Neither of them seemed particularly interested in it, and neither of them visited it as far as he knew. It had become his own space. His father was dismissive:

– Oh it was one of your grandfather's many eccentricities, he said, when Darius questioned him once. He said it was where he got all his ideas. Probably why they came to nothing. Not grounded in the real world, poor old Dad.

That wasn't how Nana had described Down There. To her, it was a sacred place, and the first time she took the young boy down the steep, winding path, she held his hand and every so often looked at him with a mixture of excitement and awe. They had walked slowly, as she told him she no longer had the energy to make the trip very often.

– I discovered it myself by accident, when I first moved here after your grandfather and I were married, she said. I try and keep the path clear, but it gets more and more difficult every year. If you like it too, perhaps you can help me keep the path cut, dear.

As Darius inhaled deeply sitting now on the plinth, he remembered that first time six years ago when he and Nana had finally emerged from the path into the clearing. It was a defining moment. The sudden impact of this strange enclosed space seemed to take over his entire being – it was overwhelming to the boy. He almost felt an urge to cry, but little Darius had already learned by then about being brave, and he just kept hold of his Nana's hand as they stood quietly, taking in the silent mystery of Down There.

It was as though they had passed through to another country, another world even. A world where none of the rules and rituals of the Range applied. This was a world stripped bare of all human artifice – this was pure Nature. Standing there beside his Nana, he had felt in awe of everything around him: the trees, the grass, the birds calling one another, the river flowing endlessly and heavily in front of them. This was a magical place where Nature held sway. Gloomy, still, deep shades of green and brown, the strength of the bordering branches and foliage, the smell of the leaves – everything combined into one single impression. He understood it instantly.

As he began to prepare a second joint, Darius paused for a moment, still cross-legged on the plinth. He shut his eyes and felt the occasional whisper of the breeze on his face. He could hear the gentle lapping of the water and he could smell the faint moisture in the air which was the dew preparing to arrive. He breathed deeply and felt himself disappear into it all.

What or where did he disappear into? He never knew and he had never really analysed it; he didn't have any reference points, Down There just exerted its influence upon him as he suspected it had done on his grandfather and on Nana. There was definitely a sense of removal, of travel to another place, but beyond that, he had been unable to create much sense out of it. All he knew was that the place he visited in his head was more real to him than most of the rest of his life.

After a while, he shook his head, ran his hand through his long dark hair, rubbed his face with his hands. It was time to head off. He jumped off the plinth and walked over to the edge where the old rowing boat nestled into the bank. He undid the rope which was tied to an exposed tree root and pushed out through the screen of willow branches.

Darius always loved that moment, emerging from the hidden spot into the wide flat silence of the Thames. It was impossible to see anything of Down There from the river itself because of the tree cover: the stretch of waterfront which constituted the limits of the Range estate appeared to be impenetrable, made up entirely of thick undergrowth. He pulled on the oars, and slipped quietly across the water. As he looked back, he could see the manicured lawns on either side of the Range's wild stretch of woodland, the neighbouring houses having been built on the traditional

Thames principles of facing onto the river. Only the odd geography of the Range with its steep slope and the cussedness of his great-grandfather in commissioning Lutyens to build at the top of the hill looking away from the river explained the continued hidden secrecy of Down There.

He rowed slowly. The sun was still quite high over to his right. He was alone on the river and the oars creaked on the rollocks as he pulled. Two swans were drifting downstream to his left towards the island where an old man still lived on his own in a rundown shack. The current was strong, and he had to pull hard and keep in a diagonal direction across the river to make sure he kept on course for the bank opposite. The rugby club was on the eastern outskirts of Marlow and the pitches ran almost down to the river – Darius was not always the only one to arrive by rowing boat, but this evening he had the Thames to himself.

The surface of the water had begun to glow like bronze, the lines of current sculpting patterns that twisted and flowed all around him. A splash over to one side as a fish took a fly. Beneath him, beneath the planks of the old rowing boat, he felt the presence of the living water, the waving reeds embedded in the mud, the submerged ancient life of the river. This he would miss, when he left. None of the rest of it, but this – Down There, the woods, the mysterious river – this would always be a part of him.

He guided the boat towards an old landing stage, tied up and headed off towards the playing fields. He could see a few figures already on the pitch. Late again. He began to trot towards the brick changing rooms.

The following day was Friday, and Darius dutifully turned up to school. He had learned just how far he could stretch the school's patience in terms of playing truant, and where possible he tried to avoid his Father being summoned for yet another lecture in the headmaster's office.

He spent most of the day with his friends, discussing the party that was due on Saturday night. At one point he caught the eye of the red-headed girl.

– Hi, he said. My name's Darius. You're new here, aren't you?

She nodded.

– You coming to the party tomorrow night?

– Might be.

– Cool, said Darius. I'm bringing treats.

She laughed.

– I heard, she said.

I bet you haven't heard about the acid, though, he thought. He'd only confided about his new cache to one person, his closest friend Dave, who played with him in the first XV. Dave had grinned.

– You absolute nutter, he'd said.

That evening, he was under strict instructions to be home for dinner. His mother had spent the day preparing a feast in honour of Francis's friends. An hour after he'd got back from school, Darius was smoking a quick joint, his head poked out of his bedroom window overlooking the back of the house, Kraftwerk pounding relentlessly from the speakers. He had already ignored one yell from downstairs for him to come down. Now his bedroom door burst open and his brother marched in.

– Jesus, Darius, he said, shaking his head and walking over to the amplifier to turn the music down.

Darius took one last draw on the joint, then stubbed it out on the window ledge.

– Didn't you hear Mum calling? asked Francis, irritably. It's dinner.

– I was coming, said Darius.

– Amazing they haven't smelled that stuff, said his brother. How many have you had?

– Oh for Christ's sake, Francis.

– Christ's sake nothing. You're rotting your fucking brain, you idiot.

Darius smiled. Although he was three years younger than Francis, he was taller than him, and his long dark hair hanging off his shoulders emphasised the difference between them. Francis stood with his hands on his hips, his neat haircut framing his angry, glaring face.

Now Darius laughed.

– Chill out brother Francis, he said. You're looking tense as fuck. You should be chilled. That Belinda, she's cute.

– Shut up.

– Have you?

Francis reddened slightly, then marched back out of the door.

– I'm coming, I'm coming, said Darius, still laughing. He hasn't, he thought. The silly sod hasn't even touched her.

Dinner was held in the main dining room, which lay beyond the sitting room at the front of the house. Another huge low-ceilinged Lutyens room, it contained a long mahogany table which was an original from the birth of the house in 1904. Violet had asked one of their cleaners, a young girl from the village called Katie, to stay on for the evening to help serve the dinner, and she was now passing out plates to everyone.

– Where's Nana? asked Darius, as he took his seat. His brother had already sat down, and the only space left was opposite him, next to Belinda.

– She's too tired today, she's gone to bed early, his mother called out as she carried over a bowl of roast potatoes from the sideboard. His father was carving a huge joint of lamb at the head of the table. Annabel had the seat next to him.

– She is a fascinating lady, your mother, she said to Richard. I spoke to her at tea. What a life! And she's written so many books. I'm ashamed to say I haven't read any, but I would love to while I'm here.

– Well, I don't think Mum's novels ever reach the Cambridge syllabus, Richard chuckled. Not highbrow enough, really. Lots of heaving bosoms and all that.

– Now that's not fair, Richard, his wife scolded, as she carried vegetables over to the table. Felicity was a big seller in her day. *Antonia's War*, *Marianne* – she was a bestseller in the '30s and '40s.

– That's true. Probably more popular in her field than poor old Dad was in his, he said, passing out a plate of lamb.

– I would love to know more about your father, Sir Richard, said Belinda. I'm studying the postwar Labour government next term.

– Richard, Richard. You can't call me Sir if you're staying here all week. So you're the historian, Belinda, is that right?

– Yes, Belinda replied, taking the plate that was passed to her. We start specialising in the Second Year, so I'm doing a term on the Attlee government.

Richard nodded.

– Plenty of interest there. Sadly for Dad, that was the moment when his flame died out. The war years preceding that – 1940 to 1945 – they were his moment.

– Was his party called Level Ground? Belinda asked.

– That's it. Won five byelections during the war, had a membership up to 400,000 by 1944. Swept like wildfire around the country: meetings in town halls packed to the brim, pamphlets, books, radio broadcasts. For a moment, people seriously considered that Level Ground could form a government at the end of the war.

– And it was very left wing, wasn't it? continued Belinda.

– Oh God yes, said Richard. Common ownership of the land, the means of production, all industry state-owned, equal pay – the whole caboodle. Churchill even formed a secret sub-committee to try and undermine it. The whole thing tapped into the wartime sense of insecurity and fear. People wanted all the suffering ultimately to be worth something. Everyone got quite carried away with it.

– I'd have voted for Level Ground, said Darius.

– Minor technicality, his brother said from across the table. You're not old enough to vote.

There was laughter, and this time it was Darius's turn to blush. Francis and Richard both started talking about the postwar Attlee government – Francis was reading politics and economics at Cambridge – and Belinda turned to Darius.

– Margee targeoo, she said quietly.

Darius looked quickly at her. She laughed quietly.

– I worked it out, she said. You and Francis. Your secret language. You put "arge" in between every syllable.

Her dark brown eyes were twinkling.

– As in, nargeot bargead.

Darius blushed again.

– It's just from when we were kids, he muttered. It annoys Francis now. I usually only use it now to annoy him.

Belinda laughed again. The conversation between Francis and Richard was animated and quite loud, and Violet was booming interruptions.

– I like it, she said. She was still looking at him. You're not very like Francis, are you?

– I'm the thick one, Darius replied.

– That's obviously not true, she said. You're just different.

– Well, I'm not going to Cambridge, that's for sure, he said, the defiance back in his voice.

– What are you going to do?

– Me? No idea. Never thought about it. Apart from experiencing all the pleasures the world can offer me, I haven't got much further than that.

Belinda's eyes widened slightly, the curl of her smile still playing on her lips.

– My my, she said.

The following afternoon, Darius was weeding the verbascum beds in one of the ornamental gardens on the front lawns. Felicity sat on a wheelchair nearby watching him. Richard was up in London – the *Chronicle* was a Sunday newspaper, so Saturday often required him as editor to arbitrate over spats between the senior journalists all jostling for front page leads. Violet had gone up into town with him to have lunch with friends. Francis had taken the two girls out boating on the Thames for the afternoon, allocating a day off reading studies.

– Don't be too rough, dear, Felicity called out. Those verbascums are quite delicate.

– I know, Nana. His parents employed gardeners to ensure that the gardens were kept to Felicity's standards, but he knew she liked to spend time with him like this. He had pushed her wheelchair around all the gardens earlier, inspecting the work of the gardening staff.

After a while, he straightened up and came back to where she was, sitting down on the dry ground with his back against the old brick wall. The sun shone on them both. Darius closed his eyes. After a while he opened them again, and saw his grandmother was looking down at him from her wheelchair.

– All right, Nana? he asked.

– Yes dear, she smiled. It's kind of you to take me out. I know you want to go off and see your friends.

– Plenty of time, Nana, he said. I'm going to a party later. Don't need to see anyone till then.

He reached his hand up and placed it gently on her sleeve. Her arm was so thin. She closed her right hand over his.

– I don't know, really, she said, looking away from him back at the garden.

– What don't you know, Nana?

Felicity gripped his hand tighter.

– Everything, she said. These gardens. This house. It all meant so much to your grandfather.

– He loved it here, didn't he?

– It wasn't just that. It all meant something. There was a purpose. Zachary meant to change things. He thought he could help the world become a better place, and he planned it all from here, and I believed in him so much. And then none of it happened. None of it.

Darius could see her lip trembling, and he kept his hand on her sleeve.

– And now it's just like it always was, worse really, she

continued. All these people jostling for power, no-one caring about anything. Now there's someone called John Smith, and before that there was someone called Kinnock, and next there will be someone called something else and none of them want anything other than power.

– Didn't Grandad want Level Ground to win, though? asked Darius.

– Yes he did, dear, desperately. We really thought it might happen, for a while.

– I don't know enough about it, said Darius. I should read more. Be more like Francis.

He was smiling, and she looked down at him again and now she laughed a little.

– Don't read anything, my darling boy, she said. You have the goodness of your grandfather in you. Perhaps you in your own way will find what Zachary couldn't. Perhaps he was wrong, perhaps the times just weren't ready for what he spoke about. Perhaps he was trying to force something to happen when he should have waited.

They sat in silence for a while.

– I might go away for the summer, Nana, Darius said after a few minutes. I might head down to Biarritz with a couple of my friends. Go surfing.

– Surfing, Felicity repeated. How wonderful. What does it feel like, when you're standing on that thing?

Darius laughed.

– Surfing's the best, Nana. I wish you could try it. When you swim onto the crest of the wave and you pull yourself up and you're balancing on this incredible rolling water and it's carrying you, like you've joined its body and you're locked into its energy. It's like…it's like you're not a human being any more, you're part of the water which is part of the earth and you're just completely free.

Felicity looked at him, smiling.

– You see, you dear boy. That's when you sound like your grandfather. You should go, she said. It's exactly what you should do. I will try and dream about surfing with you. In fact, I will dream about surfing with Zachary.

Then she laughed.

– No, I won't. That would be too ridiculous. Zachary would not have made a successful surfer. Go and do our surfing for us, Darius. Go and conquer the waves.

The acid that Darius had bought in Soho turned out to be much stronger than any he'd had before. He'd only experimented a couple of times, but this batch seemed to come from a very different production line. At the party in Marlow on Saturday night, he and Dave split a tab just before midnight, with Darius planning to find the redhead and share some with her. But unlike previous times, when he'd had to wait for about half an hour to feel the effect, the impact of this was almost immediate: within ten minutes, they were looking at each other and grinning madly.

– Oh my God, said Dave.

Out in the garden of the house where the party was, the two of them lay on the grass and looked up at the cloudless sky.

– Can you see it? said Darius. The sky. Can you see it? It's on fire.

– Man.

The bright full moon was a burning furnace, and the flames leaped across the sky, almost reaching down to lick the roof of the house. People were walking in and out of the house through the French windows and it seemed to Darius that they were entering and exiting a massive oven, and the electric lights of the house were like flamethrowers. A girl stood in the doorway looking out at the garden, and when she waved, her hand trailed sparks and jagged embers. The speakers in the front room were blaring out Oasis, Blur, Pulp and the beats rang in his head in a completely new way, as though they were being beaten out for him on drums in the jungle, sending him messages, speaking in tongues.

For what seemed like hours, the two of them lay on the grass, initially pointing out the streaks of fire to each other, then relapsing into silence, overwhelmed by the vision. Eventually Darius fell asleep, and when he woke up, he was cold, lying on his own in the garden, the chill of dawn around him.

He got up and walked back into the house. It was dark, and the music had finished. He could see some couples here and there lying asleep on the floor – one of them had long red hair covering a man's denim jacket. He picked his way through the room, opened the front door and left.

It took an hour to walk back home from Marlow – even Darius knew not to drive his motorbike to a party like that. The long walk up Quarry Hill was tough after a night like that, but he was strong and young and although he liked the idea of bearing off into the woods for a sleep, he kept going. When he reached the iron gates at the entrance to the Range, it was six thirty, and the sun far over on the left was already casting long shadows from the trunks of the elms lining the drive. He walked slowly down the curving drive, tripping here and there on a stone. He felt thirsty. Oh well. It was Sunday. He didn't have to do anything today.

He let himself in the front door and walked quietly over to the door on the far side of the octagonal hallway. The house was silent and he padded slowly down the corridor towards the kitchen. He closed the door carefully behind him, then went over to the sink to pour himself a glass of water. He stood there for a while, looking out the window at the thick hedging beyond the edge of the rear veranda. He refilled the glass, and slowly sipped water.

Smoke on the water. Fire in the sky. He hummed the old Deep Purple song. He'd always thought it was just about the fire at the Montreux Jazz Festival.

The kitchen door opened. Belinda crept in and turned to make sure the door closed quietly. She hadn't seen him down the far end of the long kitchen, and he watched her place her left hand up on the door to stop it making a sound as it closed. She was wearing a white cotton nightgown, not very long, and her legs were bare. As she finished shutting the door, she reached up as though to make sure there would be no noisy final click, and as she did so he saw her right bare foot arch up so that for a second it balanced just on her toes, and the back of her leg quivered very slightly as she stretched up.

She turned around and immediately saw him.

– Oh!

She stopped and instinctively crossed her arms across the front of her body, then tugged the white gown down at the hem with her left hand.

Darius beamed.

– Morning, he said.

– I didn't think anyone would be up. I just came down to make a cup of tea. I woke up early.

– That's OK.

She still didn't move, and Darius laughed.

– I'll make you a cup of tea, he said, and turned to one side to fill the kettle. He heard her move quickly and heard a chair draw up. When he turned back round she was sitting the other side of the long wooden table.

– You're up very early, she said, looking a little more composed.

– I just got in, he said. I took some new acid at a party in Marlow and passed out in the garden.

– Acid? You mean?

– Come on Cambridge student, I've heard all about student life.

– No. I mean, gosh no, I've never taken acid.

– Really? Are you kidding me? Never?

Now she smiled, and Darius saw again the slight dimples on either side of her lips.

– Never, she said. Pure as the driven snow. Too many history books to read.

– Wow, he said. He leaned back against the sink and put his hands in the pockets of his jeans. He kept looking at her as the kettle began to boil.

– Is that where you met my brother, he asked, grinning.

In the library?

– Actually no, she said, smiling back. It was at a meeting of the University Labour Party.

– Jesus Christ, said Darius. Not you as well.

He turned to make her tea.

– You come from a famous political family, she said. He could hear the humour in her voice. You're supposed to approve of things like that.

He threw a teabag into a mug.

– I'm the black sheep, he said. I think we've already established that. Milk, sugar?

– Just milk please. Francis worries about you.

He brought the mug of tea back to the table and sat down opposite her, pushing the mug forwards.

– Thanks, she said.

– Francis doesn't worry about me, he said, rocking back now on the back legs of the chair. Francis doesn't like me. Francis just worries that I will embarrass him in front of his hot new girlfriend.

She took the mug and sipped the tea, even though it was still scalding. Her dark hair fell down around her hands.

– Sorry, he said, after a moment's silence. Then:

– What's your name?

She put the mug down and looked back across at him.

– Weiss. Belinda Weiss. Reading Modern History at Magdalen College, Cambridge. Going out with Francis Frome, son of Sir Richard Frome, ex Labour MP and now editor of the Sunday Chronicle.

– Brother of Darius Frome, the waster everyone wants to get rid of. Is your surname really Vice?

– Weiss. W E I S S. It's a Jewish name.

– Oh.

There was another silence.

– Probably not many Jews around Marlow, she said after a bit. We tend to stick around north London.

– I don't care about all that, said Darius.

– About what?

– You know. About what people believe in.

– I don't believe in anything, Darius. I just said I'm Jewish.

– I know.

She smiled again.

– You are funny. You know, you don't even look much like Francis, or even your dad. With all your hair, I mean. And – she waved one hand around in front of her, framing him – with all this going on.

He glared at her.

– With all what?

– Oh you know what I mean. The James Dean rebel thing.

– Who's James Dean?

Now she laughed.

– You really are funny.

– Ha bloody ha, he said, not laughing.

She lay the hand she had been waving down across the table, touching his sleeve.

– Sorry, she said. I'm not being rude. You're just very different.

Darius looked down at her hand. There was another moment's silence, then she took it away.

Darius pushed back his chair and stood up, yawning and pushing a hand through his hair.

– I'll let you finish your tea, he said. I'm going to get a bit of sleep. We're probably all on parade today for Sunday lunch, it's a big thing here. Every bloody Sunday. My mum likes playing the hostess with the mostest.

– I've noticed, said Belinda, looking up at him.

The dimples were back, he thought.

– Thank you for my tea. Sleep well, she said.

That afternoon, the four young people – Darius, Francis, Belinda, Annabel – lay out on the grass lawn at the front of the house, the sun still strong over their heads. They all lay on their backs, looking up at the sky. Francis and Belinda were holding hands.

– I can't believe how stuffed I am, Annabel said, rubbing her stomach. Do you always eat this much here?

– Always, said Francis. It's why Darius is so fat.

– Fuck you, said Darius.

– We should have helped wash up, said Belinda.

– It's fine, Francis said. My mum likes being superwoman. She'll be writing to the vicar soon and arranging next week's flowers. She's unstoppable.

– Do they all go to church, then? asked Belinda.

– It's ridiculous, said Darius.

– It's part of Dad's thing about tradition, said Francis. I don't mind it.

– It's ridiculous, Darius repeated.

– I think your granny is really, you know… Annabel said, sitting up. I read some of her World War Two novel, *Marianne*, this morning in bed. There was a copy on the shelf in my room. I mean, it's not – you know – it's not...

Francis laughed.

– Literature. You mean it's not literature.

– No, no, Annabel said quickly. I mean, it's brilliant. She's a storyteller, she has a real gift for pace and you really want to keep reading. The Marianne character is like this really strong woman operating inside a dominant male structure, with Robespierre and Marat and all these other Revolutionary characters all strutting about in Paris, and she's this powerful force for good.

She leapt to her feet and adopted a pose: her left hand on her hip, and her right pointing up to the sky, her head held back and a proud and insouciant look on her face.

Belinda clapped.

– Bravo! The Statue of Liberty herself!

Darius looked at her. It was true: with her blonde hair glinting in the sunlight and her tall slim body standing straight, she could have been standing at the entrance to New York.

– Why isn't it literature? he asked. Nana's sold millions

of books.

– Oh you can't say anything against Grandma with Darius around, Francis said.

Annabel dropped her pose and knelt down.

– Oh I'm not saying anything at all, she said. I think it's great, it's a really successfully plotted popular novel.

Francis laughed again.

– I think you're digging yourself a bigger hole, Annabel.

– I'd like to see you try and write a bestselling novel, Darius said to his brother.

– I don't want to write a bestselling novel, Francis replied. Anyway, we're proud of her. She's a Frome.

– Good grief, said Belinda. You make it sound like a football team.

Darius laughed.

– I'm not saying she's not a brilliant writer, Francis persisted. That novel was massive during the war, it became a symbol of resistance here against the Germans. I'm just saying, I understand Annabel's critique.

– Anyway, I like it, said Annabel. I'm going to carry on reading it tonight.

They were quiet again. Then Belinda said:

– Why don't we go for a walk? Why don't you show us that secret place, Francis? The place you told me about down by the river?

– Oh God, you mean Down There? Did I tell you about that? I probably shouldn't have. I'll get in trouble with Darius again.

– You can tell people what you like, Darius said, yawning. I don't give a fuck. I'm going to leave here soon. You can have Down There.

– He doesn't mean it, said Francis. He's the gatekeeper. Dad and I are hopeless, we're all three of us supposed to keep the path down to it clear, but it's only Darius that looks after it. Isn't that right, little brother?

– Stop being annoying, and show us, said Belinda. She stood up. Come on, I think we should all go.

Twenty minutes later, Francis was at the head of the line of all four of them, stepping carefully down the final steep stretch of the path, each of them holding their hands out to either side to steady their progress by touching the snipped ends of the branches on either side.

Darius was at the back. He had only had a few hours' sleep and combined with the weight of the Sunday roast, he was feeling sleepy and disconnected from his brother and the two girls. They were talking in excited whispers all the way down the path, and Francis had been giving a rather patronising account of how their grandfather had spent time developing his political philosophy in this secret place.

As the final twist in the path came up, together with the last really steep drop down in the incline, Belinda – who was ahead of Darius – paused to steady herself by gripping a branch. As Darius closed the gap between him and her, she put out her other hand behind her without turning round, and took hold of his hand and continued the descent.

Darius felt shocked by the contact, his senses lurched out of their dulled state, and now he felt the warmth in her fingers as they gripped his hand. Ahead, Francis called out:

– Here we are!

At that, her fingers closed tighter around his and suddenly he felt a rush of sensation, a current through his body and a keen awareness at last of everything around him: the dappled light inside of the woods, the smell of the leaves, the knowledge of life.

Belinda let go of his hand as they entered the clearing, and ahead of them Annabel was pacing around the circular grass lawn.

– Oh my God, this is so amazing, she was saying.

Francis lent against the stone plinth and smiled at Belinda as she approached him and then reached up to kiss him on the cheek. Darius stood back at the entrance to the glade and watched them.

– This is like a magic den, Annabel continued.

– It is magical, Belinda said, and turned to smile at Darius.

Darius could hear the river lapping against the shore the other side of the plinth. He listened to the birds communicating in the trees above and he felt the slight breeze coming off the Thames.

– How often do you have to clear the path to keep it going? Belinda asked Darius.

He shrugged.

– Every now and then. Nana used to do it herself but she can't get down now.

– I did some cutting last year, Francis said.

– Bollocks you did, said Darius.

Francis laughed.

– OK, I lied.

– So who knows about this place? asked Annabel.

– Well, me and Darius, Mum and Dad and Grandma, said Francis. And you two now.

– Oh my God, said Annabel. That's so cool. Can you see it from the river or is it hidden by all these trees?

– It's hidden, said Darius. Nana said Grandad found it when he was exploring the river in his rowing boat.

Annabel walked around the plinth.

– And what is this thing? There's no markings on it.

– I don't think anyone ever found out, said Francis. It might be a tomb for all we know.

– Oh that's too much, said Annabel. The tomb of a wandering knight. I love it.

Darius walked over to the plinth and then lifted himself up. He sat down cross-legged on the surface and pulled out his tobacco from the back pocket of his jeans.

– Anyone fancy a joint? he asked, not looking up but starting to spread the paper out on his knee.

– Oh my God, are you serious? said Annabel. Francis, your brother is a hippy!

– Tell me something I don't know, said Francis. Darius, don't be a moron.

Darius continued to construct the joint, spreading the tobacco out along the long line of glued paper.

– Why don't we? said Belinda. It will be fun. I've never had a joint before.

Darius looked up.

– Francis, you want to try some at last? he asked.

– Oh do let's, Francis, cried Annabel. Belinda wants to. I've never had any either.

– I can't believe you girls, said Francis, but he was laughing.

A few minutes later, Darius passed the joint down to Annabel, who took it and tentatively inhaled.

– Keep it in your lungs for a bit, Darius said. That's where it does it.

Annabel coughed and passed the joint to Belinda.

– It tastes sweet, she said.

They passed the joint around, not talking very much, until it was finished.

– Makes me feel a bit funny, said Annabel, wandering away from the plinth.

– I like it, said Belinda. What about you Francis?

– I can feel it rotting my brain already, he said. Ridiculous.

Annabel called out from the far side of the clearing.

– Who does the archery?

She was standing about twenty feet away beside a straw-filled circular target with arrows sticking out of it, a bow lying on the grass.

– It's mine, Darius called back. I practice down here. It's out of the way.

– Can I have a try?

– No, Darius laughed. Arrows and dope don't mix. Another time.

Belinda was smiling.

– Why have you got a bow and arrow, Mr Hunter? she asked.

Darius was starting to roll another joint.

– Oh God, said Francis, he read a book about Zen. Don't

get him going on it.

– Shut up, said Belinda. Tell me, Darius.

– Not much to tell, said Darius, not looking up from his preparations. I just like it. Francis is right, as he always is. Zen masters use archery as a way of teaching. It's all about the eradication of the self, or something. Anyway, after they've practised for years, they can hit the target with their eyes closed every time. It's like they lose their sense of self and become one with the target and the bow.

– Can you hit the target with your eyes closed?

– Sometimes.

Annabel came back to the plinth.

– More, she said. I like it.

Darius passed round another joint. The smoke hovered above the plinth and Darius watched the late afternoon sunlight play on the drifting fumes. He lay back down on the stone surface and closed his eyes. He could hear the three of them talking quietly on the grass. He thought of the sea and how the waves would be in Biarritz, and he could hear them thundering down onto the shore and he felt himself balancing in the air. He felt lighter, and lighter.

When he woke up, the light had changed. He sat up and looked around, but the others had gone.

Later that evening, everyone was sitting around the kitchen table. There were plates of bread and cheese and ham in the centre, and Annabel was asking Felicity about the plot of *Marianne*. Violet was questioning Darius about school.

– There's not much point even going in, Mum, he was saying. We've done all the exams. I've just got the one bit of coursework to finish and that's it.

– It's Monday tomorrow Darius, and your father and I want you to go to school.

– Do as your Mother says, Darius, said Richard, not looking up from the newspapers spread out at the far end of the kitchen table.

He was about to reply when he felt a piece of paper

being pushed into the pocket of his jeans. Belinda was sitting next to him, and she was part of Annabel's conversation with Felicity about the novel, but Darius saw her left hand quickly come back up to the table top.

Later, upstairs alone in his bedroom, he pulled the piece of paper out. On it was scribbled:

– I want to see Down There at dawn tomorrow. Meet me there.

Darius held on to the last branch at the bottom of the path as he stepped down onto the grass. The grey early morning light gave the clearing a completely different look, a mono-chrome stage, silent, completely still. He could feel the damp of the dew through the canvas of his sneakers. The tangled undergrowth surrounding the circular lawn looked solid and impenetrable, a wall that shut out the world.

He walked slowly across the grass and could see the sil-houetted figure sitting with her back to him on the plinth. Darius was aware, fiercely aware, of the presence of the natural world around him. Perhaps as never before, he smelled the impact of the dew upon the wakening grass, a chilled cocktail of essential elements: carbon, nitrogen, phosphorous. And the pure water of the dew, connecting the clearing intimately with the silent water beyond the fringe of trees. He felt the strength of the interlocking branches and fronds of the woods, the twisting knotted fingers bearing living leaves, the ivy coursing through the vegetation like a snake. The air was filled with stirring life.

As he came around the edge of the stone monument, he could see that she was looking out towards the river, smiling. She was hugging her knees and her brown hair gathered on the shoulders of a thick sweater. Darius noticed her fingers interlaced upon her knees, and realised how delicate they seemed.

– I've never been anywhere like this before, she whis-pered, not turning her head.

He stood still, watching her face. A sudden cry of a bird

came from the river, and the sound of beating wings followed by the clatter of entry into the water. A swan, probably. She turned to look at him, her eyes wide with excitement. She held her hand out, and he clambered up beside her.

– This is like magic, she said, still whispering, and she lay her hand on his jeans as he sat cross-legged beside her. This is like coming to another world.

They sat in silence, and through the trees at the edge of the lawn the river flowed heavy like lead. Darius thought about being down here on Friday evening, pushing the boat out from under the willow branches to row over to the rugby club. They could take the boat now, explore the river in the early morning light, come back to the clearing for breakfast, stay here all day, never leave. He suddenly wished more than anything that they could stay here, like this, hidden from a world from which they had escaped, alone in this perfect world of green and brown, of water and air, of nature in perfect equilibrium.

– It is another world, he said.

– It's a beautiful world, she said.

– It's different today, he said. It's…more perfect.

– I know, she said. I can tell.

– You understand it, don't you? said Darius.

She nodded, still smiling.

Darius closed his eyes for a moment, and he could feel himself inside of the clearing, weightless and as free as the life all around him, in the earth, on the branches, in the water.

He opened his eyes and Belinda turned her head to look at him. She lifted up her hand and gently pushed at his chest, and he lay back down on the stone. She uncrossed her legs and turned to sit on top of him, using both her hands to smooth her dark hair back up from her forehead.

Then she pulled off her blue sweater and lay it beside her, and began to unbutton the white shirt. A moment later, she stood up and unzipped her jeans. She put all her clothes in a pile at the edge of the plinth, and lay down carefully on

117

the stone surface next to Darius.

He turned his head to look at her. She kissed him.

– Now, she said.

Later that day, at school, Darius thought about Belinda. He thought about her face with its eyes closed, he thought about her pale ivory skin in the half light of Down There, he thought about that little cry she gave which seemed to linger inside the clearing – the call of something unknown, something primitive and wild.

He couldn't concentrate on anything and he didn't really hear any conversations.

– You're fucking weird today, mate, said Dave.

He didn't answer. He just thought about getting back to the Range, finding her. Darius didn't even think much about Francis. What was he to do with anything now? She didn't want him. Everything had changed. Nothing was the same. All he could think about was her face, her dark brown eyes, her skin.

When he got back home about five o'clock, the house was quiet. He found his mother in the drawing room writing letters.

– Where is everyone? he asked.

– Your father had to go to town, said Violet. Francis and the girls have gone to Oxford for the night, they're going to a party. They'll be back tomorrow.

He felt dumbstruck. She hadn't said anything, just gone off. He went upstairs to his room to see if she had left him a note, but there was nothing. He wandered down the corridor to the guest bedroom where she was staying. The thick blue sweater that she had worn that morning was lying on the bed. He lifted it up and pressed it to his face, smelled the trace of her on it.

Why hadn't she told him? Maybe she didn't know, maybe it was just some dumb surprise that Francis dreamed up. That was probably it. Of course she didn't want to go, but the others made her. He left her room, walked slowly down one of the back staircases, thinking of her face staring at him.

In the kitchen, Felicity was slowly chopping the ends off runner beans, her hand shaking slightly as she cut through each one. Darius sat beside her and watched her, picked up a couple of the ends which had fallen on the slate floor.

– Thank you, dear, she smiled. She looked at him. What's the matter?

– Nothing, Nana, he said.

She turned back to the chopping board.

– They seem very nice, Francis's friends, she said.

Darius didn't reply.

– Very pretty, that dark-haired one, she continued.

– I wouldn't know, he muttered.

– Very pretty, she repeated. I knew a girl like that on the Riviera in the '30s. Caused all sorts of trouble.

– What sort of trouble?

– Oh, she had men falling in love with her left, right and centre. I don't think she meant them to. They just did.

– What happened to her?

– She ended up marrying a bank manager.

Darius laughed.

– Lucky bank manager, he said.

– She never had to work, that's for sure, Felicity said. But then she was killed in the war, poor thing. A bomb landed on their house in Kensington Square.

Darius was silent. Felicity looked at him again.

– You look exhausted, Darius, she said. Haven't you been sleeping?

– Not a lot, he said.

She went back to cutting.

– No good not sleeping, she said. You're still young, you need your sleep.

– I'm not that young, Nana, he said.

– You are, she said, cutting into another bean. You think you're older than you are. You're sixteen, Darius.

– You sound like Mum, he said.

– No I don't, she said. I sound like your grandmother, and I'm telling you, you need more sleep and less of...you know.

– What?

Felicity put the knife down, and laid her old hand lightly on his on the table top.

– Don't hang around here, she said. Not now your exams are over. Go and do what you said you were going to do, go and surf those waves in France for me. Come back at the end of the summer and tell me lots of stories about your adventures.

– I'm going to, he said.

– I mean it, Darius, she said, gripping his hand. I mean it.

Tuesday 25th June came hotter than the previous days, a languid, still summer day. Violet had left early with her husband to go into town, making Darius promise before she left that he would not be late for school. As soon as the car had driven off from the front of the Range, he went back to his bedroom and rolled a joint. He had no intention of going to school.

Mid-morning, he took a cup of tea and two shortbread biscuits into his grandmother's room, but she had gone back to sleep. He left the tray by her bed and tiptoed out. He felt out of sorts, and wandered along the long, stone corridors of the house, trailing a hand against the chalky walls. He went back into the guest bedroom where Belinda was staying, and poked his finger into the messy pile of clothes in the open suitcase on the sideboard. He could smell her scent still.

He went back downstairs and lay down on the grass outside the front of the Range and smoked more joints under the morning sun. He drifted in and out of sleep and listened to the birds chattering in the branches of the elder trees over by the drive.

Just after midday, while he was making himself a sandwich in the kitchen, he heard a car door slam out the front of the house. He sat down at the table and began to eat.

A couple of minutes later, he heard the sound of laughter, and then the kitchen door burst open. Annabel and Belinda came in.

– Hi Darius, said Annabel. We weren't expecting to see you.

He shrugged. Francis followed the girls into the room.

– Oh God, are you mitching off school again, Darius? he said. Mum'll find out.

Darius shrugged again, and carried on eating. His feet were up on the kitchen table.

– I'm starving, said Belinda. We didn't get any breakfast.

– I'll make us some sandwiches, said Francis.

– What was the party like? asked Darius. He was looking at Belinda.

– Dullsville, said Annabel. Dull dull dull. Bloody Oxford types.

– Oh it wasn't that bad, said Francis. I met an interesting chap whose thesis is on voting patterns in marginal constituencies.

– Exactly, said Belinda, and both girls laughed.

Once the sandwiches had been made, they sat down at the table.

– What did you do last night, Darius? asked Belinda. She looked at him for the first time.

– Can't remember, he said. He stared at her, but she had already looked down at her plate. Her dark hair fell over her face as she began to eat the sandwich.

– It's so hot out there today, Annabel said. I think we should go swimming. Can we swim from your place down by the river, Darius?

– From Down There? Yes, you can get into the water OK.

– It's the Thames, though, grimaced Francis. Bloody dirty.

– Oh don't be such a spoilsport, said Annabel. There are swans and ducks on it, they do all right. It'll be fine. I want to.

– Me too, said Belinda, looking at Annabel and smiling. I'd love to go in the water.

– All right, all right, Francis laughed.

Half an hour later, Belinda was leading the group down the path at the back of the house. Darius was at the back, and not keeping up with them – the morning's dope had spaced him out. He could hear them up ahead, laughing and shouting. By the time he got to the clearing, the three of them had already stripped down to their underwear and Francis was cautiously stepping into the water, holding branches aside to allow the two girls to step past him. As Belinda stepped into the river, she turned and waved at Darius, beckoning him to join them.

– Come on Darius, don't be scared! she called out. He watched as she turned and let her body into the water, watched as the space between her thighs was consumed by the Thames.

He took off his shirt and jeans and shoes and socks, and followed them in. They were already twenty yards ahead of him, swimming in the clear sunshine. Once he was past the overhanging branches of the shore, he ducked his head and swam underwater, the chill sweeping through him, cleansing him suddenly and bringing back his awareness. He felt down and touched the reeds at the bottom, then came back up for air.

– It's freezing! Annabel shouted, laughing.

– I warned you, said Francis.

They were closer to Darius now, and had stopped swimming. Belinda splashed water and they started a mock fight. Darius ducked down again and swam closer, then emerged amongst them and scooped water at them all. The girls shrieked, Francis splashed back.

Later, they all stood with towels around the plinth on the clearing, the girls on one side, the boys on the other. They turned away from each other instinctively to take off wet underwear and put their clothes back on. They were laughing and talking as they did so.

Annabel was the first to be dressed.

– Darius, make us one of those naughty things, I want another one now, she said. That was such fun.

Darius looked at Belinda, who had her arms up in the air letting her T-shirt fall down over her naked back. She turned and looked at him directly, smiling.

– Yes let's, she said. That will warm us up too.

The plinth was big enough for all four of them to sit cross-legged on it, and they passed the joint around. After a while, Darius made another.

– I can't believe I'm actually doing this, said Francis, but he was smiling.

– Chill brother, said Darius.

Belinda laughed.

– Belinda said you had acid as well, said Annabel, laughing too. She told me. Have you?

Francis looked at Belinda.

– How the hell do you know that? he asked.

– She caught me sneaking in on Sunday morning, Darius said. I was still high, I think.

– You told me the sky had been on fire, Belinda said, and laughed again.

– Oh my God, that sounds fantastic, said Annabel.

– Seriously Darius? said Francis, looking back at his brother. You've been taking acid?

– Oh come on, said Belinda, now you're sounding like his father. It was only a bit of acid.

Francis turned to her.

– As though you'd know all about it, I suppose, he said. The acid freak of Magdalen.

– Well, what if I haven't tried it? she said, blushing slightly. Have you?

– Of course I haven't. I leave my dopey brother and his surfer mates to all that. I actually don't want to ruin my life, strangely.

– But how do you know, if you haven't tried it? Belinda persisted. How do you know it would ruin your life?

– That's true Francis, said Annabel. It's not empirically sound to make an assumption not based on evidence.

– I think there's plenty of evidence, Annabel, Francis replied.

– I don't think you know of any evidence at all, she said. I think you're just scared.

– Why would I be scared? I'm not scared. It's just stupid.

– So why don't we? asked Belinda, looking at Darius. Why on earth don't we? If not now, then when? Why don't we just try it? Can we Darius?

Darius looked at his brother, just raising his eyebrows. There was a moment's pause. He could hear the river behind them, gently lapping against the shore. The heat of the day was penetrating now even into Down There, and he was feeling slightly sleepy again after the exertion of the swimming.

Francis lay back down on the stone surface, closing his eyes.

– Oh for God's sake, all right.

Annabel clapped her hands.

– Yes! Darius, have you got some here?

Darius nodded, and pulled a crumpled paper package from the pocket of his jeans. He laid it out on the plinth between them, and gently poked at the collection of small yellow paper squares. He picked one out and, using his thumb nail, split it in half, then did the same with another. The four halves were then in the palm of his hand.

– Just half, he said, looking up. To start.

Belinda's eyes were wide open.

– What do we do? she whispered.

– Take one and put it on your tongue. Let it dissolve, said Darius.

Both girls took one of the tiny paper shapes each and placed them on their tongues. Annabel closed her eyes. Belinda nudged Francis.

– You too Francis, she said.

Francis sat up.

– God, he said, wearily, but he took one too. Darius put the final half into his own mouth.

– What now? said Annabel.

– Just wait, Darius replied. It took about twenty minutes to kick in properly on Saturday.

Now Darius lay down on the stone, and closed his eyes. The other three were talking quietly, and he felt his own mind slipping in and out of a haze. The heat of the sunny afternoon felt like it was getting stronger. He could feel the presence of the trees and shrubs surrounding the clearing, the tangled branches overhead encasing them in this still tomb.

After a while, he felt fingers gently combing through his long hair. He opened his eyes. Belinda's face was right by his – she was standing on the grass behind the plinth, her head pressed close to his. She licked his forehead lightly, then whispered in his ear:

– Did you like what we did yesterday?

He pushed himself up. He could hear Francis and Annabel on the other side of the clearing, laughing. Sitting up, he could see them now, over by the archery target. Annabel was striking a pose in front of the roundel, her Marianne pose, but this time she was holding the bow. Francis was pretending to worship before her. Both figures seemed to be sliding, as though they were on ice. He could feel the trees twisting round and round, and the grass lawn was rippling like the river.

Darius turned around. Belinda put her hand on his thigh.

– Well?

– You know I did, he said.

She smiled, looking up at him, her hand pressing into his leg.

He put his hand out to lift her back up onto the plinth, and she took it. When she was beside him, they both looked over at Francis and Annabel's performance.

Belinda laughed, and called out:

– Beautiful, Marianne! You're beautiful!

Annabel inclined her head, and Francis made an elaborate sweep of his arm.

– I feel crazy! Annabel called out, and began to laugh again.

Now Belinda lay down on the stone and closed her eyes.

– Darius, come here, Annabel called out. I need another centurion to worship me. I am divine!

Belinda giggled and pushed at Darius, who swung his legs off the plinth. The clearing was spinning around him now. He walked over towards Annabel and Francis, slowly and staggering a little as he went. Francis suddenly let out a howl like a wolf.

– Ah ah ah! shouted Francis, grinning at his brother. Ah ah ah!

– Submit to me, you slave! Annabel called. She aimed the bow at him, although there was no arrow in it. Her blonde hair was a little matted now, and her face was sweaty. She was unsteady on her feet.

Darius lowered his head and spread his arms out wide.

– My name is Marianne, and I am to be obeyed, Annabel continued, her voice slurred. I am divine. I am to be adored. Which of you is to win my approval?

Francis raised both his hands up high.

– My lady Marianne, he cried, then he giggled, a high-pitched giggle.

Darius was making shapes in the air with his hands. He felt the world spinning around him, he saw creatures which looked like giant birds looking down at him from the canopy of leaves, huge things with great eyes staring down at him.

– My lady Marianne, Francis said again. We should compete, this worthless fool and I, we should compete for your divine approval.

He staggered slightly.

– Yes, said Annabel. That is correct. I must be shown… I must be shown…

– Respect, your majesty, said Darius, and they all

laughed again.

– Here, said Annabel, thrusting the bow at Darius. Take this. I shall be the judge. You shall both fight for my...for my, yes, for my approval upon the target. Whosoever shall hit the target with his arrow, shall have my blessing.

Francis stumbled over to the round straw-filled target, and grabbed several arrows which lay on the grass underneath it.

Darius shot first. His arrow disappeared into the thicket behind the target. Annabel was standing behind them, and she called out:

– Fool! she cried. Next supplicant!

Francis took the bow and lay an arrow on the fingers of his left hand, stretching the string out with his right. Like his brother's, the arrow shot into the trees.

– My God, said Annabel. I am failed by my knights. I shall give you one more chance before you are punished for your lack of respect.

She pushed past the two boys and meandered towards the target to find more arrows. She bent down on the grass and felt her hand around her, looking for spare arrows. She found one, grabbed it, put both hands on the grass and lifted herself back up. She staggered slightly then seemed to lose her balance. She lurched to the left, giggling as she tried to stay upright. She turned around clutching the arrow and was about to speak, when an arrow flew straight into her eye. She fell, without any noise, and her body lay on the grass with one denim-clad leg twisted badly behind her, half of the arrow shaft sticking upright out of her eye. Blood began to trickle down her cheek. She was still. There was no noise. The clearing was absolutely silent.

Then Francis said:

– Oh my Christ Darius. What have you done?

Part Three

Chapter Thirteen

– This house is all wrong.

Darius said this aloud, although he was sitting alone at the top of the lawns looking down towards the Range. Over to one side he could see Tink playing with James and Alice, who were back from school, taking it in turns to do handstands on the grass. Belinda and Francis, who had got back from London half an hour ago, were still in the kitchen, he presumed.

He had been about to go into the kitchen himself ten minutes ago, and had walked halfway down the long white corridor at the back of the house when he had heard raised voices from beyond the closed kitchen door. Belinda and Francis were arguing.

– How do you know he sent the cards? he had heard Belinda yell. You don't know. For all I know, you sent them.

– Don't be so bloody stupid.

His brother's voice was angry.

– You don't know him like I do. It's classic Darius. Always doing what he wants. He stays away for years, he leaves you and me to look after Dad, he swans around the world doing his ridiculous hippie crap, and then he decides he wants some fun. Well, I'm not fucking having it. He's a dopehead, he's a bloody loser. He's only got half a brain left after all the shit he's consumed.

– Oh for Christ's sake Francis. He told me he hasn't taken any drugs since he left prison. He's been clean for twenty years.

– Why are you taking his side? That's what you did before, isn't it? When it all happened. You took his side. You didn't even bloody know him but you liked him all right, didn't you? Don't think I didn't notice. Is that what this is about?

Darius heard Belinda's laugh, a little ragged with tension.

– Are you still jealous, after all this time? Are you jealous of your brother? Is that why you never wanted to see him? Because you thought I might flutter my pretty little eyelashes at him? For God's sake, Francis.

– I didn't want this ridiculous weekend because I didn't want the past raked up again, Belinda. We've got a family, in case you'd forgotten. Do you think Alice and James are going to be pleased to find out about what their lovely Uncle Darius did when he was a boy? What's the matter with you?

– What's the matter with me? What's the matter with me? How can you say that? Look at us Francis. Look at us. What's the matter with us? Tell me that: what's the matter with us?

– Oh for God's sake, don't start all that again.

– Don't you dare patronise me, Francis. Just don't you dare. Take a good look at yourself. Your face is screwed up with fury. Maybe you sent the cards because you're trying to confront something. Maybe that's what it is. What is it you want, Francis? What is it you want so bad that you had to ask your brother to come back home?

Darius heard the smash of china then. Something hurled against a wall.

– I didn't ask him back, you stupid bitch.

There was a silence. Darius turned and walked quietly back the way he had come. Now he was up here alone at the top of the lawn. He looked down over the gardens, and wondered again at the decline. Patches of weeds had taken hold in various parts, in others the grass had been invaded by moss. Why hadn't they fixed the peeling render on the front of the house? Why had they let the elm trees entangle themselves so much along the drive that they must almost touch the roof of Francis's

Range Rover when he drove in and out?

– It's all wrong, he repeated to himself.

There was obviously a problem in their marriage – that was clear even before he had overheard their argument. But the feeling he was getting was deeper than that, connected with the house himself, with his father up there in that lonely bedroom.

Yet again, Darius questioned himself on why he had accepted the invitation and why even he had come three days early. Tink had been surprised when he had told her that he planned to go, and that he would like her to accompany him.

– Of course I'll come with you, she had said. But are you sure you want to go? Are you sure it's not more to do with getting away from here?

She had been right, of course. He hadn't been thinking straight. What on earth was he doing coming back here? This wasn't part of his problem. His problems were to do with Level Ground, with the valley, with the fallout between them all. Maybe he had overreacted when the police first arrived two months ago. That was the view of his two co-founders.

– How come you're taking the side of the police, Darius? they had shouted. All we're doing is growing our own grass. It's our land. Isn't that the point of what we're doing, claiming back the land? And you think they've got the right to march in and stop us just because they don't like cannabis?

Now, sitting here with the lawns sloping down before him towards the house, he was unsure again. Had he overreacted to the police raid? Maybe his reactions were more to do with his own past rather than the present. Maybe his friends were right: he should be supporting them in resisting the police, putting together a defence, rather than lying down and letting the law trample over everything they had achieved. It was a mess.

Now it felt like he was being drawn back into a family

from whom he had cut all ties a lifetime ago. And it seemed to be trying to reach out to him, to want him to take some action. Only he didn't know what that was.

He imagined his younger self sitting down on the lawns in front of him twenty-five years ago. An arrogant 16-year-old, confident, rebellious, charismatic. In America, they would have called him the Boy Most Likely To, the Year favourite – not academically of course, but in terms of popularity, of appeal, certainly.

He found it difficult to align that young man with his persona now, his 41-year-old self. Not so much in terms of his attitude – he knew he retained that certain swagger, it was a part of him, one of the reasons he had learned how to survive prison – but more in relation to his aimlessness then. He remembered that summer, when it all happened, as a period of rootlessness, of lack of knowledge, of a generalised dissatisfaction with his place in life. He knew his Nana had been worried about him, had thought that a summer as he had planned surfing in Biarritz might shake him out of his complacency.

The death had put an end to all that. Over the years, he hadn't found a better way of terming it, other than just that: the death. He didn't like to think of Annabel's name, although the endless therapy sessions in prison had forced him to address everything about her: her bereft family, her unfulfilled potential. He had been obliged to accept his responsibility, to recognise the direct link between his aimlessness and its associated drug use and her death. The drugs rehabilitation programmes he had attended as part of his overall parole plan had been effective in weaning him off all drugs for good, and he had never succumbed in the twenty years since he had left prison.

His attitude to his family had been a different matter. He had known from the first night in his cell in the Juvenile Facility that he could survive, but that survival would require him to depend entirely on his own Will. Any weakness, any sentimental dependence on a family

– other than his grandmother – for whom he had previously had no respect would endanger him. It would make him weak, and he could tell from the cold grey atmosphere of his first night under lock and key that weakness in that environment would be fatal.

So he ignored them. He ignored the requests for visits from his mother and father, explained to the social worker attached to his case in the early days that he would prefer to build a new life in isolation from them. He tried to explain this to his grandmother in the letters he sent in response to hers, and he believed that she understood, although the sadness behind the upbeat tone of her letters was the most difficult of all for him to bear. In many ways, her death within a year of his incarceration came as a blessing.

He remembered those first few months in the Facility. Posh boy, they called him. One of the warders had taken a dislike to him early on, told the other boys that he was the son of a baronet. The loneliness he felt being hurled into that bleak environment became compounded by a daily ritual of taunts and provocations. He remembered now, he was almost beginning to close down, to feel that his life could go no further. It was just the massive shock of that sudden displacement, the contrast between these gardens he was looking at now and the ugly, sour-smelling daily violence of where he had found himself.

He shook his head. How had he survived? Had there been a cost to that survival? The twenty-two-year-old who came out of prison six years later was not, in his memory, very recognisable to the youth who had sat down on the grass below him smoking joints and thinking about girls. But they were linked, they were the same person; he could see that, however difficult the transition in his mind might be. That at least was one benefit so far of this strange visit. In all the years of travelling, he had cast aside the teenage rebel but now here he was, facing up to him. How would he greet him, here on this lawn, if the tall, strong, confident 16-year-old were to stroll up to him, give him a slightly mocking

135

smile? Up until now, he had assumed he would turn away from his younger self, but the fractured air of the Range and its current inhabitants made him feel that perhaps he might give his young alter ego more benefit of the doubt. Why had he been so keen to leave back then? Why had he been so determined to get away that summer, to leave for France and maybe never come back? Was there something that he sensed even then, something about the place which was encouraging him to go?

– You're looking thoughtful.

He turned and saw Belinda standing beside him. He immediately saw that her eyes were slightly reddened, and she looked exhausted. She sat down beside him and lay down on her back.

– I was imagining seeing my younger self down there on the grass, rolling joints and thinking about parties and surfing.

He looked down, and saw her smiling, although her eyes were closed.

– Tell me about the young Darius, she said. I never got to know very much about him.

– It's strange, he said. I've been sitting here thinking that maybe he wasn't the complete prat I always thought he was.

– I never thought he was, she said. Why did you?

– Well, there's a pretty obvious reason, Belinda.

She shook her head, her eyes still closed.

– No, she said. Then she sighed. But don't let's talk about that right now.

They were quiet for a while. Darius looked down on Tink playing with the children.

– Was it very bad? she asked, after a while. Being in prison?

– I was just thinking about it. Prison wasn't so bad – I was eighteen when they moved me to an adult prison. I'd got used to it by then. The first two years though, in the Juvenile Facility… That wasn't great.

He felt her hand rest on his arm.

– I'm so sorry, she said softly.

– I survived, he said. You either learn in those places, or you don't. If you don't learn, you go under. So I learned. It wasn't that complicated. It was pretty physical. But I learned.

He felt her body beside him on the grass quite rigid for a moment, but neither of them said anything.

– Tell me what you did, when you left prison, Belinda said, after a while.

Darius looked back down at her. Her eyes were still closed. He suddenly remembered that early morning, twenty-five years ago, when she lay so quiet and beautiful on the plinth. He looked away again down towards the house.

– I got on the first plane I could find, he said after a while. Dad had arranged for me to have a bit of money in an account for when I came out, and I applied for a passport in my last few weeks in prison. I spent months before in the prison library, looking up about places around the world. I wanted to go somewhere that was as unlike this place – he swept his arm around in front of him – as possible. So I got a plane to India. I flew straight to Mumbai, and I found the British Embassy there and went to ask them about how I would go about getting paid work in India. They could see from my passport that I was an ex-con, and for some reason that seemed to make them think that they should help me. They rang up a few hotels and I got a job washing dishes in a hotel in Chennai. Took me three days to get there by train from Mumbai. I was sick as a dog by the time I got there.

– What were you, twenty-two? I must have been twenty -five by then. I was still at home with my mum and dad in north London. You didn't know about all that. I'll tell you. But there you were, in the middle of India on your own, washing dishes. I had no idea.

He looked down and she was smiling again, her eyes still closed.

– Funny, isn't it? he said. I loved it. I stayed for ages there, then I moved around India a bit, managed to avoid all the hippies in Goa, then I met a girl who said we could both get a job in South Africa working in a safari park so we just left.

– I bet she was good-looking, said Belinda, still smiling.

– She was actually. Fabulous arse.

Belinda kicked him, and they both laughed. She sat up and they both watched Tink and the children doing handstands. They didn't speak for a while.

– Then what?

– With the girl?

– No you idiot. What did you do then?

– I'd started reading a lot when I was in India. I wasn't much of a reader when I lived here, if you remember.

– You did seem to rather pride yourself on that aspect of your character.

– Well, I got very interested in Indian mysticism. I liked it, it was very different to what I'd grown up with I suppose and I was wanting to build something far away from this place. So I read a lot. I still do, you'll be amazed to know. But it led me on to other stuff. The more I read, the more I wanted to explore places that were further and further away from here. In South Africa I started learning about shamanism and the teacher I had there said that he thought I'd benefit from going to Mexico. So I went to this little village in Durango with a letter of introduction from my teacher in South Africa, and I started working as a sort of apprentice to the village elder who was from a long line of shamanic healers there. Stayed there for three years.

– I never knew, said Belinda. I don't think your brother knows either. At least he's never told me.

– No, there's no reason why Francis would have known what I was doing.

– You'd be surprised what he knows.

They were quiet again.

– That's really interesting, though, she continued, looking at him curiously. We do lots of work in South Africa and Mexico, at World Action I mean, but I've never been out to either place once. I'm not like you – I'm a bit of a scaredy-cat.

– I don't think so, he said, smiling. You were just smart enough already. I had to go out and find stuff out for myself.

She shook her head.

– No, she said. I'm not that smart, Darius. That stuff you said earlier about Richard, though. Is that what you mean, is that what you spent your time studying?

He shrugged.

– Some of it. A lot of those cultures, whether you're in India or Mexico, if you go back to the traditional beliefs, they share a pattern of thinking about the cycles of life and death. It's very different to Western ideas, heaven and hell, all that stuff. We see death as an ending, other cultures see it as part of a much longer journey.

– Why did you say what you said about Richard?

– It was one of the core techniques the elder in Durango used, to allow the person to tell you whether they wished to begin the journey, the crossing over. That's what I found in Dad this morning. It was very clear. It doesn't mean he's physically ill, or there's something that the doctor can or can't sort out. It's of his own choosing. It's something he wants to do.

She was silent for a moment, then:

– Don't you think that's strange, that you should come here now, after twenty-five years, and get that sense, whatever it is? I'm not saying I don't believe you, but don't you think it's strange?

He nodded.

– I don't think what Dad is going through is strange. But there is something here that is very out of sorts. I've felt it since I got here. Something in this house.

She sighed.

– I know, she said. It's worse than it used to be.

– But everything, Belinda. The gardens, look – he pointed over to the formal gardens – they're in such a terrible state. And the house. Look at it – the render is coming off all over the front. The trees over the drive have almost taken it over. I never thought it would be like this. I always imagined it in my head like it was when I was here, when Nana was still alive.

– God, now you're making me feel guilty. Is it that bad?

He looked at her.

– It's not bad. It's just what it is. It's a representation of something, isn't it?

– Is it? I don't know. I just thought that neither of us is very green-fingered, we're both ridiculously busy with our jobs and with the kids, and neither of us really spends much time thinking about the garden or the render. I suppose we should.

Down below, Tink looked up as she held James's legs in a handstand, and with her free hand she waved at them. They both held up their hands and waved back, then were quiet again.

– She's nice, said Belinda.

– Tink is special, said Darius.

– How long have you two been together?

Darius looked at her.

– Together? In that way? Oh, I see. No, Tink and I aren't together like that, Belinda. I should have said.

– Aren't you? Oh God. I'm so sorry, I just presumed. But I put you in the same room, I'm so sorry.

Darius laughed.

– I do believe you're embarrassed, he said. That's so sweet. Honestly, it's fine. Tink and I are just really close, but we're not like that. It just never happened between us that way. I only met her a few months ago and she was looking for somewhere to stay in England for a while. She'd ended up in Cornwall after a festival went wrong, and I invited her to come and stay in the valley. We're a bit more like brother and sister, if anything. Tink carves her own path in life but she's also part of the faery movement, if you know anything about that. I think she finds me an interesting challenge.

– She's not wrong there.

– She's very unusual, Tink. She's some sort of ancient

spirit. She has a lightness about her. She was really great about this whole weird weekend thing, after I got that invitation. I asked her to come with me, partly because I was so freaked out about it. I didn't know what to do, and she was the one who said I should go.

– Really? Good for her. Do you mean you wouldn't have come if it wasn't for her?

– Oh God, I don't know. You know what I'm like.

– Do I? said Belinda.

He touched her arm.

– I think you know you do, he said.

They watched Tink standing on her hands with Alice and James running around her.

– She's amazing with the kids, said Belinda.

They sat and watched the scene below for a while.

– I heard you and Francis arguing in the kitchen just now, Darius said.

– Oh.

She leaned back on the grass and looked up at the sky.

– That probably didn't sound great, she said.

He shrugged, but didn't reply.

– It's been getting worse, Belinda said after a while. The last year has not been good.

– I'm sorry, he said.

– I don't really care any more. About him and me, I mean. I just really care about James and Alice and I want to protect them from it. That's the hardest bit. I've made him promise not to let them be aware of what's going on with us. That thing in the kitchen just now doesn't happen much. We're very civilised about our unhappiness.

– That all sounds quite exhausting, he said.

She sighed.

– I suppose it is. I'm used to it.

He looked down at her. Her eyes were closed again.

– Are you? he said.

She opened her eyes and looked up at him. Then she smiled.

– Are you doing it to me now? Examining my inner thoughts?

– I'm not a magician, Belinda. It just sounds like quite a big thing to just get used to.

She closed her eyes again.

– Sorry. I wasn't being flippant, she said. Or maybe I was. I don't know. I am sort of used to it. I'm used to the idea that I don't like him very much any more.

– That's a shame.

– Is it? I'm not sure I ever did like him that much. I realised that when I met you.

Darius looked down at her. Her eyes were still closed.

– I thought you were beautiful, she said softly. Really beautiful. I'd never met anyone like you. And then the world fell in, and I never saw you again.

After a while, he said:

– I thought about you. All the time, in prison. For ages, you were about the only thing I thought about. Then after a while, I taught myself not to think about you. I survived better that way. And I thought that you must have regretted it, that you must have been trying to forget about it too. You were older than me, you were clever, you were going to be successful. All I'd thought of doing was going off to Biarritz to spend the summer surfing and smoking dope.

She smiled and opened her eyes.

– I'm not that much older than you. You make me sound like the wicked stepmother.

– You know what I mean.

She nodded.

– I thought it was all my fault, she said. Everything. I thought it might just as well have been me holding that bow and arrow. I thought I should have been in prison, not you.

He frowned.

– I never imagined you thinking anything like that, he said. I thought you'd just gone back to Francis, got on with your life.

She looked at him.

– Don't you know? No, I suppose you don't. I didn't have anything to do with your brother. After the horrible court thing. He just went straight back to Cambridge next term, carried on as though nothing had happened. I went home to Mum and Dad and never went back. I stayed at home with them for five years, I never saw him again. I fell to pieces, Darius. I wasn't strong like you. It took me a long time to come back.

– I had no idea.

She smiled and touched his tattooed arm.

– There's no reason why you should have, she said. You were busy ravishing beautiful aid workers around the world.

– Seriously, he said. I didn't know. I thought you'd stayed with him. What happened?

– Well, I was at home with Mum and Dad for about five years. I didn't get my degree because I never went back to Cambridge. I spent a lot of time reading when I wasn't having therapy. I read up about your grandfather, Zachary, and it got me interested in the charity he set up in the '50s, World Action. I got a job as a volunteer there eventually, it was my first step back into the world. And it turned out I was quite good at it. They made me a director, after I'd been working there for a few years. Then about ten years ago, I was at a fundraiser in New York and Francis was at the same table as me. It was the first time I'd seen him since we were all in that bloody courtroom – she reached out and touched his arm again – sorry, she said. I hate thinking about that. Anyway, there he was, now the rich hedge fund man who was one of the Labour party's biggest donors, pledging God knows how much for World Action that night.

She shrugged.

– It just happened. It seemed exciting somehow. We both knew lots of the same people. He seemed to me to have some sense of idealism still, he seemed to believe in the power of capital to make change for good. We had all that shared history. I don't know. It was a whirlwind thing. We got married and we had Alice a year later. And it was about that time that we heard that you had come back to the UK, that you'd bought this place in Cornwall.

He shook his head.

– When I got that first letter from you, when was it, seven or eight years ago? I just assumed you'd been with Francis all that time, ever since it happened. And you'd only been back with him for a couple of years.

– I don't regret it, she said. I've got Alice and James. I've got my work. And I've got a lover as well, now I'm telling you everything. He's a poet. I see him in London. He hasn't got any money, and he doesn't talk about money, and he's got a beautiful smile.

Darius raised his eyebrows.

– And before you ask, I'm not going to tell you anything about him, Belinda said. Her eyes were closed, but she was smiling. Nothing at all.

– We'll see about that, said Darius. But let's leave the poet for later. You and Francis: are things that bad between you?

– Things between me and Francis? Are they bad? Yes, I suppose. I don't know whether he was really like this ten years ago and I chose not to notice, or whether he's changed. It's the obsession with money, the glorification of it, the wallowing in it. I can't bear it. I think of your grandfather, and I feel the poor old thing turning in his grave when I hear your brother crowing about some deal. I don't want the children to grow up thinking that money is something to be worshipped.

– Is he really like that?

She sat up fully and put her hand on his arm again.

– You're going to have to work that out this weekend. I've been trying for years. I've reached my limit.

– Don't expect too much, he said. I'm trying to keep up already.

She turned to face him and put her elbows on his knees, looking up at his face.

– This is a strange weekend, Darius. I kind of want you to look after me. Does that make any sense?

Chapter Fourteen

The summer of 1943 was another of those wartime summers that were remembered years later: month after month of still, hot summer days, the skies now mercifully free of dogfights and the drone of incoming bombers. The everyday privations – the lack of food, the disappearance of more and more everyday items from the shelves, the terrible news from Europe and the fear of the knock on the door and the postman bearing a telegram – all these were somehow suffered a little easier now that the bombs weren't dropping.

Felicity certainly felt that. With the Blitz two years in the past, she no longer dreaded her husband telling her that he planned another trip to Plymouth. Zachary was much caught up in the huge task of healing the wounds of the onslaught on his constituency city but – and she felt selfish even thinking such a thing – she no longer panicked when the telephone rang at the Range during one of his trips to the south west.

That Friday morning, she woke early. Zachary was still asleep, having been up late the night before writing speeches, and she crept out of their room and out down the corridor to the nursery. She pushed the open door ajar and stood over her sleeping son, Richard. He would be four years' old on Sunday. It would be an odd birthday for him, because the Range by then would be filled with people. She would need to make sure that the day still somehow remained his, despite all the noise around him.

The third annual conference of Level Ground was to take place this coming weekend. As in the past two years, Zachary had decided to hold it at the Range but the huge strides taken by the party over the last twelve months meant that many more delegates were expected. She left the nursery and carried on down the corridor, looking into all the rooms to check that everything was in place. Each room was filled with green canvas Army camp beds – they had borrowed 150 of them from the Guards barracks at Windsor.

Level Ground had won three byelections since the last Conference, and with her husband's defection from the Liberals, that made four MPs standing in the Commons under the party standard. Each victory had been a triumph, whether it be against Tory or Labour incumbents, as voters turned their backs on the "London men" who were seen as somehow responsible for the war and voted instead for the new visionaries who spoke eloquently about a future where everything was held in joint ownership.

Felicity went quietly downstairs and made herself a cup of tea in the kitchen, then stood outside the back door looking out over the small kitchen garden at the back of the house. The sun had not yet appeared above the trees over to the right, and the air was clear and clean. She walked along the length of the house and out to the front, where the lawns were dominated by the pale cream marquee that was to host the weekend's speeches and meetings. The gardens looked perfect – the grass newly trimmed, the box hedges surrounding each of the enclosed plantings finished off with sharp edges.

She sat down on a bench under one of the elms and drank the rest of her tea. This was what they had worked together for since they had first met five years before. Zachary's vision of a new England, personified here this weekend at the Range, was now a reality. It wouldn't be long, surely, before Churchill summoned her husband to join the wartime coalition government to make plans for when the war ended. Level Ground had arrived. Nigel Jenkins was bringing down proofs of Zachary's new book that morning.

– It's not going to threaten the sales of *Marianne*, Jenkins had said yesterday on the telephone. But it will do a decent number. We sold out of his first one, remember?

Marianne had been a bestseller for eight months. It seemed somehow foolish now, her scribbling, in the light of these immense social changes they were helping to usher in. She didn't want to talk about it this weekend, she didn't want attention taken away from the themes of the conference. It was bound to come up, of course – people would bring their own copies for her to sign. Perhaps in some ways it did have its place here, the story of hope and strength against seemingly impossible odds. But she would downplay it. It was just a story. This was a new world they were helping to usher in.

And this was just the stage in which to do it. The house and the gardens looked better than they had ever done in this early morning light. Her team of gardeners had worked all out to have the estate looking pristine in time for the conference. Nothing was out of place. Nothing was superfluous.

– It's wonderful, my darling, absolutely wonderful!

Zachary was striding out across the lawns from the house. He kissed her cheek as he sat down beside her on the bench. She took his hand.

– This is your moment, dear Zachary, she said. This is what you have been working so hard for. This weekend will be a triumph for you, I know it.

He shook his head.

– For all of us, he said. It is our triumph: you, me, all the fine men and women who will begin to arrive today, all those we have yet to meet. That is the marvel of Level Ground: we have achieved our successes jointly, fairly, by working as one. We have proved our very philosophy by our actions. There is no one source of power, no Churchill or Mussolini, but a true mass force, an unstoppable force which consists in the simple notion of man embracing his fellow man.

He looked around at the glittering gardens in the early morning light.

– And it began here, my darling, he said. Under these trees, on this ground, beside this river. You have helped me more than you will ever know. You have created the stage on which our play is to unfold.

He swept his arm before him.

– You have painted a masterpiece. This is England, this is the England for which our fellow countrymen have yearned, an England free from the cruelties and violences of the past.

– I do believe Nature herself is in approval with your ideas, said Felicity. She sanctions your vision with her beauty.

– You understand it, I know, he said. I so wanted the Range somehow to reflect what we are here to talk about. Everything, everyone working together for the common cause. Everything and everyone being as good as they can be, being as useful as they can be.

He turned to her.

– You know, my darling, that the time for me to make the announcement about our beloved Range is imminent? You know that I must announce our handing of the place over to the nation?

– I know, she said. And I support you absolutely and always will, my dear Zachary.

– You have helped me come to it, my darling. Without you, I could never have got us to this point. Without you, the Range would not be what it is, a living expression of faith. Nor what it can become for future generations.

They sat in silence for a moment, her hand squeezing his, and she felt an immense tranquillity.

The delegates began to arrive at the Range after lunch that day, and by evening, most had come. The house rang with voices, shouts, laughter, and Felicity had had to stay much longer with Richard in his nursery before the child would sleep. On the Saturday morning, Zachary had arranged for long wooden trestle tables to be laid out in the early morning sunshine in front of the house, and mugs of tea and bacon sandwiches were served by the local servants they had re-cruited for the weekend.

Now Felicity stood at the back of the marquee with her arm around her son's waist – she had stood him up on a box so that he could see over the seated audience towards the podium where his father was speaking. Nigel Jenkins stood next to her, that ironic smile never far from his lips.

She was wearing a tightly buttoned white jacket over a navy blue pleated skirt, and her blonde hair and red lipstick marked her out very clearly. The audience was predominantly male: schoolteachers, public servants, the occasional serviceman in uniform. Here and there, young women without hats, scribbling notes into pocket books, nodding vigorously. There must have been almost 200 people in the marquee, and both sides were crowded with those standing without a seat.

– I say again, Zachary was calling out, his slightly high-pitched voice almost querulous with emotion. I say again, this Coalition Government will fail to deliver on all of its promises of a new Jerusalem, its much vaunted pledges of a new land for our returning heroes, if it does not address the fundamental issue of our time, which is that of private ownership.

Hear Hears rang out, and a pale-skinned young man in a suit too big for him shouted:

– Common ownership for all!

– I commend you Sir, shouted Zachary. For without common ownership of the land on which we walk, the land which offers up the food which sustains us, the land on which we build our homes, without that common ownership, we return from one fight overseas to a new fight on our own shores. An unnecessary fight, a debilitating and soul-destroying fight, in which those who claim prior rights of ownership seek to perpetuate a system of injustice which has brought us to these perilous times.

– Shame, another called out.

– Shame indeed, Sir, Zachary replied. Shame upon our governors – Tories, Liberals and Labour too – shame upon them for conspiring to deny every man, woman and child of this country the simple dignified right of sharing with his neighbour what this precious earth of ours holds in store for us.

– What we need now is the adoption, in our public and political life, of those elementary ethical principles to which we have long paid lip-service in our churches. We no longer need to bind ourselves to nonsensical party politics, to the machinations of the Parliamentary parties, to the moribund ways of the past. Level Ground is not a political party, my friends, it is a movement, it is a belief in the common good, it is a religious faith every inch as ecstatic as the original teachings of the son of Joseph of Galilee!

A great roar from the crowd.

Nigel Jenkins leaned into Felicity's ear.

– The old boy's pushing it a bit there, my dear.

– Be quiet, she hissed.

Jenkins smiled, then pointed towards a man standing against the canvas at one side, a notebook and pencil in his hands.

– Greene will love this, he whispered. He loves a bit of religious demagogery.

Felicity looked over towards the rather bored-looking man taking notes.

– Who is he? she whispered back.

– Graham Greene. The novelist. He's probably reporting for *The Times*. You'd better be nice to him later.

Zachary continued from the stage.

– My fellow delegates, he said, a different tone in his voice now. At this, our third annual conference of Level Ground, I wish to put into practice the principles of which I speak, which we share in our discussions and our pamphlets and our speeches all around the country. I hereby announce that on the successful election of a government led by Level Ground, I shall pass over this house, the Range, and all of its land and estates to the public so that it may become a permanent education facility for future generations. This remarkable place, which I had the entirely arbitrary good fortune to possess through the outmoded principle of inheritance, has stimulated my thinking over the years in ways I cannot now count. I hope it has exerted some of its mysterious influence upon you all too. And so let it continue that influence into the future as a home of teaching for our young so that they may learn at an earlier age than I how private property is the enemy of progress.

A great roar from the audience, who got to their feet to give him a standing ovation.

When the talks ended for lunch, everyone trooped back over to the tables in front of the house, where towering plates of ham and cheese sandwiches were laid alongside jugs of beer. Felicity was putting cheese sandwiches onto a plate for Richard, who nervously held onto her skirt in the noisy throng of people, when a voice behind her said:

– Lady Frome, I believe we have met once before.

She turned round and recognised the writer Jenkins had pointed out.

– Mr Greene, she said, a little flustered. I'm sorry, my hands are rather full with sandwiches and sons, otherwise I would shake your hand. We have met, you say?

– In St Tropez, before the war.

She steered Richard back away from the table, trying to remember all the time. They sat down on the grass amongst the other diners.

– Mr Connolly was giving one of his performances in a little bistro, Greene continued. We spoke only briefly.

– I'm so sorry, Felicity said. Life before the war seems like a strange country to me now. Forgive my appalling memory.

– There is nothing to forgive, he said, gravely. Then: I must congratulate you, Lady Frome, on the success of *Marianne*. You are the talk of London, yet you are never there.

She cut a sandwich in half and passed it to Richard.

– Who is this man, Mummy? the boy asked. Does he work for Daddy too?

Felicity laughed.

– No Moley, don't be silly. Mr Greene is a respected writer, and we are delighted to have him here.

Greene looked idly at the child.

– The child is called Moley?

– Oh, I'm sorry. That's our nickname for him. He's Moley, from *Wind in the Willows*. Because he's so sweet. He's actually called Richard.

– How very charming. You never come to London? he persisted.

She looked at him.

– Very rarely, she said. I am kept so very busy here.

– A shame, he said.

– You are reporting on the conference? Felicity asked.

– Yes. He yawned. *The Times* wanted the inside track on your husband's remarkable rapid rise. Might I speak to him?

– Yes of course, I will find him for you. Will you look after Richard for a moment?

– Oh there's really no hurry, he answered, grimacing. I will introduce myself later.

He took a drink of beer from the glass in his hand.

– So you are buried in the country plotting to overthrow the capitalist system? he continued. Quite a journey from your friends in St Tropez. I seem to remember a rather more louche political philosophy being espoused then.

– You make fun of me, Mr Greene. But you cannot doubt the sincerity and passion of our people here. Do you not sense a change in the air?

– Oh I don't doubt your schoolteachers and nursery-maids are sincere enough, Lady Frome. They adore your husband. But it is, I am afraid, an adolescent venting of the spleen. Life will return to normal when the war is over. Life always returns to normal.

– I believe you are wrong, Felicity said quietly.

He looked at her.

– Then come up to London and debate it with me. They still find some oysters at Wiltons, you know.

He got up.

– I shall go in search of your husband. One has copy to file.

Felicity was livid. The impertinence of the man! She

gathered the empty plates beside her and was about to lift her son up when Jenkins walked over, a grin on his face. He sat down.

– And you can take that ridiculous look off your face, Nigel, she said crossly.

Now he laughed.

– I do believe you are blushing, Felicity, he said.

– Your friend Mr Greene proved himself to be extremely rude, she said. First he denigrated Zachary's work, then he had the temerity to invite me to eat oysters with him in Wiltons.

Jenkins laughed even more.

– Oh that's priceless, he said. That's absolutely priceless. Of course you must go, we need more filthy gossip in London.

– I am not amused Nigel, she said firmly, now picking a rather sleepy Richard up in her arms. Jenkins stood too, and placed a hand on her arm.

– I'm sorry, he smiled. He's jealous of you, of course. Professionally, I mean. *Marianne* has sold a hundred times more copies than *The Power and The Glory*. He probably wants to pick your brains about how to write a bestseller. Very worthy, his stuff. All a bit too serious, I think. He's a rum one, that's for sure.

– Never mind Mr Greene, she said. We shall overcome him. But I must warn Zachary to be on his guard when he speaks to him.

She walked off with Richard's head on her shoulder and empty plates in her hand.

The Times article which appeared the following week under Greene's byline was a savage piece.

"The delegates who gathered under canvas in the grounds of the fabulous Lutyens mansion owned by Sir Zachary Frome and his glamorous popular-novelist wife Felicity were a mixture of pipe-smoking London intellectuals and star-struck teachers from the provinces, some of whom clutched copies of their leader's histrionic volumes setting out his case for the abolition of private ownership. Others could be seen furtively carrying a copy of *Marianne*, the latest pageturner produced by Lady Felicity, presumably in the hope of securing an autograph. It was a curious event. Even a hardened cynic such as your correspondent found it impossible to dismiss the sincerity of the adolescent yearnings for fair play and equality on show at the conference, but to call Level Ground a political movement is rather like suggesting that the Home Guard – admirable though they may be – might be called upon to tackle Field Marshal Rommel in the Arabian deserts."

Zachary, reading the article with his wife in the drawing room of the Range, was unperturbed.

– I can't imagine why *The Times* of all people sent some minor novelist down to report on the Conference, my dear. Why, he's hardly sold any books, has he? He's not what I would call a proper writer, not like you my darling. What a strange choice. Anyway, it doesn't matter. I am convinced that our colleagues are more committed, more impassioned than ever. They will have gone back to their homes determined to spread the word still further. With four MPs in the House and a national party that is growing week by week, we will very soon be unstoppable. It is the will of the people of this great country that will prevail, of that I have no doubt.

Felicity agreed with her husband, and told him how supportive and excited all the delegates to whom she had spoken over the weekend had been. She looked at him sitting across from her on the other side of the fireplace, his eager, almost childlike enthusiasm lighting up his face, and she hoped that he was right.

Chapter Fifteen

Darius sat between Alice and James at the long kitchen table while they ate their supper. Tink was chopping carrots further down the table, and Belinda was stirring a big casserole pot on the Aga.

– Where's Francis? Darius asked.

– Oh, he'll be in his study, phoning America. He always spends an hour or two phoning America when he gets back from London. He'll come down and join us when we eat later.

– Why does he phone America every day? Tink asked.

– Daddy has investors in America, Alice said, seriously.

– Oh, said Tink. That sounds very grown up. I don't think I'd be a very good investor. I don't have any money, to start with.

Darius laughed. Alice glared at him, baked beans sauce around her mouth. Darius smiled at her.

– I'm sure Daddy's American investors are very nice, he said.

Alice looked at him for a second, then carried on talking:

– Tink hasn't got any money because she is a faery, Mummy, she said. She told us.

– That's very nice darling, said Belinda, putting the lid back on the pot. Would you like your uncle Darius to tell you a story when you go to bed?

Alice nodded.

– Will you, Darius? asked Belinda. Then Tink and I can have a glass of wine.

Upstairs, while he waited for the children to finish brushing their teeth in the bathroom, Darius sat on James's bed. It was his old bedroom. He hadn't been in here since they arrived. It looked different of course: the wallpaper wasn't the same, he didn't recognise any of the furniture. He looked over at the window in the corner, and remembered leaning out of there and smoking joints.

That brought it all back. The sick fear in his stomach. All the noise: the crying, the shouting. The police appearing. The barking of dogs, the flashlights everywhere. His father talking to some uniformed man. How they brought him up here to get a jacket before putting him in the back of a police car. He'd seen a glimpse of Nana's face at the window of her bedroom, pale, terrified, as the car drove him off to spend the night at Marlow police station.

He was back the following day, this time sitting in the back of his father's car, the lawyer who had arranged bail in the front passenger seat. The two men had spoken quietly and seriously all the way back to the Range, and Darius remembered looking out at the lawns as they drove under the elder branches down the drive, thinking then how different everything seemed, as though they had come back to the grounds of a different house.

He couldn't recall how long he had spent back at home before the trial. He supposed it must have been weeks, but he had no memory of it. Was he sleeping back here in his bedroom? Presumably, but sitting here now on James's bed, he couldn't picture it.

All he could remember was the trial. How the bow and arrow were brought into the court, how diagrams showing positions were shown to the jury. They seemed to know everything: someone had found the motorbike, even his rugby friend Dave appeared in court and didn't look at him, but told the court about Darius's drug dealing in school, how he'd bring the drugs back from London.

He remembered Belinda giving evidence. Her head was bowed so that her hair fell down over her face, and she spoke in a soft voice giving brief answers to the questions. He tried to make eye contact but she never looked at him, and after a while the judge decided that she had had enough and dismissed her from the witness box.

Francis had seemed nerveless. While not deliberately blaming his brother in any way, he made it clear that he had never known of Darius's drug habits and had never indulged himself, not even at Cambridge, where he was a successful and influential student. The judge seemed to like him. Francis regretted the impulsive decision to accept Darius's offer of dope and acid, swore that he would never make the same mistake ever again.

I find you guilty of manslaughter. He remembered now looking at the judge as he said those words, then looking over at his mother and father whose faces stayed impassive, only Francis next to them returning his look with a hesitant lifting of one hand. His father appeared a couple of hours later when he was down in the cell underneath the court room. Darius remembered the moment his father came into the cell, he remembered the look of embarrassed disgust on his father's face, the clumsy attempt at a hug which ended up as a handshake before his father turned and left, and Darius was escorted out to a van to be driven away.

He felt his hands gripping the bedspread so tightly that he had creased it. He shook his head, smoothed out the blanket and stood up. He wiped a hand across his brow, smeared the sweat into his long dark hair. Just then, both children came running into the room.

– James didn't finish doing his teeth properly, Alice shouted.

– I did so, you liar, James called back.

They stopped in front of him.

– What's wrong, Uncle Darius? asked Alice.

He swept his hand over his face again.

– Nothing, nothing.

He smiled.

– Do you always make this much noise when you clean your teeth?

– Can you tell us a story here and then Alice goes back to her room? asked James.

– That's not fair, said Alice.

Darius leaned down and patted the bed.

– You both sit here tonight, and then tomorrow night I'll tell you another story in Alice's room, OK?

They sat down, and he sat down on the floor opposite them, his back against the wall.

– What was I going to tell you about?

– The men who catch fishes, Alice said.

– Oh yes. The fishermen who catch the dreams of fishes. You didn't believe me, did you? I don't blame you Alice, most people don't believe it either. But you have to believe it, because it's true.

– Where are they? asked James, pulling a blanket over him.

– They live in a place called Madagascar, which is a big island in the Indian Ocean off the coast of Africa, a long, long way away from here.

– Why were you in Mad...Mad...

– Madagascar, Alice. I lived there for a couple of years. I was working in the kitchen of a restaurant on one of the beaches. We used to cook the fish that the fishermen brought in on their boats every day. They used to take the boats out early in the morning, little wooden boats with oars, and they used to row out to sea with their fishing lines wound up on wooden sticks.

– Did you go with them? asked James.

– Sometimes, when I had a day off, sometimes I would go out with one of the men and help them row while they fished. That's when they told me about it. The dreamer fish, they called them. It was just one kind of fish, quite a small one with a shiny orange back. I don't know what everyone else calls them, but the fishermen called them dreamer fish. They said that dreamer fish created dreams for all the other fish, who were too busy rushing around and eating and playing and shooting in and out of caves on the bottom of the sea.

– Dreamer fish were different to all the other fish,

because they spent all their time dreaming, and they shared their dreams with all the other fish who were too busy to dream. They spread their dreams around the sea and the other fish felt happy when they bounced into one of their dreams, so they would give the dreamer fish food to eat, because the dreamer fish were always too busy dreaming to be able to look for food.

– And when one of the fishermen caught a dreamer fish – which wasn't very often because there aren't many of them and they don't usually take a hook because they're too busy dreaming – they would very carefully take the hook out of the fish and then they would hold the fish in front of them and put his mouth up very close to their mouth so that the fish's dreams escaped into them, and then they would put the fish back into the sea so that he could carry on dreaming.

– Did you ever catch a dreamer fish? asked Alice.

– Only once. A fisherman I was with caught one and instead of putting the dreams into his own mouth, he pressed the fish up against my lips and the dreams came into me before he put it back in the sea.

– What was the dream? James asked.

– It was a very strange dream. Dreamer fish don't dream like human beings dream. It was a dream about swirling bright blue and green and yellow colours, all spinning in the water like long scarves, and there was music in the dream, which wasn't like music we listen to but was like sea music, with lots and lots of tiny noises all making sounds at the same time so that it sounded like an orchestra with a million players in it.

– What else was in the dream? asked Alice.

– Were there sharks in the dream? asked James.

– I don't think there were any sharks, said Darius. There were lots of different patterns and shapes and colours, and the music all sort of moved around and got louder and quieter and closer and further away. It was a very beautiful and happy dream and it lasted in me for a few minutes before it drifted away, like dreams do. And that's how I

159

found out about how fishes dream.

– Is that a true story? asked Alice.

– Yes, it's true, said Darius. When you're older, maybe we can go to Madagascar and try and find the fishermen again. They're probably still there, and the dreamer fish will still be there. You'd like it in Madagascar.

– Can we? said James. I want to go and find the dreamer fish. Do you think there are dreamer fish in the river here?

– Maybe, James, although I've never seen one. Now go to sleep. Try dreaming about dreamer fish. You know, everybody and everything in the world dreams. Trees dream, and stones dream, and waterfalls dream and bumble bees dream. Dreaming is what we all do when we're not so busy being who we are.

He took Alice's hand and walked with her to her bedroom opposite.

– Good night Uncle Darius, she said sleepily.

– Sweet dreams, he said.

Chapter Sixteen

Felicity and her father were wrapped up in heavy overcoats and blowing the steam from two mugs of tea. They were sitting on metal chairs at the back of a school assembly hall in Dartford, Kent. The hall was filled with people, most of them sitting at long low tables with boxes and piles of voting papers in front of them. Large signs had been erected at various stages over each of the tables, giving the hall a hectic air which together with the constant buzz of conversation was beginning to exhaust her. Over in a far corner she could see Zachary deep in conversation with a group of men, his hands thrust into the trouser pockets of his suit. The men were listening to him earnestly as he talked, the light from the overhead lamps flashing on his glasses every so often. He looked vulnerable to her, almost schoolboyish. She knew this was not how others saw him, certainly not the group of acolytes standing around him, but to her he retained an innocence which filled her with a wish to protect him.

It was now two years on from the calamitous General Election of 1945. She thought again of that awful night in the Plymouth Devonport Guildhall, as it became clear that Zachary was on course to lose his seat to the Labour candidate. All the effort of the previous years, the endless campaigning, the joyful conferences at the Range, the radio talks, the speeches across the country: all of it had come to nothing. Level Ground had been demolished by a Labour party promising a New England after the war years. Only one Level Ground MP retained his seat out of twenty four candidates which the party fielded and Zachary himself had tendered his resignation to the shell-shocked Level Ground Committee three months later.

– Penny for your thoughts.

Her father's gruff voice beside her interrupted her reflections.

– Oh Daddy, I couldn't help thinking. About two years ago. It only feels like yesterday.

Her father nodded, and squeezed her hand. She noticed these days that his grip, always so fierce and strong, was becoming weaker.

– He's been through a lot, he said. I take my hat off to him. He's no quitter. I'm not sure I'd have had the strength of mind to get back in the ring after what he went through.

She squeezed his hand back.

– Oh, you! There's no ring you wouldn't climb back into, you old scrapper.

He shook his head.

– You're wrong. It takes a particular kind of strength to lay yourself out for the public like your Zac did. I do my fighting behind closed doors. He's had the whole world looking at him for all that time and then they go and slap him in the face. You've got to be tough to want to go back in again after that.

– I do worry about him, she said. He takes on so much. He thought for such a long time about whether he should do this, join Labour I mean.

– That's what surprised me. I thought your Zac thought Attlee's mob were as bad as mine. All of us out to take what's rightfully not ours from the innocent working man, all that stuff. You know I don't agree with him, but at least I thought I understood his position. Now here he is standing as a Labour man.

She sighed.

– Everyone wants a little piece of Zachary, she said. They want some of his magic to rub off on them. Those awful Labour men – Mr Bevin, Mr Dalton –

– Hah! her father exclaimed. Don't even mention their bloody names to me.

– I know, I know, Daddy. But they need Zachary. They're

such ghastly types, they know the public don't really like them. They want Zachary to bring them some popularity. Even though Level Ground failed, the voters always loved Zachary. He makes people feel there might be a cause to hope.

– I recognise that. But it's a gamble for him, if he's not really behind their thinking. What's in it for him?

– He thinks there is more of a chance of introducing his ideas into the Labour government from the inside than from standing at the sidelines. That's his phrase. He says he will offer them his voice in return for them listening to his.

– I've no doubt about his sincerity, her father replied solemnly. He's one of the most decent men I've ever met. Deluded as dandelion, but bloody decent. I just hope that he doesn't find the soup at the Westminster table too bitter.

– Oh, my poor Badger, she said softly.

Her father raised an eyebrow.

– Badger? he said.

Felicity felt herself flushing.

– Oh dear, that's my name for him. Badger. Because he's always the one who everyone needs to sort everything out, like Badger does in *Wind in the Willows*.

Her father grinned.

– And who are you, petal?

Felicity looked seriously at him.

– He calls me Ratty. You're not to tell a soul.

Her father laughed out loud.

– Badger and Ratty, he chortled. I've heard it all now.

– Actually, you haven't, Daddy. You're included too.

– I am? Her father looked pleased. Who am I?

– I'm afraid you're Mr Toad.

Chapter Seventeen

Darius left Alice's door open and walked on down the corridor. He wasn't ready to go back down and join the others in the kitchen. He carried on, passing the old portraits which hung on the walls, the faded carpet muffling the sound of his steps. A skateboard was propped up against the wall. He felt like picking it up and trying it out, but thought better of it.

He stood outside his father's room. He hesitated for a moment, then pushed the door open quietly. The old man was asleep in bed, the sound of his breathing just audible in the still room. Darius sat on a chair beside the bed and watched his father's face, papery white and run with thin blue veins. There was a book beside the bed – Annie, the daycare assistant, must have been reading to him today. He picked it up. Agatha Christie, Murder on the Orient Express.

– Are you going to get to the end of this, Dad? he said aloud. Have you worked out who did it yet?

He placed the book back on the table. He watched the slight movement of the bedclothes as his father breathed in and out.

He thought about the times in Mexico when he had attended end-of-life ceremonies with his teacher, the holy man in the Durango village. He had learned how to distinguish between those who were ill, and wanted help, and those who had made the decision to go. His teacher rarely addressed him directly, and never explained anything to him, but had been willing to let him observe and learn. Others in the village would explain things to him afterwards, or give other stories of previous ceremonies, so that he built up a knowledge of the subtle differences in the ceremonies which reflected the wishes of the individual in question.

That was always the key: those attending and conducting the ceremonies had an obligation to assist the dying, to make their journey into the next life as peaceful and as tranquil as possible. Those who passed through without help ran the risk of taking with them unsettled grievances or negative emotions which would remain with them and cause their next life to be more difficult. The soul had a right to be set free from the troubles of this earth, and it was the responsibility of those who stayed behind to assist in this.

He was sure that his father, whom he had not seen for over twenty years now, was preparing to leave. That had been the overwhelming message he had received this morning, when he had first laid his hand on him. The dry desert, the fire whose flames had finished and which was sending up a spiral of smoke into the sky. It was a familiar symbol. Once more, he lay his hand very gently on the old man's forehead and closed his eyes.

Almost immediately, the same imagery presented itself: the desert hills, the blackened embers of wood in the stone fire in the sand, the wisps of smoke curling up gently.

Was this why he had been called back? Was this why he had responded to that strange invitation a week ago? He hadn't needed to accept. He'd had nothing to do with the family for so long. But he'd felt little doubt about it: he had to come. Perhaps his father somehow had reached out to him.

– Did you call for me, Dad? he asked quietly. He watched the old man's chest moving very slightly up and down as he breathed thinly in his sleep. Obviously his father hadn't sent the cards, but somehow this gathering here, twenty-five years after the death, somehow it had been originated by his father. He felt sure of that now.

– We have no more trouble between us, Dad. I've come back.

Chapter Eighteen

This was to be their tenth Summer Garden Party. The first, in July 1946, had been Felicity's idea: it had been her way of replacing the excitement and drama of the annual Level Ground conference at the Range once the party collapsed after the 1945 election. A much smaller affair, this was a Frome family and friends celebration with the annual theme of a passage from *Wind in the Willows*. It gave them all a chance to dress up, a practice into which Zachary in particular always threw himself with great enthusiasm.

The family always dressed as the characters they knew each other as: Zachary as Badger, Felicity as Ratty, Richard as Mole, Bill Drummond as Toad. As Felicity sat in her dressing room upstairs, applying whiskers to her cheeks with a mascara pencil, she smiled as she listened to Zachary and Richard laughing outside on the lawn as they set out the markers for the sack race, always a favourite item on the list of activities at the party.

– I'm sure I've won more of the races than you, Moley! she could hear Zachary taunting their son.

– Dad, I was only seven when we had the first one. I don't think the odds were even.

– Nonsense, my dear boy. Each man must be held to account. It is a grimly serious business.

– It's a ridiculous business, Richard replied, but she could hear the pleasure and laughter in his voice.

– When you go up to Cambridge next year, you will thank me for instilling the virtues of a competitive spirit inside you.

That mention of Cambridge gave her a familiar twist inside: she was still not accustomed to the thought of their son leaving home. She did not worry so much for him. He was a confident boy, clever and industrious, determined to follow the father he so admired into politics. He was in so many ways so much more practical, down to earth, than both his parents. The imaginative flights which took her into her fictional world and Zachary into his idealism had never taken hold with Richard. Indeed, he often seemed to both of them to view them with a certain amusement which left them wondering who was the grown up.

She knew also that Richard was particularly worried about his father following Zachary's defeat at Dartford two months before. The 1955 election had not been such a cataclysmic event generally as previous votes but Richard's defeat by the Conservative candidate at Dartford had been noteworthy. He had resigned from the Labour party several months before the election, continuing as an Independent until the general election, and father and son had debated the issues surrounding his resignation at length over suppers at the Range.

For Zachary, the Labour party's support for the Churchill's government's nuclear defence policy had been a step too far. Ever since his election in 1947, he had doggedly taken the Labour party whip on a number of issues with which he felt uncomfortable, only because as he said there was still a chance that his views might influence the party. With their support for the Tories' programme of nuclear weapons, he had found himself unable to continue, and had resigned. Richard, on the other hand, filled with youthful confidence from his recent success with the Debating Club at school in Marlow, had for the first time disagreed openly with his father and had told him that he thought Attlee's support of the policy an acceptable pragmatism.

Hearing them now through the window joshing with each other in the gardens, she was glad that their close relationship did not seem to have been damaged by their first political disagreement. But she too worried about Zachary: how many more defeats could her husband shoulder?

– Toot toot!

She turned around and burst out laughing. In the doorway of her dressing room stood her father, leaning heavily on a thick wooden walking stick and wearing a three-piece green checked suit topped off with a leather helmet and driving goggles.

– Mr Toad! she cried.

– The very man. Her father bowed carefully, holding on to the door jam for support.

– Oh, I think you've reached a new pinnacle of Toad fashion this year, Daddy. Where on earth did you find that suit?

He walked slowly to an armchair and sat down.

– I've been sorting out our clobber since your mother died, he said. She kept everything, God bless her. Everything. I bought this suit about forty years ago and she kept it in mothballs. That's the pong. I had to have it let out a bit, of course. Not as slim as I was.

He looked at her.

– But you look exactly as you did when you left home, young lady. You never age. That's the Corby iron in you.

– I'm glad you came, Daddy. The tea party wouldn't quite be the tea party without you here.

– What, with old Badger marching around telling everyone what to do? I don't think so, my dear. How is he, anyway? I spoke to him a little last night when I got here.

She sighed.

– Oh, you know Zachary. He's been through such a lot, but he's not slowing down. Has he told you about World Action?

– This charity thing? He mentioned something last night. I told him I didn't think much of it. Charity begins at home, I told him. He just looked at me in that way he has.

She smiled.

– The two of you are like chalk and cheese, but sometimes I think you could be brothers.

Later that afternoon, after an exhausting round of

cricket, rounders, the sack race and hide-and-seek, the party sat on rugs on the lawns above the house, drinking tea and eating scones and sandwiches. There were about 25 in all, made up of family and friends and several of the tenants who lived on the edges of the estate. All had made an effort to dress up, and Felicity was trying to gather them all into a smaller group so that she could photograph them.

– You all look so splendid, we must have a photograph, she was calling out. You weasels, stop running around and come and sit down there in the front. Where's Pan gone?

– I'm here, the vicar called out, waving a pipe from the back.

After the photographs, Zachary walked over to where the camera stood and clapped his hands, facing them all. He slipped the fur coat from his shoulders.

– Do you mind? he asked. This fur coat is so hot. I'm not sure Badger himself ever really liked to engage in these exhausting games. However, congratulations to everyone and – pointing to the children sitting at the front – in particular to the weasels who I think have this year held the day.

After the applause had died down, he continued.

– I would like to thank you all – family, friends, neighbours – for contributing to our nonsense for yet another year. The Summer Tea Party is in its tenth year this year and it remains an enormous pleasure to Ratty and I to see so many familiar faces. As you know, my own circumstances have changed this year which will result in my spending far more time here at the Range than before. I shall no doubt be put on gardening duty by my indefatigable wife and, if I am honest, the forking up of thick clods may well come very easily to me after eight years of dealing with the Labour Party.

After the laughter had died down, he carried on.

– I shall look forward to seeing more of many of you, and hopefully will encourage you to take an interest in our new charity, World Action, which we launched last year. In addition, I have some news too, which may or may not please our young weasels here at the front. With our own son, Richard, set to leave us next year for Cambridge, I shall have no-one with whom to debate and unless I find some suitable adversaries, I shall find myself banished to the vegetable gardens for good by Ratty.

– You can always pick up the telephone if you need a good argument, Zac, called out his father-in-law.

Zachary bowed his head.

– I can always rely on you Bill, I know that. But to keep me in fighting form for our discussions, I am happy to tell you all that I am returning to the profession I enjoyed many years ago, when I first had the good fortune to meet my beautiful wife.

He reached out and took Felicity's hand.

– The headmaster of Marlow School has very kindly invited me to return as a part-time history teacher and I shall start next term. I look forward immensely to exploring the great moments of our country with these fine young people. If I may not have had the success I sought in bringing about change amongst my contemporaries, then perhaps I may do better in inspiring the next generation to pick up the challenge.

He raised a tea cup.

– To the future!

Chapter Nineteen

The four of them sat at one end of the long table in the dining room: Belinda and Francis one side, Tink and Darius the other. Belinda was spooning out casserole onto their plates, Francis was opening a bottle of red wine. He was smiling.

– I've been wanting to try this for a while, he said, pulling the cork out gently. Needed an occasion.

He turned the bottle around to show the others the label.

– It's an Hermitage, 2000, the hot year. From the Barbantier Domaine. They only make 200 cases a year. Remarkable. Try it.

He began to pour the wine.

– Thanks, but I don't drink, said Darius. Tink will, she drinks like a fish.

Tink laughed, and took a gulp.

– Tink approves, she said. Thank you Francis.

– That's a shame, said Francis, frowning. It's a very rare vintage.

He swirled his glass, held it up to the light and tilted it, thrust his nose in so that his metal spectacles clinked on the edge of the glass, sniffed the wine then, after a little shake of his head, took a sip, keeping the wine in his mouth and tasting it with his eyes closed and the liquid making little sounds as his lips made puckering movements. He swallowed, and opened his eyes.

– Superb, he said. You're missing something, Darius. This is about the most prestigious estate in the Hermitage region. We brokered the sale of it to a Chinese family last year. They paid an astonishing price.

Darius looked at his brother. The last time he had sat

opposite him for dinner at this table had been twenty-five years ago. Belinda had been there too. She had flirted with him. Nargeot bargead, she had mocked him gently. He looked at her but she was busy ladelling out boiled potatoes.

– It's very nice, said Tink, taking another gulp. Do the Chinese family like making wine? Are they going to pick the grapes too? I did that once, in Cornwall. It's backbreaking. And you cut your fingers all the time. I wouldn't buy a vineyard. I'd like to have my own meadow though.

Darius laughed and squeezed Tink's arm.

– Faeries aren't supposed to do hard work anyway, Tink, he said, still chuckling. It makes your wings go all oily so it's difficult to fly.

– That is very true, she nodded.

Francis was staring at them, still frowning.

– What on earth are you talking about? he said.

– Tink is a faery, Belinda said, handing her husband a plate. She looked at Tink and smiled. I think it sounds wonderful. They have faery gatherings, Francis. Is that right, Tink?

– We do, said Tink. Only every now and then. To be honest, I'm not the most dedicated of faeries. I just like the dressing up.

Belinda laughed.

– I think you must make an excellent faery, she said.

– And what may I ask do you and your faeries do? said Francis, peering at her through the thick lenses of his glasses.

– Oh, whatever you fancy, said Tink, taking a plate from Belinda. The gay men like to do lots of hugging so there's lots of that when we meet. But it's mostly about dressing up.

Francis looked at his brother.

– Don't tell me you're a faery too, he said.

Tink laughed.

– Oh, Darius is much too serious to be a faery, she said. And he hasn't got the body for it, too big and muscly.

– I think I could make it as a faery, Darius protested.

Tink shook her head.

– No, you'd be analysing us all the time, she said. We like to spend our time singing and hugging and dancing.

– I can do that, he said.

Tink ran her hand through his hair.

– You can do lots of things, Darius, she said, smiling. But those wouldn't be strong points for you.

Belinda laughed again.

– Is he terribly serious all the time? she said.

Tink nodded.

– Very.

– So's Francis, said Belinda, picking up her fork. Must run in the family.

They were quiet for a moment as all four began to eat the casserole. Darius looked around the room as they ate. It hadn't changed much. The long table was the same one that he had sat around as a child. The extravagant mirrored glass above the fireplace had invitation cards tucked into its sides, just as his parents had done. On the far wall was a painting he didn't recognise. Beneath a bold blue swirling sky, several cartoonish figures seemed to be dancing on a green hill. The sky was decorated in white patterns like leaves.

– That painting's new, he said.

– Picasso, said Francis. 1959. It's called Bacchanale. It's one of 50 prints which he made himself. He was developing his own technique for linocutting then, apparently. I bought it in Sothebys in New York. It was a birthday present for my wife.

– Come to think of it, said Belinda, it looks a bit like one of your faery meetings, Tink.

– Fancy, said Darius. Having your own Picasso.

– I don't think fancy is the term I would use, said Francis.

– No, said Darius. I'm sure not.

– I'm thinking of auctioning it, said Belinda. I know you bought it for my birthday darling, and it was very nice of you, but I've never particularly liked it and we're doing a big World Action auction next year for the 65th anniversary. I thought I might put up the Picasso. You don't mind, do you?

Darius watched his brother. He looked like he did mind, but he remained silent.

– I'm thinking of holding the anniversary event here, Belinda continued. You know, as a kind of homage to the Level Ground conferences your grandfather and grandmother used to stage here. They used to put big marquees up on the lawn, didn't they?

– I don't really know that much about it, Darius said. I was such an ignorant kid, I never paid much attention to the family stories.

Belinda continued to talk and Darius watched his brother's studious indifference.

– I found some photographs in one of your dad's old albums, she was saying. There was a picture of him as a little boy holding your grandmother's hand outside a big white tent, and lots of people milling about in suits. I thought I might host a similar kind of thing here. We're doing a big new drive next year to raise new donors. We need a bit of glamour.

– You'll need to smarten the garden up a bit if it's glamour you're after, said Darius.

Belinda smiled at him.

– That's where you'll come in, Darius, she said. Don't worry, you've got twelve months to get it spick and span.

– Belinda tells me you have concerns about Dad, said Francis.

Darius looked back at his brother, who was glaring at him across the table.

– What exactly are you concerned about? Francis continued. You realise we have been looking after him here, since the onset of his dementia, and that we have daily care and regular nurse and doctor visits? You realise that I have made sure that the best medical care has always been made available to him?

– I don't have any concerns about Dad, said Darius.

– That's not what I was told. Belinda said that you thought there was some problem. I can assure you that if

Dad had a medical problem, it would have been brought to my attention.

– I don't think Dad has any problem with his physical health.

– Then what have you been talking about? said Francis, staring at his brother while angrily forking a boiled potato.

– I haven't particularly being talking about anything, Francis, said Darius calmly. I can tell you what is going on with Dad if you want, but if you don't want me to, then I have no need to discuss him with you. You seem strangely defensive for some reason.

Francis put his knife and fork down on his plate and sat back for a moment. He took off his glasses, wiped them with his serviette, and put them back on.

– Let me explain something to you, Darius, he said, more quietly this time. While you have been spending the last few years globetrotting or surfing in Cornwall, I have been responsible for looking after Mum and Dad. When Mum died, I decided that Belinda and Alice and James and I would move back to the Range to make sure that Dad could be looked after properly. There were signs of dementia even before Mum died, but her death certainly accelerated it. Since then, he has not wanted for anything. I have Power of Attorney over Dad and I am the sole executor of his Will. There is nothing about Dad's life that I do not arrange, and I can absolutely assure you that his dementia is managed in a highly professional manner. There is nothing to give you any cause for concern. You may carry on living your extended teenage rebellion for as long as you wish and wherever you wish to indulge it, but please do not make the mistake of thinking that you have any role to play in the management of the Frome household.

He picked up his knife and fork and continued eating.

– What a pretty speech, said Darius. I imagine you talk to your staff like that. Tell me Francis, how many deaths have you witnessed?

Francis looked up again.

– Just one. And I wish I hadn't had to. She wasn't even twenty years old.

– Even for you, Francis, that was cheap, said Darius. But I'm talking about natural deaths. How many natural deaths, deaths from old age, have you witnessed?

– None. I assume you are going to tell me that you have attended many.

– That's right, Francis. Many. I have studied under people whose job it is to help those who are about to die leave this earth in peace. And I can tell you two things: Dad is very close to death, and he is not at peace. There is something disturbing him, and if I can help him to overcome that before he goes, then I'll do it.

– Listen Darius: I don't care if you want to sit by Dad's bedside and recite some mumbo jumbo that you've picked up from some of your hippy friends. It will make no more sense than his own speech these days, so I'm sure he won't mind. And when you've finished you can go back to Cornwall and Belinda and I can carry on looking after him as we have been doing.

– Oh stop quarrelling, it's boring for Tink and I, said Belinda.

– I wasn't aware I was quarrelling, said Francis. A difference of opinion, yes. All right Darius, let's leave it. Feel free to do what you want while you're here. I have no wish to stop you.

– Can I have some more Chinese wine, said Tink. It's delicious.

– It's an Hermitage, my dear girl, said Francis, pouring more into her glass.

– Anyway Francis, said Darius. Belinda's right. Let's make an effort. We may lead very different lives but there's no reason why we can't find a bit of common ground. I haven't seen you for a long time. Tell me what you've been doing.

Francis poured himself and Belinda more wine, then sat the bottle carefully back down. He picked up his glass, and sniffed again. He smiled, then looked up.

– Doing? What do you mean?

Darius waved his hand around.

– All this stuff, he said. The Picasso, the wine. Presumably they come from somewhere. What do you do for a living?

Francis laughed, and picked up his fork again.

– A living! I'd never really thought of it like that. You mean my company?

– Yes. Magenta, isn't it? How long have you been running it?

– I set it up about fifteen years ago. I'd been working for Tony at Westminster for a few years –

– Who's Tony?

– Blair. I worked as a policy adviser during Tony Blair's first and second governments.

– What were you advising him on?

– Oh, mostly industrial strategy, attracting overseas investment, manpower and union stuff. I didn't get involved in foreign policy. Not much, anyway.

– Why didn't you become an MP? You always said you were going to be an MP like Dad and Grandad.

Francis shrugged.

– I saw a lot of MPs close up when I worked for Tony, he said. I saw what they did, what influence they had, how they operated. It seemed to me to be much less of a useful occupation than I had imagined when I was at Cambridge. They had little autonomy, and not enough time to think. Constantly rushing up and down the country to their constituencies, being hustled into TV studios for half-baked interviews, endlessly lobbied by PR companies, only ever able to absorb bite-sized chunks of arguments. I was usually the one who was preparing the arguments for them into those handy bite sizes, and I came to see that the role had become antiquated, not fit for purpose in the modern world. I thought it would be a waste of my skills.

– What did Dad think? When you told him.

– Dad? Maybe he was disappointed, I don't know. He'd

retired from newspapers by then and he missed all the Westminster gossip. I don't think he really understood my reasoning. But he was from a different generation.

– He was disappointed, said Belinda. He said he thought you could have become a Minister.

Francis shrugged again.

– And wasted even more time, he said. Most Ministers don't know what they're doing half the time. It's a sham, a circus. It's not where the power lies.

– And where does the power lie? asked Darius.

– Power lies in the arms of those who wield it, said Francis. In today's world, it is the corporations which oversee the lives of the world's populations, not the governments. Governments exist to provide the bureaucratic function of administering the decisions of global corporations.

– Well, at least we've found something we can probably agree on, said Darius, smiling. Only you probably think that's a good thing, and I don't.

– It is neither good nor bad, Darius. The very fact that you use such terminology shows how little you understand. It just is, and it will continue to be. There is no other way for the world to operate. Marx was the one who foresaw it, ironically. Obviously he failed to draw the correct conclusions, but his analysis was correct: he who owns and controls the means of production, owns and controls the world.

– But what about democracy? asked Tink. What about people standing up against things they don't believe in?

– My dear girl, virtually every democratic uprising globally over the last fifty years resulted from corporate ambition. From South America to the Arab Spring, these were carefully orchestrated endeavours by corporate leaders to effect changes within global business interests. And those symptoms of democracy which you might be referring to, such as standing up for this or that, well, they pass through into law only so long as they do not disrupt the corporate worldview. A corporation doesn't care whether you're a faery or a fireman, as long as you buy its coffee and drive its cars.

– It's all pretty bleak, Francis, said Darius. Don't you think it's pretty bleak? There doesn't seem to be much room for the individual in your scheme.

Francis sighed.

– You are a romantic, Darius. The notion of the individual as you probably understand it was just another invention of modern capitalism. When all Model T Fords came off the production line in black, and all men wore suits and ties and hats to work, then it made sense for people to be encouraged to wish to be like one another, to be part of a mass. That was one of the many mistakes our grandfather made: he thought he could get everybody behind a mass spiritual movement. But people didn't want to change as a group – they wanted to be the same as each other and the easiest way to express that was by buying things. Then when industrial technology developed so that variations could easily be made in manufacturing, it became more convenient to peddle this notion of individuality. That's what the '60s counterculture revolution was all about: the creation by capitalism of a new and more compliant consumer who was encouraged to believe in his or her individuality.

– Actually I don't necessarily disagree with you, said Darius. I think human beings set too much store on their sense of individuality. I think they should spend more time on identifying with the natural world around them. From what I do know about Grandad, that was his big thing too. Nana used to tell me.

– That is of course not a conclusion that I would reach, but I am glad to see that we may have some common ground. We are, after all, brothers.

– In name, Francis. Let's not pretend that you and I are bound up in family feeling.

– I can assure you, Darius, that I never pretend anything. I am just stating a fact.

– There you go, all bleak again, said Darius. What do you make of your family, then? Of Mum and Dad, of Grandad

181

and Nana, what they all seemed to believe in? You seem to have come a long way from them all.

– I am proud of our family, Francis replied. Both our father and grandfather were diligent public servants. Our father was an excellent journalist. Grandma was a successful novelist. They were all do-ers. They made things happen. Mum did too, in her energetic organisation of Labour party affairs. I see myself very much like them.

– But Grandad's beliefs? persisted Darius. Level Ground, the abolition of private property, the commonwealth of man. Doesn't that hold any meaning for you?

– Frankly, no. I think all political parties encourage messianic movements every now and then, and our poor deluded Grandfather's party was a temporary aberration under extreme wartime conditions.

Darius shook his head.

– I don't believe that at all, he said. I think it is possible for human beings to live in harmony with each other and with the world. I don't think those corporations which you seem to love so much will hold sway for ever.

– They may not. And that's when you should really be fearful, because that's when war takes over. If I were you, Darius, I would continue to live the self-indulgent life which the world affords you and not worry about how things are arranged on your behalf.

Darius smiled.

– I'll do my best. Anyway, tell us all about Magenta. What does it do?

– It's a fund. Or rather, a fund of funds. It's grown over time. Put simply, we take investment decisions, we work as an activist investor in some cases, in others not. We cover most areas, most parts of the world, notably the US. We have an office in New York and one here in London.

– I still can't imagine what you do. Tell me what you're working on at the moment.

– It's not really your sort of thing, Darius. But as we're being polite with each other, I've just commissioned an analysis of all the social housing stock in Belfast.

– Why are you interested in that?

– Because I'm planning to buy them.

– Buy what?

– All the social housing in Belfast. All of it. Every single residential property which the council currently owns – I'm going to buy it all in one go.

– Why?

Francis looked irritated.

– Well, why do you think? Because it's massively under-rated. Belfast is booming, there are going to be thousands more jobs there over the next few years. Unemployment will be going down. People will be earning more, and those workers who live in social housing will be able to afford to pay higher rents.

– Why on earth does Belfast council want to sell all its houses to you?

– Why does anyone sell anything, Darius? Because they haven't got any money. They can't afford to build the roads which the city will need to transport the materials to the factories which are going to be built. They're effectively bankrupt.

– How come you get to buy them?

– Because I took the time to look into it. It's not rocket science, anyone could have found out what I found out, but I just happened to be the one who did.

– So you're going to buy all the council houses and then you're going to put the rent up?

– To a sustainable level, yes. It only makes sense to buy the houses if the yield increases over the next twenty-five years. There's quite a few houses there – I'm going to have to invest a lot of money to buy them. I need to show a return.

Darius shook his head.

– None of that makes any sense to me, he said.

– Well, before you start preaching at me, consider this: if I don't buy the houses, the council can't afford the upkeep on them, so they will gradually decline and people will be forced out of their homes because they will become uninhabitable. This way, Belfast keeps its housing stock and people have somewhere to live so the city will be able to attract the employees which the buoyant industries there require to meet their growth demands. You're not, I presume, opposed to people having jobs and somewhere to live?

– I just don't get it, that's all.

– There's no particular reason why you should get it, said Francis. There's not many of us who do this sort of thing.

– Who works for you?

– Not many. Fifteen in the New York office, twenty over here.

– Do you employ ex politicians too? Does Tony Blair work for you now?

Francis smiled again.

– The world really is a simple place to you, isn't it Darius? I think that's enough about my business. What about you? What sort of life do you have?

– You know where I live. In Cornwall. You and Dad lent me the money to buy it.

– We did indeed. Although I wouldn't worry about it. It was remarkable to me even ten years ago how little a valley in Cornwall cost. And don't worry, I shan't be buying anything else near you – Cornwall is one of those places that will be forever outside of the interests of global capitalism.

– Thank God for that. Anyway, I'll pay it back.

– As you wish. And what happens to you and Tink in Cornwall?

Darius caught the amused smile on his brother's face. It annoyed him and for a moment made him forget the problems back at the valley. Instead, he felt a swell of passion for where he lived.

– We try and live a life which is as diametrically opposite yours as possible. I called the valley Level Ground, which I'm sure must give you pleasure.

– I did have a smile when I heard that, yes.

– Well, we call it that because we want to try and live

in a way which challenges everything you stand for. We all own the valley equally, we grow our own food, we look after each other. We trade with people in Penzance, we exchange food and skills for things we can't deliver ourselves, like electronics or medicines. Although we're doing our best to live without both. But we have a harmonious relationship with our neighbours, I'd like us to get more land in due course, attract more people.

– And how many inhabitants does Shangri La currently have?

– Fourteen of us at the last count. Tink is our most recent arrival, aren't you Tink?

Tink raised her glass.

– It all sounds very charming, said Francis. And, to use your terminology, what do you do for a living, Darius?

– Various things. I make charcoal in the winter, I work the odd festival in the summer.

– Doing what?

– Putting up teepees. I used to do Glastonbury every year, but I only do smaller festivals now. There are too many people like you at Glastonbury, Francis.

– That is a pleasure which still awaits me, said his brother.

– I'd like to go to Glastonbury, said Belinda. I've never been to a festival.

– We're going to one in Cornwall next month, said Tink. You can come, Belinda and bring the children. They'd like it.

– Maybe I will.

– I suspect that whenever your festival is, I shall be in New York, said Francis.

– That's a shame, Francis, said Darius. I mean it. It might do you some good to see life through a different lens sometimes.

– I have to say, you don't strike me as a particularly compelling example of what I might be missing.

– Perhaps we'll kidnap him, Belinda, said Tink. When he's had lots of this Chinese wine and he doesn't know what he's doing, me and James and Alice can kidnap him and bring him to the festival. I can dress him up like a faery, he'd like that.

Belinda laughed. Darius looked at his brother, who was staring at Tink with incomprehension. What was it about Francis? This atmosphere in the house, in the gardens, this sense of decay, of decline: did it come from him? If so, why would he be content with it? Why would he want to live like this? There seemed to be a disjoint between his world vision, a world of corporate efficiency and ruthlessness, and the ramshackle nature of the Range today, the shouting that he had overheard outside the kitchen. Was the Range somehow Francis's weak point? Was there something here that scared him even?

– Why are you letting the Range get so run down? he asked. The gardens are a mess. Even the outside of the house needs repairing. Why are you living here like this?

– I'm busy, said Francis. Belinda is busy looking after the children and Dad. We have responsibilities Darius. Tending to Grandma's gardens comes quite a way down the list. When Dad does finally go, I'll probably bring some people in and get the place spruced up. I don't want to do it now, it will disturb him if he sees lots of activity going on.

– I would have thought Dad would be pleased to see someone looking after his mum's pride and joy, said Darius.

– I don't think you know very much about what Dad would or wouldn't like, said Francis. You've not really been a part of this family for a long time, Darius. I do advise you not to make the mistake of thinking you can turn up after twenty-five years and sort us all out. We're actually getting on pretty well without you.

– Are you? said Darius. He looked at Belinda, but she had stood up and was gathering the plates.

– Oh please, Darius, said his brother. Let's not beat around the bush. I have no idea why you have come this weekend, or what your intentions are, but please do not insult us by pretending to know or care about anyone here.

You walked away from this family. You refused to see any of us while you were in prison, then as soon as you were out, you disappeared. What is it you're trying to achieve with this ridiculous reunion?

Darius stood up and walked over to the window. The gardens out the front lay in darkness, just the silhouette of the trees over the driveway picked out by the pale moon-light. He suddenly felt exhausted. He knew he had nothing that he was trying to achieve here. But all the same, the sense that he had been called here for a reason was strong within him.

– Maybe it's not me that's trying to achieve something, Francis, he said quietly, not turning around and still looking out of the window. He stayed there for a while, hearing the noise of plates being gathered at the table behind him, Tink and Belinda talking in low voices. He heard the door open and close. Beyond, out in the darkness, he felt the land calling to him and he had a desire to go out and lie down on the earth in the dark and feel the sustaining energy of the life beneath him: be supported by the thousands and millions of different forms of life pulsing and changing and growing and dying. He felt like digging his hands into the soil, burying himself in it, disappearing into the warm dark ground.

– Listen Darius. His brother's voice was different, less strident. Darius turned around slowly and looked at him. He was still sitting at the table, holding a glass of wine.

– Let's stop messing around, Francis said. This whole thing is ridiculous. I accept that you didn't send the cards, and as I know I didn't, then maybe you're right, maybe sometimes things happen and we just don't have an expla-nation for it. All right. But let's not take this any further. We don't like each other, we have nothing in common with each other. You never planned to come back here, you just felt that you should because of the wretched card. Without it, you'd have carried on living your life in Cornwall and we'd carry on here and maybe there might have come a time when we'd have wanted to get back in touch with each other, but it's obvious, isn't it, that we're not ready now?

Darius continued to look at him but didn't say anything.

– This whole thing is just stirring up unnecessary past unhappiness, Francis continued. You know, don't you, that Belinda is by no means as strong as she seems? I know she seems very capable now, what with her role in World Action, managing the house, looking after Dad and the children. But the tragedy with Annabel affected her very badly. I don't know whether you know. Before she and I met again, she had suffered a quite severe breakdown. Her parents had to look after her. Even now, she has anxiety attacks. But she's happy here.

– Really? said Darius. You're sure about that?

Francis shook his head.

– Drop it, Darius. Don't you see? We're just opening up old wounds, and for what reason? You've got a life you want to lead and so do I. Just go back to it. Take your friend with you. I'll order you a taxi tomorrow morning, you can be back home in Cornwall by the afternoon. There's nothing here for us together at the moment. Maybe one day, but not now.

Darius pushed himself away from the window and came back to the table, sitting opposite Francis again.

– I can't do that, Francis. It's too late. Something is happening. I can feel it all over this house, all over the grounds. I can't ignore it. It's all got something to do with Down There, and I can't just walk away from it now. The 25th is the day after tomorrow, it's Sunday, that's all we have to wait until. Then I'll go.

– Darius, Down There doesn't even exist any more. There's no path to it. Dad used to cut it occasionally out of sense of loyalty to Grandad, but I haven't touched it since I've been back here. The path grew over years ago. It's gone. It's a part of our lives that we don't need to resurrect, a very painful part. It's ancient history. Just leave it be and go home.

– The card specified Down There. The 25th June. I'll

find the path tomorrow, it won't have disappeared, I know it. Then on Sunday we can all go there as we've been asked. We can't ignore the invitation, Francis. We just can't.

– Oh for God's sake, Francis muttered. He poured the last of the wine into his glass. He got up and walked over to the mantlepiece beneath the huge glass mirror.

– Sometimes I wish I'd never brought Belinda back here, he said. We could have moved to New York. I was thinking of it. I don't need this ridiculous building. It costs me a fortune just to keep the bloody thing heated. You're a sentimental character, Darius, you have feelings about this place because of Grandma, I understand all that. But I don't. I might just sell it when Dad dies. Then you can buy lots of valleys in Cornwall and I can get a decent place back in London and we can just all move on. You're right, I don't look after it. I have no interest in it. I'd walk out tomorrow if I could.

– But you don't, Francis. That's the point. You're here, and now I'm here too. When I was a kid, I used to think that you could just create whatever life you wanted. That summer, before it happened, I was going to go to Biarritz for the holidays. I was going to go surfing and I was thinking that I just wouldn't come back. I didn't tell any of you because I thought I'd get a new life and everything would be different and everything would be fine. But that's not how life is. Everything is connected, every grain of earth, every tree, every person, every piece of stone that makes up this house – it's all just one. It's life. And we're travelling through it, maybe not together but we're connected, Francis.

– So no, I'm not going to go tomorrow. I'm going to find the path, and I'm going to open it up, and on Sunday we'll do what we've been asked.

Chapter Twenty

– I'm not sure I have any novels left in me, Nigel, said Felicity.

They were strolling through the gardens of the Range, as was their habit each time her publisher came to see her. She reached out and dead-headed a rose.

– Another summer's coming to an end, she said. They come by so fast now, don't they?

– Nonsense, he said. Don't you dare try and get maudlin with me. I've known you too long. Write me another novel.

She laughed.

– You have always had such faith in me, Nigel.

– Of course I have. You're a great writer. I know we didn't do so well with the last two, but my dear girl – it's 1965! It's an exciting new era. We need a big novel from Felicity Drummond to define this modern world.

– You mean you want another *Marianne*, she said. I think the world is very different, Nigel. We all needed hope then. We needed to believe that the war would end one day. I was lucky to capture that mood, but I don't get the impression that these young people have any fears at all. I'm not sure I would know what to say to them.

– But why feel you have to speak to them? *Marianne* inspired a whole generation of young women in the '40s – they're still around you know. They still read books, they still have dreams. Maybe they're waiting for you to tell them what to make of this strange new world.

– Oh dear, what a responsibility, she said, yanking off another rose head. I don't think so, you dear man. You should have signed up that ghastly Mr Greene, he seems to be doing very well for his publishers now. Am I to conclude, she said, leaning into a hedge to pull out a weed, that my sales are beginning to cause concern?

– Nonsense! Jenkins cried.

– Ah, but you flushed just a little then, Nigel. Don't worry, I understand. But I really don't think I have much left. I hate to disappoint you. I'm sixty years' old, Nigel. I'm an old maid.

– If you are an old maid, my dear Felicity, then there is no hope for any of us. We might as well fold up the tents and call it a day.

She laughed.

– You're incorrigible, she said. Are you still managing to behave appallingly, or has that very pretty wife of yours put an end to your gadabouting?

– Oh, one has one's moments, my dear. London is rather a rackety place at the moment. It would amuse you. Rather like the twenties again. Lots of pretty girls.

– How awful, she sighed. Zachary refuses point blank to go up at all. I'm going to have to force him next week to come up with me to see Richard. He's just been made Westminster correspondent for the *Guardian*. I promised him we would take him out to lunch to celebrate.

– I heard, Jenkins said. Congratulations. He's well in with the new Wilson mob, so I hear. What does Zac think?

– Oh, Zachary says he is prepared to give Harold the benefit of the doubt.

Jenkins laughed.

– That bad, eh?

– Well, he says that Harold has sound principles and good intentions, it's just that they have a tendency to slide off him rather like eggs off a plate.

Jenkins laughed loudly again.

– Excellent! he said. I do miss Zac, send him my regards.

– You'll see him for lunch, said Felicity. He only teaches part time now, and he's home today working on a new book. He's looking forward to seeing you. And don't worry, he's not expecting you to publish it.

They ate in the kitchen, the three of them gathered around one end of the long wooden table, sipping the mushroom soup which their housekeeper had prepared earlier.

– I've been telling poor Nigel that I'm all washed up and he shouldn't expect any more novels. Perhaps it's not too late to take up cooking? I never really mastered it, and one has more time on one's hands now. I could write you a cookery book, Nigel.

Zachary looked at Jenkins and winked.

– I always think it's rather rash to make sudden changes at our age, my dear. Besides, I do still recall the goulash you made me when we first met. I'm sure Nigel will be persuasive, won't you, my dear chap? We can't have her mucking about in the kitchen, now, can we?

– You're very rude, she pouted. Nobody explained you didn't put the whole pot of paprika in. It wasn't my fault.

– I was telling Felicity that Richard's getting himself quite a name in London now, Zac, said Jenkins. Is he aiming for a seat?

– Oh yes, I think so, said Zachary. He's taking to politicking like a duck to water. He's already writing some of Wilson's speeches in his spare time. He tells me the *Guardian* rather like having their man inside the government tent, but I would think they will try and find him a seat to contest before too long. He's an ambitious young man.

– Like his father! said Jenkins.

– Perhaps, perhaps, said Zachary, examining his spoon. He is certainly talented. But he and I tend not to wade too deep together into the waters of the Wilson administration. He knows my concerns. I have voiced them already in his own newspaper, so I can hardly pretend to be entirely uncritical.

– Is that the subject of your new book? Felicity tells me that at least one of you is still writing.

Zachary laughed.

– Ah, I wouldn't worry my dear chap, my talented wife will not find herself content to spectate from the grandstand for too long. Why, I am sure I spotted her bringing back a fresh pad of writing paper from Smythsons the other day.

– Ha! said Jenkins, triumphantly. I knew it!

– You are both being ridiculous, Felicity said, gathering their bowls. I have merely being making lists of the planting requirements for next Spring. I think, for what it is worth, that Richard will make an excellent MP. He is an old head on young shoulders.

– I agree, my dear, I agree. His constituents, when he finds a seat, will be most fortunate in their choice, of that I have no doubt. He is an excellent young man.

– You just don't agree with his views? Jenkins enquired.

– If I only knew what they were, said Zachary. If I only knew what Harold's were. You know Harold and I go back – he helped me set up World Action all those years ago. He was a very different man then, full of excellent intentions. He understood, or I thought he understood, the need to take a global view of poverty. But now it seems to me that his administration, if you ask it to remove its very colourful Carnaby Street coat, is wearing the hand-me-downs of the previous Tory government. They say they are the government of the working man, and that they will control the means of production through nationalisation, but what does that mean? Does their idea of democracy and equality extend to the landowners, to the factory owners, to the newspaper owners? Of course it doesn't. This is the same Labour talk of Attlee and Cripps, it is the managerial administration of a fundamentally inequitable and corrosive system of private ownership which in the end always sets man against man.

– But Wilson says this is a new kind of world, said Jenkins. The white heat of technology, all that sort of thing. Perhaps they are right, Zachary: perhaps progress will deliver equality.

– My own vision is much expanded now, Jenkins. I see the world more completely now, from our little bunker here beside the Thames. I see a global crisis of politics, not just a national one. We are seeing suffering all over the world, especially in those countries that were our former colonies, and the colonies of the French. My book is about the coming crisis in Africa where so many of the new administrations, so glorious in their early days, are heading down the same familiar path of wealth being restricted to the few and denied to the many.

– My son thinks I am impractical, he thinks politics is a terrific contest to achieve the best possible outcome from a battlefield which has already been set. I admire his tenacity, and I applaud his dedication. But I have walked away from that battlefield, I have lain down whatever colours have been given to me. Although my horizons now are wider, my concerns remain as they were when you were kind enough to publish my first books: there has never been a human system of government which can provide for human happiness as the meadow provides for the butterfly. This white heat of technology of yours is a chimera; beneath its sheen, people still in their hearts yearn for a return to a simpler, more equitable life.

– One day, I still believe it will happen. I just hope that we don't destroy all that we have before we realise the truth.

Chapter Twenty One

The path, at first, didn't want to give itself up to Darius. He had walked up and down the thick hedge at the back of the house several times after breakfast on Saturday, without finding the original entrance point. The thick brown and green wall refused him entrance: silent entwined branches, the fronds of ivy and convolvulus wrapping themselves around spidery hawthorn limbs, the thorned barbs of bramble waiting to tear his fingers.

Breakfast had been quiet enough – all of them seeming to have decided to put the arguments of last night's supper behind them. Francis was organising a trip for Alice and James to the swimming pool in Marlow, Tink was out the front of the house somewhere now with her yoga mat, Belinda was upstairs with Richard and Annie. Darius had wandered into his Nana's old garden room down one of the corridors from the kitchen, and had found secateurs and shears and an old pair of canvas gloves.

He sat down on the low wall that ran all along the back of the house bordering the stone terrace. He closed his eyes. He could picture his Nana now: her silvery hair tied back and tucked in with a silk headscarf, her creamy foundation smoothing out the lines in her cheeks, her bright red lipstick glinting as she smiled at him. He imagined her coming out of the back door and walking towards him, the pockets of the long coat she wore now even on summer days bulging with gardening tools. He felt her brush past him as he sat there on the wall, smelled the Dior perfume she always wore, heard the very soft hum of her voice as she quietly spoke to him.

– Down There, Darius. Down There.

He opened his eyes and looked over at the hedge. About twenty yards away, he noticed a slight dip in the ground at the foot of the thick vegetation, no more than a couple of feet wide, but it was there, clearly now: the original point of entry into the path.

– Thank you, Nana, he said aloud, and jumped off the wall. He stood in front of the hedge where the ground had a change in the level, and he peered into the darkness inside. His eyes took a moment to compensate for the change but then he realised he could feel the outline of the old path, waiting mutely. He leaned back out, grabbed what felt like a honeysuckle branch, pulled it taut and cut it with the secateurs. It fell to the ground, and he grabbed another, then another.

After an hour, he was deep inside the wood and on familiar ground – the path felt as he remembered it, and was not as obscured as he had first thought. It was as though all the effort had gone into camouflaging the entrance; once inside, much of the old path was still intact and untrammelled. He was already into the steep slope, snapping branches with his hands here, chopping them with the shears there.

He thought of Francis as he methodically pursued his way through the branches. He wondered whether he had seemed so alien, so distant to him when they had been boys here together at the Range. He remembered their games on the lawns, racing each other on bicycles down the long stone corridors of the house, swimming in the river. He remembered too the disdain on his brother's face when he began to smoke, his condescension about his rugby friends. They had never really exchanged truths with each other as boys and the coded language they exchanged had been Darius's idea which he had forced on his older brother.

Perhaps that was part of it. Perhaps there was a mutual antipathy between them which led one to always be attempting to outdo the other. He had never been jealous of Francis's learning and had always deliberately swaggered his physical strength in front of him, always ready to climb the higher tree, throw the largest stone into the water. Francis, on the other hand, had sneered at Darius's lack of knowledge, looked down on his dutiful apprenticeship in gardening with their grandmother.

But despite all that, had they really been as foreign to one another as they seemed last night? He had no understanding of the finances and economics behind his brother's Magenta business and he had no desire to; he knew instinctively that at some fundamental level, it represented everything he abhorred. There was more reality and more truth in his cutting up wood in Cornwall and turning it into charcoal in the old kiln in the woods than there was in all of Francis's schemes. He didn't believe that the world needed those schemes; it could survive without them. It couldn't survive without the processes of life and growth of which his charcoal-making was a part.

A voice behind him startled him:

– Tea break.

It was Tink. She was carrying two mugs of tea, and smiling at him in the gloomy light.

– I'll come back up to the top, he said.

– No, I like it here, she said, and crouched down on the ground. This is your secret path, isn't it?

She handed him a mug, and he sat down too. There was just enough room for them to sit cross-legged, and they faced each other.

– Thanks, he said, and sipped the tea. Yes, it's still here. It's not as difficult as I thought it would be. I reckon it'll only take me another couple of hours.

– Do you remember it? Her voice was soft in the enclosed, shaded space, and he was conscious of the smells of the freshly cut branches crowding around them.

– Oh yes. Completely. My grandfather, Zachary Frome, he was the first one to cut this. Nana told me. I never really knew him, I was only four or so when he died. She said he found the clearing one day when he was out on his boat when he was a kid, and he took it upon himself to cut a path

199

back up to the top.

– So he was coming the other way?

– Yes, I'd only just thought of that. Perhaps I'll meet him halfway.

– I think you already have, said Tink.

He looked at her, but she was looking around her inside the cramped path, peering through gaps in the branches into the dark interior.

– It's quite spooky here, isn't it? she said, turning back to look at him. Not just this path, I mean. All of it. Your home.

– Well, it was my home, Tink. Doesn't really feel like my home any more.

– Is Cornwall your home, Darius?

He thought for a while.

– I thought it was, he said.

– You know I haven't said anything to you about it, she said. It's not what I do. But I think I've got to. You're wrong about it, Darius. You're wrong about them growing cannabis and about the police and everything. It's up to them what they want to do with land that they look after. And it seems to be up to the police and the law to do what they want to them when they find out. But it's not your responsibility. It's not something you need to control. It wasn't your decision, and they didn't ask you for permission. That's why they're upset with you, because it just looks to them as though you're on the side of the law for no good reason. It doesn't matter whether you think cannabis should be legal or illegal. What matters is that you've broken your friendship with them just because they did something which somehow touched a nerve with you.

– It's not that. Darius felt a flash of anger. It's not that, Tink. I was angry with them because what they did is going to bring the law down on us, and that could threaten the whole future of Level Ground. All that we've been working for. Of course I don't care if they grow cannabis, but not in the valley. Not somewhere where they could ruin all our plans. They should have thought about it.

– Why should they have thought about it, Darius? Not everyone is like you. Not everyone wants to plan everything out, be in control all the time. I'm not criticising you, I'm just explaining that sometimes people do things because they want to do them, and they don't necessarily think about anything more than that.

They were quiet for a moment and sipped their tea. Then she said:

– Why didn't you tell me before about her, about Annabel, about what happened? Tink continued. You told me you'd been in prison, but you never said what for, and I would never ask. It's not that I mind, you know I don't think like that. But I think it must have been so hard for you, having all that in your head and not talking to anyone about it. You were just a child, and a terrible event happened to you which wasn't something you meant to happen. That's such a burden. No one can cope with everything, Darius, not even you.

– I just decided, when I was in prison. I just decided that I had to build a life that wasn't based on what happened, that I had to learn from what I'd done but not take my identity from it. It was like that in prison. If you let someone feel they were stronger than you, then you got into trouble: they'd try and exploit your weakness, increase the threats. I didn't want the death to have a hold over me. I became obsessed with getting out into the world and trying to discover meanings in the world which would make more sense than everything which had led up to that afternoon twenty-five years ago.

– Haven't you told anyone? Haven't you told previous girls, like that pretty one you said you went to South Africa with?

– No one. You're the first person I've ever told. It seemed to make sense to me, Tink. I was wiping out the stupidity that had led me to kill that poor girl: the drugs, the selfishness, the arrogance. And I was wiping out this place too: my family, who never really liked me anyway, and the house, which represented some kind of dream for my grandfather but which I never knew anything about. I banished all of it. I told the prison psychiatrists that that was what I was going to do, and they kept telling me it was dangerous, that I was going to build up bigger problems. But they were wrong. I knew they were wrong. As soon as I got to India when I was out, I knew I could spend the rest of my life discovering everything about the world in my own way.

– You can do anything, she said. I know that's true. But even so, all this history here, Darius, it's still in you. It's still affecting everything you do.

He shook his head.

– I don't know, he said. Maybe.

They sipped their tea.

– Why is your brother so angry all the time? she asked.

– It's not what I was expecting. I don't know what I was expecting, but it wasn't this. I thought he'd invited me here, I thought he'd sent that card to me as some kind of message, something he wanted to say to me. But he doesn't seem to want to, he doesn't even seem to be happy that I'm here. I don't get it.

– He's very unhappy.

– Is he? Why's he unhappy? What's he got to be unhappy about? Surely this is everything that he wanted: living here, nice kids, married his university sweetheart, earns a fortune, knows a million important people. He's a proper power broker. Isn't that what he wanted?

– Maybe he's jealous of you.

– What? Are you kidding? Jealous of me? He thinks I'm a freak. He thinks you and I are hippy wasters.

– I think Francis was always jealous of you, Darius. But he hasn't had to confront it for a long time. Now you're here, and you're making him feel ashamed.

– Ashamed of what?

– Something. I don't know.

They drank their tea.

– It's connected with my Dad, he said. That's what I feel

most strongly. Dad and I were never close, not like him and Francis. They were like buddies. I just exhausted Dad. But now Dad wants something. He really wants something Tink, I know that. It's behind the reason why we've come here. He wants to tell me something and I need to make sure that he can. Before he passes. It's why we've come, I'm convinced.

– I think there's lots of reasons why you've brought us here, Darius. But I'm glad you did. It was the right thing to do.

– Was it? I don't know.

She nodded, reaching out to stroke his long dark hair.

– It was. Sometimes you don't know everything. By the way, I like Belinda. She's nice. She likes you. She's pleased you've come.

– You know she and I had a thing, when we were kids? Darius said. It was really sudden, it was the weekend when it happened. I never saw her again. She had a bad time after it and I never knew. She only told me yesterday.

– Be nice to her, said Tink.

– I am being nice to her.

– She wants to tell you something too. I can tell.

– It's complicated.

– You're complicated, Darius. You're the opposite of Tink.

He smiled.

– Who's the ying and who's the yang?

– I don't know what it's like to be complicated, Darius. You're all complicated here. Even those children are complicated.

– Are they?

– They're lovely. Especially James, he's really sweet. But he frowns sometimes, and I can see he's thinking something terribly important, and I want to take his frown away and tell him to go and fly to the moon.

Darius laughed.

– Is that what I should do as well?

She smiled.

– Maybe.

Tink took his empty mug and walked back up the steep slope of the path that Darius had cut. He turned and continued pulling down branches, cutting them with the secateurs or shears, always keeping to the outline of the path that was still visible in the gloom of the vegetation here.

After a while he noticed the incline of the path steepen, and he remembered this as one of the last stages of the route towards Down There – he must be close now. He snapped some more branches and pulled down a canopy of green ivy, and then he saw it: the glimpse of green grass further down ahead. Now with renewed energy, he tore down the last remaining obstacles and stood, for the first time in twenty-five years, at the edge of the grass clearing.

It was mid-afternoon by now and the summer light was at its strongest, giving the clearing a shimmering aura underneath the canopy of trees above. He felt an overwhelming sense of recognition and immediately looked towards the centre, where the plinth remained exactly as he remembered it: solid, grey, stained with moss, its flat surface with a scattering of leaves and sticks upon it. He walked towards it and put both hands on the stone, feeling how cold it was. He brushed the leaves from the top, and remembered the rough feeling of the stone surface on his hands.

Darius walked around the plinth, looking at the circular grass clearing. Nothing had changed – the grass was still short, so the rabbits must still have been doing their job. He looked to the edge, and through the hanging branches of the willow trees he could see the glint of water. He knew it was there: he'd smelled the river for the past ten or fifteen minutes, had sensed the change in the atmosphere. Now here it was, and he walked towards it, pulling aside the willow branches to be able to see the flat weight of the water stretching out from the bank, felt the power of its bulk moving silently, just the occasional lapping against the mossy bank.

He felt exhausted, suddenly completely exhausted. How

long had he been cutting the path? A few hours? That wouldn't explain how he felt. It hadn't been as difficult a job as he had been expecting. This was a different feeling: a sense of being overpowered. Everything around him was alive, watchful, alert, but his own senses felt dulled, soporific. He walked back to the plinth, lifted himself up onto the top, and lay down.

He was dreaming, although he was sure he was still awake. His eyes were closed, but he could hear music and he could see figures moving about. A laugh suddenly, and then quiet again. It was as though someone was trying to say something to him. He could see a face, distinctly now, but not recognisable. The face was smiling at him, it was a woman's face, and her lips were moving in speech although he couldn't hear what she was saying.

He opened his eyes. Belinda was standing beside the plinth, her head close to his.

– So you made it, she said gently. I thought it might be too difficult to get through.

– How long have you been here? he said, sitting up.

– Not long. You were dreaming – your body was twitching. What were you dreaming about?

– I don't know. Somebody.

Belinda pulled herself up onto the plinth and sat next to him, her legs dangling off the side. She looked around.

– I've never been back here, she said.

– Neither have I.

– It's the same.

– Yes.

– We were all young then.

He didn't answer.

– I told Tink about you and me, said Belinda. About that morning, here. You can tell Tink anything, can't you? How does she do that?

– She's a faery. What did she say?

– She asked me if I enjoyed it.

– What did you say?

– I told her I did.

Darius closed his eyes and for a moment imagined Belinda, twenty-five years ago, pulling off her clothes on the plinth.

– I wonder what would have happened? he said.

– With us?

– Yes.

– I used to think about that a lot, she said. Sometimes when I was lying in my bedroom in my parents' house, I used to imagine you and I had gone to Biarritz that summer, and I'd watch you surfing. We'd have lived in some kind of wooden house near the beach, and I'd make big pots of food for you and your friends, and some of them would have French girlfriends and we'd have cool parties and you'd think I was the prettiest of them all.

– Did you think that? I did think you were the prettiest of them all. I thought you were beautiful Belinda. I didn't know what you saw in me though. When you were thinking those things, I was still in prison, thinking that I'd never see you again. You were three years' older than me, and you weren't just beautiful, you were clever. You were a Cambridge student. I was a rugby-playing drug dealer who didn't know what day it was.

– I wasn't a Cambridge student. I told you: I never went back after it all happened. It was imagining being your French girlfriend that kept me going in those early years.

– I'm sorry, he said.

She shrugged.

– Me too. I'm sorry I didn't try and make contact with you when you were in prison. I think I wanted you perfect in my head. I didn't really think what was actually happening. We were all just kids, Darius.

They were quiet for a while.

– I did think somehow that it wasn't serious for you, Darius said. I thought that I'd been a fool, misunderstood what you were thinking. I ended up convincing myself in prison that it was all a part of my own stupidity: that you were just a very confident person who felt like playing around but it didn't mean anything to you. And I was this idiot who got everything wrong, who thought he was really cool but in fact turned out to be a moron who caused this terrible tragedy.

– Well, now you know: none of that was true, Darius. Maybe it's taken you as long as it's taken me to get over it all.

– Are you over it all? How it affected you afterwards, I mean.

She sighed.

– I thought I was. There was something comfortable about being back here at the Range. I like Richard, he's a kind man really and before his dementia got so bad he was nice to me. The children love it here. My mum and dad could still come down and see me every so often, I could get up to London easily for World Action meetings. My colleagues liked coming down here too, because of the connection with Zachary. I just didn't realise how tough things would get between me and Francis. I suppose that's when I realised I wasn't over it all.

– I still don't really get the thing with you and Francis.

– That's what the poet says. I think I used to get it, but maybe I don't get it any more now either.

– I might have to have a word with the poet.

She turned to him and smiled.

– Oh, I don't think I'm introducing him to you. He's out of bounds.

– Where did you meet him?

– Paddington Station. He flirted with me in a Pret A Manger.

– I'm definitely having a word with him.

She laughed, then slipped off the plinth and walked over towards the water. Darius watched her as she peered through the willow branches. She turned round and smiled at him.

– We all went swimming, didn't we? she called out to him. You, me, Francis and Annabel. In our knickers.

She walked back towards him.

– I thought it was my fault, for a long time, she said. I thought I'd done something to make you want to show off to me or something. I thought I'd put you up to picking up the bow and shooting the arrow without looking. I wished I'd gone to prison, not you. I thought that for ages. I thought of you being in prison when I should have been there.

– Do you and Francis talk about it?

– Never. When we met again, he said that if he and I were going to have a life together, we would have to agree never to speak about it, because there was no point and it would hold us back and stop us from being happy. He said that over dinner one night in London, quite soon after I'd met him at that fundraising dinner. That was how he was: super confident, always knowing what was the right thing. I accepted it. I'd spent so many years thinking about it that to be honest it was quite a relief, as though I'd been given permission to stop thinking about it. And then we got married and we moved into a house in Fulham, and the children came along and everything seemed quite exciting.

– You know when you started sending me letters? After I got back to the UK and settled in Cornwall? I used to read them endlessly. I thought it sounded as though you both had it all sorted out. I had all these visions of you and him leading this perfect life.

– I suppose I thought I did for a while. But we were just so busy: the children, Richard, my work, his work. Those years just flew by and I didn't really think about whether everything was all right. It just flowed along.

– Then what happened?

She looked away.

– I don't know. It was a bit like a painting starting to peel off and you find another one underneath. I started to realise that Francis actually didn't care about anything other than that bloody business and all his cronies. Sitting around slapping each other on the back as they make more and more money. For a while, I bought that whole story about needing to be in control, that if you controlled the money you could do good things with it. But when you do my job, you know that's not true. People keep dying all over the world because people like Francis take decisions. That's the reality.

Darius thought about the difficult supper the previous evening.

– You don't think he was always like that? he asked.

– Maybe. Maybe I just didn't see it. But I think he's changed. And something Richard said last year made me think about it even more.

– What did he say?

She shook her head.

– Don't want to talk about it now. I'll tell you later. Or maybe I should tell Tink.

– You know, I only told Tink about it yesterday. About Annabel, I mean.

– She told me she knew there was something you wanted to tell her, said Belinda. She said you call out in your sleep sometimes. I used to do that. It used to scare Mum and Dad.

Darius looked around at the clearing. They were probably the first people to be here in years. It had sat here quietly, waiting. The implacable plinth he was sitting on, the willows, the grass, the thick vegetation around the sides. He imagined his grandfather sitting here all those years ago, looking around at exactly the same scene.

– There's something happening, isn't there Belinda? he said. Here, I mean. This weekend.

She nodded.

– We've been brought back here, all of us, Darius continued. None of us has talked about it for years. We haven't even seen each other. Now we're all here.

He looked around the clearing again, and this time he felt that same sensation as he had on the first evening, an impending violence in the air, in the ground. It was almost as though he could feel the agitation in the branches of the trees, hear the urgent whispers of the leaves.

Belinda looked up at him.

– I think something is going to happen, she said. I don't know what. But I think something is going to happen. And I think we're going to need for you to be strong, Darius.

– Why me?

– Because you're important.

She rested her hand on his on the surface of the plinth.

– I'm sorry about everything, she said. But if you're strong, then we all can be.

Chapter Twenty Two

Felicity looked at her husband as the telephone rang.

– It will be Richard, she said.

Zachary nodded. He looked around the book-lined walls of his study, illuminated now by the early morning sun streaming through the window. It was six thirty. In the corner of the room, the television was still showing byelection results coming through, but they had turned the volume off a while ago.

– He will want to speak to you first, dear, she said.

He nodded again, and she passed the telephone to him, sitting it on his lap as she sat down next to him on the sofa. They were both wearing dressing gowns. Zachary picked up the receiver.

– Zachary Frome.

There was a slight pause, then:

– I lost, Dad.

– I know.

Another pause.

– You fought an excellent campaign, my boy. You fought decently. You have everything to be proud of.

– It's a bloody disaster. You know that, Dad.

Zachary didn't say anything.

– Thatcher's got a clear majority. We could be out for years.

– You don't know. New governments get unpopular very quickly. There could be a byelection any time.

– There's too many of us lost seats, Dad. There'll be a queue to get back in. There won't be another election for five years, it'll be 1984 then. Your man Orwell's year. I'll be 45 by then.

– That's nothing, Richard.

– But the boys are still young Dad – Francis was six last week. I've got to think about a new career, I've got to be able to feed my family. I can't just hang around hoping for a seat.

– You can't give up. Take some time to think about it. You're exhausted, you must all be exhausted. Your mother and I didn't sleep either.

– I'm sorry, Dad. I'm sorry I lost. I wanted to match your record, but I didn't get near it. You did twenty years, on and off. I managed five. And now I'm out.

– You served your country, my boy. We're all very proud of you.

– I'm going back to Fleet Street. I've already been offered the *Telegraph*. But the *Chronicle* want me too. Sod Westminster. You never really liked it anyway, did you? Sod the bloody lot of them. Give my love to Mum.

– And ours to Violet. Is she with you?

– No, she's back home with the boys. School day today, Dad. Life goes on. I'll come down and see you at the weekend.

Zachary put the phone back on the receiver. Felicity put her hand on his.

– Poor boy. Did I hear him say that he'd wanted to match your record? What a thing to think.

– It's all beyond me, my darling. It's a world I don't understand any more. I don't understand this grocer's daughter and her finger wagging. But I don't understand my own son, either. It's all about power, about getting a salary, having an office. What's that got to do with it all?

– You don't see it, but he so wants to have your respect, my dear. He adores you. It's a terrible blow for him.

– He's my son, Felicity, and I love him but I don't admire what he stands for. I don't know what he stands for. This ramshackle Labour government, this cabal of cronies that Callaghan has kept in power these last two or three years – who are they? What do they believe in? What did they expect the electorate to do? At least when we failed in 1945, we failed on our own terms. We didn't fail because we wanted power, we failed because the people didn't believe our story. I failed then. I failed to articulate our cause properly, and we were punished for that failure. Our son has been punished for wanting to hold onto a job by another career politician who wanted it more than him.

He got up and walked over to the bookcase, then turned to look back at his wife.

– Don't you see, my darling? It will carry on like this now, forever and ever, like Eric's Newspeak, with one party winning, then the other, then back to the first, but all of them simply maintaining the status quo. There will never be the kind of country we once envisaged, a land of equality and shared hardships and joys. A land where neighbour helps neighbour, where children are brought into the world as equals.

– We'll have this Thatcher woman for years now. And then what? When people grow tired of her endless sermons, her bitternesses, her feuds, they will one day vote in a Labour prime minister again. Only he'll be just like her, but wearing different clothes. He'll have a glint in his eye, and his nostrils will twitch to the smell of power and money. You mark my words.

He got up from the sofa, a little unsteadily, and walked over to the bookcase. Felicity watched him, torn both by her sadness for her son's defeat and by the loss of her husband's dream. For the first time, Zachary seemed old to her.

He came back to her holding a book.

– Do you remember, my darling, all those years ago when you first came to the Range?

– Of course, she smiled. You read to me from *Wind in the Willows* and from Thomas Hardy.

He showed her the cover of the book: *Jude The Obscure*.

– They were my guides, then, he said wearily. Hardy, Grahame, Morris: a whole generation of writers who saw something spiritually profound in our English landscape. I wanted to capture their philosophy and introduce it into

213

our politics so that we might bring an end to this bitter adversarial contest, of which we have just witnessed the next generation tonight.

– I wanted the overwhelming power and goodness of the English landscape to permeate the thoughts of our people, so that every man and woman might share the same road as Jude Fawley, see the same majesty of ancient oaks, lie in summer in the shallows of the same trickling stream, wander as free as the air through the same beautiful meadow. The land of England was to become our church and all who worshipped in her were to treat one another equally before the overwhelming truth of Nature.

– It seemed for a few moments that we might achieve it, didn't it? During those terrible war years, when the bombs rained down, we did create here something which seemed to have meaning for many people in this country. We gave them hope, we gave them the right to dream of a glorious English future.

He put the book down on the floor.

– And now I fear that dream is finally over.

Chapter Twenty Three

– I'm going to go upstairs and see Dad, Darius said.

They had all finished supper in the kitchen on Saturday night. The presence of the children had prevented a repeat of the previous evening's displays of anger, and James and Alice were now helping Francis to stack dishes in the dishwasher. Tink was laughing with Belinda at the table.

Francis looked over at his brother.

– I spoke with Annie before she left for the day today, he said. There's no change in Dad. It's as I told you, he's been stable like this for some time. There's no cause for alarm.

Darius smiled.

– That's good, he said.

– I just thought you should know, Francis continued, frowning. After what you said. It's all fine.

– Yes, said Darius. I hear what you say, Francis.

Upstairs, he closed the door of his father's bedroom behind him and sat down on a chair beside the bed. His father was fast asleep, his grey face and wispy hair making little impression on the thick white pillow. As Darius sat silently watching him, the thin reedy whistle of his father's breath played quietly around the room.

– What's happening in your house, Dad? he asked softly.

Richard's breathing didn't change.

– There's something wrong here, he continued. Ever since I arrived, I've felt it. There's a grip on this place. It's not like I remember it.

– You and I, we never got on. I'm sorry about that, I suppose, although if we're honest, neither of us really cares that much, do we? But when this was your house, when Mum was here, when Nana was here, when me and Francis used to race our bikes down the corridors – it was different. I wanted to get away, but only because I didn't really like being here with you all. It wasn't the house. The house was strong back then, Dad. It contained us all, it breathed us all in and out. We lived in it.

– It's not like that now. The house is fighting everyone. Look at it. The render is falling off the walls outside. Francis is one of the richest men in the country, and he can't fix the render on his house. The garden's a mess. I know you never had that much interest in the garden, Dad, but you knew how it was supposed to look. You knew how Nana wanted it. Now look at it. It's a battleground out there. There's not a single happy plant out there, Nana's plantations are choking themselves. And you and Francis, you let the path to Down There grow over.

– It wasn't difficult to free it today, Dad. It didn't take me long. The path was waiting, like everything in this house is waiting. What's it waiting for?

He watched his father breathe, watched the slight regular movement of his chest underneath the sheets.

– Did you ask me to come here, Dad? Was it you who sent the cards?

Outside the call of an owl echoed across the lawns. Darius stood up and walked over to the window, looked through a gap in the curtains out onto the moonlit garden. It was a cloudless night, and he could see the shape of the curving drive with its elder trees over to the left and the outline of the different planted gardens dotted around the lawns. Then he noticed a figure on the gravel down below in front of the house. It was Francis. He was walking slowly up and down in front of the main door, smoking a cigarette. The moonlight had picked out his bald head, and now Darius watched his brother, saw the stream of smoke being blown out. He kept walking, up and down, and then Darius saw him pull out another cigarette and light it from the stub of the existing one, which he threw down on the gravel.

Darius carefully let the curtains drop back together

again, and he went back to the chair.

– I got over it, Dad. It took me a long time. But I got over it. It wasn't your fault, it wasn't Mum's fault, it wasn't anyone's fault but mine. It was all my doing. I was out of control. I thought I was a king – I thought that's why you called me Darius. I thought I could do anything. I didn't think any of the rules applied to me. But I was just a druggie, Dad. That's all. A fucked up, unhappy little druggie boy who ended up killing an innocent girl. I destroyed her life, I destroyed her family's life. I destroyed everything.

– I never blamed any of you, Dad. Why would I? I just wanted to cut loose from you all. I needed to deal with it myself, deal with what I'd done. I'm still dealing with it Dad, but I'm OK. I understand it. I just don't get what's happened to you all here.

There was a gentle sigh from the bed, and Darius leaned forwards to see his father's face more closely. He was still asleep – a pale bubble of saliva at the side of his dry lips flickered and his eyelids twitched slightly.

– You're dreaming, Dad.

Darius sat back in his chair and closed his eyes, his hand resting on the bed. He let his mind relax. Soon, he could see the same desert sand dunes that had appeared to him the day before. He was walking across the sand and he could see the thin line of pale twisting smoke ahead. As he got closer, he could see two figures sitting around a feeble fire on the sand, the last few sticks just glowing in a blackened circular pit. There was no flame now, just a few embers. As he got closer, the two figures looked up and he recognised Francis and his father.

They looked similar, with the same domed bald head. They were both dressed in white cloths, their hands gathered in their laps. As he got closer, Francis raised his arm and made a gesture as though he were to join them. He sat down on the opposite side of the fire pit, and he could tell there was barely any heat coming from the embers now.

He looked up and the sky was a deep dark blue black

studded with stars. It was cold, and all around them the ridge of sand dunes undulated silently. He looked back and they were both looking at him, expressionlessly. Then he could see on his father's face a tear trickle down. His father lifted an unsteady hand to wipe it away. Then Francis gathered up some sand in his hand, and he slowly let it fall over the last remaining embers of the fire. Slowly they lowered their heads and their faces were obscured and all Darius could see was the top of their bald heads.

They sat in silence for a while.

– Remember the fire in the desert, a voice said. Remember the fire in the desert.

Darius continued to sit in front of them for a while, then stood up, turned, and walked back towards the dunes.

He opened his eyes. The bubble of saliva was still playing on his father's lips, and his breathing remained quiet and steady.

The door of the bedroom opened. He turned and saw Belinda. She was smiling and put her finger to her lips, beckoning him over. When he went over, she whispered:

– The kids are insisting on other story, Uncle Darius. They refuse to go to sleep without it. Can you manage another one?

He nodded, and followed her out.

Chapter Twenty Four

"FROME, Sir Zachary Edmund, died peacefully on 3rd May, 1980, aged 74. Beloved husband and father, a true servant to his country."

Felicity looked up from her desk.

– I think that's all we need, Richard, don't you? He never liked *The Times* anyway, they were always beastly to him. Let's not give them any more money than we need.

– I'll phone it through, Mum, said Richard, taking the sheet of paper from her.

– Sit with me a moment, she said, taking his hand.

They walked over to one of the sofas and sat down. She looked up at the glittering crystal shapes soaring up the wall from the huge fireplace.

– I never liked that fireplace, she said. I asked Mr Lutyens about it, after your father and I were married. He said he thought it represented the sun in India, but he couldn't be sure. He was quite old himself, then. I suppose I should be more respectful. I always thought it looks rather silly.

– I think Dad rather liked it, her son replied.

– Oh he loved it, she smiled. He called it rococo, which always made me laugh. Darling Zachary, he had no taste at all.

– He didn't do bad in choosing you, said Richard.

She squeezed his hand.

– I'd never met such an extraordinary man, she said. I was surrounded by all these smart people, cocktail parties in Mayfair, dances in St Tropez. It was never ending, one absurd event after the other. I thought that was what my life was going to consist of, and then one day your father walked up to me and introduced himself and that was that. He was terribly unprepossessing: thick owlish glasses and thinning hair slicked back over his head – sorry darling – and a suit which didn't seem to fit him anywhere. But he was the boldest creature you could imagine. Just came straight up to me. What he saw in me I have no idea.

– A very clever and very beautiful woman.

– Don't be sentimental.

She paused for a moment, still holding her son's hand.

– He had that effect on everyone, you know. My father melted like butter in Zachary's hands. Do you remember my father?

– A little.

– He was a man of the North, made all his money himself, was probably horribly ruthless although he kept most of that from me. If he was still alive, he would think Margaret Thatcher was a communist. But he loved your father. Doted on him. Poor Zachary had absolutely no idea about money, my father very quietly cleaned up the alarming finances of the Range when I first moved here. He said that Zachary hadn't collected any rent on the houses on the estate for four years. That tickled him. But he never teased your father about it. He admired him hugely.

She bit her lip, and Richard squeezed her hand.

– He didn't suffer, Mum, he said. We've that to be grateful for. The pneumonia was kind at least in that way – it was very quick.

She nodded, lowering her head.

– You were his great love, Mum, Richard continued. He adored you to the very end.

She took a deep breath, and smiled again.

– And I him, she said.

– He couldn't have done all he did without your support. Level Ground, all his charity work after the war, his writing. This house particularly. He loved everything you did here.

– I know, she said. The Range has been such a remarkable home for us.

She looked at him.

– Will you and Violet move here? With the boys?

– He told me he wanted me to. The day before he... He said he'd always wanted the Range to go the nation, but that he wanted Francis and Darius to be as happy here as he had been with you.

– Violet would look after it very well, I know that. She is so capable.

– Let's see Mum. It's all very sudden. I just want you to be all right.

– I'll be all right if you and Violet and the boys are here. You can tuck me away somewhere out of sight.

Richard stood up, and walked over to the crystal mantlepiece above the fire.

– He's a big man to come after, Mum, he said, not looking at her.

– Rubbish, she said. Zachary was a tiny little thing.

– You know what I mean. I always felt...I wish somehow I had done more. Like him. I wish I'd been able to achieve more. Five years as an MP, that's all. Trailing round after bloody Jim Callaghan picking up the pieces. Now I'm just another hack.

– Your father was more proud of you than you think, she said. He used to tell me he wished he could write as well as you.

– I know, Mum. I loved Dad, you know that. He was just very special. What he wanted for the world, for this country: he had a dream, and it never became reality. It all fell away, all that hope and passion and excitement surrounding Level Ground. He never saw his ideas succeed. And sometimes... sometimes I think he saw my political career as a part of the rejection of his ambitions. That the Labour party I served was the party that destroyed his dreams.

– It's not true, she said. I know it's not true. He admired everything you did. And he didn't die feeling that his dreams had been destroyed. He was still working on a new book you know. He died believing that it would all come about, one day. Just not in his own lifetime. He never gave up, Richard.

Chapter Twenty Five

– I think you look positively savage, said Belinda, laughing.

Francis, Darius and she were sitting around the kitchen table. It was half past three on Sunday afternoon. There was a cut baguette on a wooden board on the table, and plates of cheese and ham and a bowl of salad. The kitchen door had just burst open and Tink, Alice and James had charged in, all shouting some kind of war cry. They were wearing feathers in their hair, they had made their faces up with mascara'd patterns, and the children were brandishing sticks.

– We're pirates, Alice said proudly.

– Aargh! shouted James, rushing up to Darius and poking his stick at him.

– Ow! said Darius, laughing too. Don't hurt me, please, I'm a friend of pirates.

– You all look splendid, said Francis. What are your names?

– I'm Captain Hook, said James, brandishing his left hand, which had a fork sellotaped to it.

– I'm Wendy, said Alice. And Tink is Tink. And we're all pirates.

– Well, you are very scary, all of you, said Belinda, still laughing. Now, you know where you're going?

– Yes Mummy, we know, said Alice. We're going to take Tink down to the boathouse and we're going to row the boat on the river.

– Lifejackets, please, said Belinda. All pirates have to wear lifejackets. Tink, when you get to the boathouse, you'll find them on a hook on the wall.

– Don't worry, she said. I am going to be a very strict pirate captain.

The three of them turned and left.

– And then there were three, said Francis, picking up his copy of the *Sunday Times* again.

– I've told Annie we're going out for a walk, said Belinda. Let's go.

Darius looked at his brother as he lay down his newspaper back down on the table. He had a slight smile on his lips, as though he knew something which the others didn't. More than ever, Darius felt the distance between the two of them, the complete lack of both sympathy and trust. It confused him. He had had no desire to renew his relationship with his brother, but now that he was here again at the Range, he found it disconcerting that there seemed to be no point of contact available between them.

There was an awkwardness amongst them at the new opening in the thick hedge at the back of the house which Darius had cut the day before. They stood as though waiting to be told who should go first. The cut ends of the branches shone palely against the deep browns and greens, their diagonal incisions raw and open.

– You've been busy, Francis said, and stepped through the gap. Belinda followed him and Darius came last.

Each of them held out their hands to protect their faces from any stray thorns and to steady themselves as the path began to descend by feeling the cut edges on either side. As they began to step downwards, the light became gloomier and the smell of the vegetation thicker. Leaves brushed their cheeks and hair as they continued, and there was also a keener sweeter smell just noticeable which Darius realised was the smell of sap from the cut branches either side.

They made no conversation as they proceeded down the sloping path. Francis was about five yards ahead of Darius, and Darius could hear his breathing, slightly laboured although the incline was taking all the strain. Maybe it was the cigarettes. How very strange, Darius thought, to be following him down this path of all paths, now, as middle-aged men.

Soon the incline became steeper, which indicated that they were close to the end. At one point, Belinda reached back to take Darius's hand to steady herself as she stepped down a steeper part.

Darius followed the two of them into the clearing. They stood still at the opening first, looking at the circular sweep of grass, the stone plinth in the centre, the drooping willows the other side and the glint of water where their ends draped the river. The light was stronger here than inside the path, although the summer sunshine was still filtered through the canopy overhead. It was silent, just the gentle unrhythmic lapping of the water at the far edge.

Slowly they began to wander apart.

– What time is it? said Francis. He was standing over to one side, looking at Belinda. There was sweat glistening on his head.

She was across the clearing, about twenty yards away. She looked at her watch.

– Five to four. Her voice was not strong as it had been earlier, it was light and nervous.

Darius wandered to the plinth, and stood with his back leaning against it, looking over at his brother. Belinda sat down on the grass.

– When was the last time you were here, Francis? said Darius.

Francis shook his head and looked away. For a moment, for the first time this weekend in fact, he looked uncertain. The clearing was silent again.

Francis looked back at Darius. His eyes were twitching behind his thick glasses.

– Not since then, he said. When it happened. And then when they brought us all down here, the police and every-one, marking it all out, measuring it.

There was a hesitation in his voice, which again Darius had not picked up any time so far over the weekend.

– When it was all over, I never came here again.

– Why not?

– I don't know if you recall, Darius, but I don't have particularly pleasant memories of the last visit.

– So you just put it out of your mind? Darius persisted. Is that why you're feeling a little tense?

Francis tried to smile again, unconvincingly.

– I'm not tense, he said. If anything, I'm slightly embarrassed to be participating in this game.

– You seem tense, Darius said. How about you, Belinda?

She was looking down at the grass, and she just shook her head.

– Is it how you remember it? Darius asked, still looking at Francis.

Francis seemed to stare at him.

– I don't remember it. I prefer not to.

– Is that it? You just don't think about it? Are you trying to tell me that you've just not thought about it for twenty-five years?

– I don't know. I mean, I've tried not to think about it. I've tried to put it out of my mind. Haven't you?

Darius looked at him.

– Put it out of my mind? Have I tried to put it out of my mind? What do you think? Of course I haven't tried to put it out of my mind. It's been in my mind every day and night for the last twenty-five years.

Francis coughed and turned away.

Darius pushed himself away from the plinth and walked around to the willows by the water. He looked through the gaps in the branches and could see the the steady flowing river. He stayed there silently for a moment, then he turned to walk back to the plinth. That was when he saw what was leaning against the other side of the stone monument.

Darius looked up over at Francis.

– Is this your idea of a joke? he said.

– What?

Francis walked over. He too came around the back of the plinth, and as soon as he saw what was lying there, he visibly recoiled.

226

– Jesus Christ, he said. He stepped backwards and turned away towards the river.

Darius continued to look at the back of the plinth. Leaning against the grey flat surface was a target, a round straw-filled target with the coloured roundel on the outward side. Lying against it at the bottom was a bow with one arrow loosely placed on the string.

– What's it doing here, Francis? Darius demanded, turning towards his brother.

Francis looked back at the plinth, then at Darius, shaking his head.

– I don't know, he said. Why would I know? Someone is playing a game, as I suspected. A not very amusing game.

Darius looked at him. His brother, for the first time this weekend, looked frail.

– Why is there a bow and arrow here? said Darius.

Francis looked at the objects at the foot of the plinth.

– I don't bloody know, he said, and his voice now sounded very strained. This is just stupid. What the hell's going on?

– It's a bow and arrow, Belinda said quietly. She had joined them around the back of the plinth, and now all three of them were staring. Suddenly it looked like a framed still life to Darius, the bow and arrow and target carefully placed by some unknown artist.

– Who put it here? Francis said, loudly now. Who?

A breeze rippled through the trees edging the water. The river began to lap more noisily against the bank, and leaves fluttered in the canopy overhead. The still air of the clearing was moving and a cold draft was now filling up the space between the thick circle of hedge and trees. The shrill insistent call of a wren could be heard now from somewhere up above, repeating its complicated set of notes over and over.

Darius strode away from the plinth back to the water's edge. The Thames sat mute and still beyond, the sun and clouds creating patterns on the still surface. Here at the bank, though, the water still lapped loudly against the moss and earth of the grass edge.

He walked away from the water and across to the other side of the clearing, looking up to see if he could see the wren, who was still singing. The branches above were moving now with the breeze, and there was no longer silence: the whisper of leaves, the creak of a tree, the wash of the water. Darius felt clearly the presence of something strange, something alive in the air, as though their solitude had been interrupted by another being.

Darius looked back over at the others, who hadn't moved. Belinda was looking at Francis, who was still staring down at the plinth.

– What time is it? Darius called out.

Belinda was motionless for a second, still staring at her husband, then she looked at her watch and then over at Darius.

– It's four o'clock, she said, her voice fragile and unconfident.

Francis looked up suddenly and shouted at Darius:

– Well? he yelled. His voice was hoarse. Well? Are you going to get on with it, Darius?

– Get on with what, Francis?

Darius could feel a cold breeze against his face now, and he looked across at the wall of willow branches which were moving erratically, their leaves stirring the water which was still lapping noisily against the edge of the grass.

Francis suddenly ran towards the opening of the path they had come down. It looked as though he was going to head back up but when he reached it, he stopped. He stood for a moment. He was breathing heavily. Then, slowly, he turned around. He looked at them.

– It's both of you, isn't it? he called out. You've all set this up.

Darius felt the clearing become quiet again. The breeze had passed, the leaves and the water were settled. The wren stopped singing. There was silence inside once more.

– Set what up, Francis? said Darius, frowning.

Francis started to laugh then, an ugly, discordant laugh

that rang out inside the clearing.

– Oh you're very good, Darius. You're very good.

He looked over at Belinda.

– Have you always known? he said.

Belinda stared back at her husband but didn't answer.

– Or was it the faery? sneered Francis. Don't tell me, her surname's Marple.

Darius walked over towards his brother.

– Pull yourself together, Francis, he said. What the hell are you talking about? What's going on?

Francis looked at him, and then suddenly he crumpled. His shoulders sagged, and for a second Darius thought he might fall.

– Don't you really know? he asked, quietly this time.

– Know what? said Darius.

Francis stared at him with a look of terrible intensity. Then he brushed past him, almost knocking into him as he rushed back over to the plinth. He stood right in front of Belinda.

– You, it's you isn't it? he said to Belinda. Of course it's you. Why didn't I work that out? You've always known, haven't you?

There was a wail from Belinda, loud and shocking in the silence of the clearing. She slumped against the plinth, her shoulders shaking as she sobbed, her hands covering her face. She was shaking her head wildly from side to side.

Darius joined them and grabbed Francis by his arm.

– What the hell are you talking about? he said.

Francis stood very still, looking straight at his brother. His face was calmer now, he wasn't bewildered as he had just appeared and his eyes were clear behind his glasses. He looked slowly down at his arm where Darius was holding him, then he looked back up, and then he smiled.

– It was me. I fired the arrow. I killed Annabel. It wasn't you.

Darius didn't immediately take on board what his brother had said. The words seemed to hang heavily in the air.

– What did you say?

Francis didn't move.

– I said I killed her. I killed Annabel.

Darius let go of Francis's arm and took a step back.

– What are you talking about?

Francis stood perfectly still. He turned his head to look at Belinda, who was still sobbing, her head buried into her arms on the plinth. Darius took in the scene but for a moment still couldn't make sense of the words. Everything seemed to be moving incredibly slowly, as though he had been plunged under water.

Francis was talking again.

– I will tell you. Now. I will tell you now, because maybe it's right now that you should know. I don't know. It's so long ago. But I'm warning you both – he looked methodically at each of them in turn – I'm warning you that I will never discuss this again in the future, and I will if I have to deny ever telling you. This conversation will never have taken place. Do you understand?

Belinda had stopped crying, but she still didn't look up. Darius felt that inside his head there was a great noise, like the roar of a gale, and he felt a little unsteady. He reached out to grip the top of the plinth with one hand.

– I'm telling you, Francis was saying. I'm telling you now. You didn't fire the arrow. That afternoon. You got us all wasted, do you remember? Me and Belinda and Annabel. We were here, and there was dope and then you had acid, and we all had it and everything went weird. We went in the river, then when we put our clothes back on we were out of our heads. You were too, even though you'd had it before. None of *us* had had it before. But you must have smoked much more dope or something, or you took more acid than us. Annabel was pretending to be *Marianne*, and she was striking poses. Belinda was lying down on the ground looking up at the sky. Annabel wanted us to fire arrows at the target, it was some game she made up about how we had to prove our worth to her or something. We took it in turns to fire arrows.

Suddenly he reached out and grabbed Darius's shirt. His face was close now and Darius could smell the warmth of his brother's breath. Still there was this roar inside his head which made it seem as though Francis were shouting to be heard over the top of it.

– It was just a mess, Darius. We were crawling on the floor most of the time. Then it just happened. It was my turn and I fired the arrow and I didn't notice that Annabel had gone back to pick up the arrows that hadn't hit the target. I just turned around and let go of the string and it was too late, she was standing near the target and the arrow just went straight into her. There wasn't any noise, she didn't cry out. They said at the inquest that she was killed immediately, the arrow went straight through her brain. She just fell down on the floor, and the arrow was pointing up out of her eye.

Francis let go of his brother's shirt and walked a little away from the plinth.

– I looked around, and you were just beside me, he continued. I think you must have passed out briefly. Belinda was further away, and her eyes were closed. I didn't know what to do. I dropped the bow. It fell on you by accident, I didn't throw it at you. It just fell on you and it woke you up and you grabbed hold of it. You got up and you were still holding the bow and I pointed at Annabel. I don't know what I said, but somehow I said something that made you think that you'd fired the arrow. You were holding the bow, don't you see? You'd passed out for a second from all the dope, and then you were standing up holding the bow and Annabel was dead and you thought you'd fired the arrow. You looked really confused and I didn't know what to say, so I didn't say anything else and then Belinda was screaming and she saw you holding the bow and then, that was it. That was what it was. It was you holding the bow, not me, and I didn't say anything else.

Darius straightened up. The noise inside of his head had

receded and instead he felt a very clear, still silence. It felt to him as though the whole clearing had been illuminated, it felt as though the sun had broken through the thick foliage above their heads and was flooding Down There with light.

– You said, Darius said very slowly, you said: *Oh My Christ, Darius, what have you done?*

– Did I? said Francis. Is that what I said? Maybe so.

There was a strange look on Francis's face. He was almost smiling, but he was looking down at the grass now.

– Yes, that's what you said, Darius repeated. I've had those words ringing in my head for twenty-five years. *Oh My Christ, Darius, what have you done?*

– I don't really remember, said Francis. I don't remember how it all happened, Darius, it was so long ago. I remember running up the path to get Dad, and I think I said something to him when I found him, something about not being sure how it happened and he was very angry and then I think I remember Mum saying at some point that it must have been your fault. I think you still had the bow in your hand when they both got down here. I remember now – Francis's eyes widened as he said this – I remember Mum grabbing me at some point and telling me that I didn't do it. She was very insistent. Dad went back up to phone the police. Mum was looking after Belinda, then she made us all go back up too. Then the police came.

– It was a tragic and stupid mistake, Francis continued. The same thing everyone said when they thought you'd done it, Darius. But it was still just a mistake. That's all it was. It might just as well have been you.

Darius was listening to his brother but at the same time, he was also marvelling at the sense of tranquillity he felt. He knew he should not be feeling this. His brother had just told him about the most devastating news which he could have relayed: not just that he, Darius, had not fired the arrow but that his own parents had conspired to shift the blame onto him from his brother.

He wanted to savour this moment. The moment when

he should have been furious, enraged, vengeful...he felt none of those things. He felt an overwhelming sense of calm and unity. He wanted to experience it fully. He looked around the clearing and every leaf on every tree, each blade of grass, seemed distinct and alive.

Belinda spoke from behind the plinth.

– This is why I sent the cards, she said very quietly.

Francis turned towards her.

– What? Oh yes, of course. I don't know why I didn't think of it. It had to be you, didn't it? The cards. Telling us all to come here. You sent them.

– I sent them, she said.

Francis began to laugh hysterically. Nobody did anything, there was just the piercing noise of Francis's laughter inside the clearing. It had a metallic edge to it, that's how it seemed to Darius – it sounded so foreign, so out of place. He wanted the noise to stop, so he moved in front of Francis and slapped him hard on the face.

The slap was like a gun shot inside the clearing. Francis clutched his cheek which immediately began to show a red weal. He stepped away from Darius, as though he were afraid of him.

– You can't do anything about it, Darius, he snarled. It never happened.

– I don't want to do anything about it, Francis, said Darius quietly. I just wanted to stop the noise you were making.

Belinda walked around the plinth and sat on the grass not far from Francis. She spoke to him.

– I knew something wasn't right, Francis, she said. About this house. About us. Darius sensed it as soon as he got here. I've known something wasn't right for years, but I've never known what it was. I blamed all sorts of things. I thought you had too much work, that you were worried about Richard. I came up with all sorts of things. I tried to talk to you, but you always said there was nothing the matter. But I knew there was. The last two or three years it's been getting worse, and then Richard said something six months ago, something which didn't make sense.

– Nothing Richard says these days makes any sense, but this was as though someone else was speaking through him. I don't know. He just blurted this out. When I was in his room, he sat up one day and looked at me, and he said: I know it wasn't Darius, but what could I do? I couldn't let Francis's career be destroyed. It would have destroyed his mother. Darius would recover. He's strong. It would have been the end of Francis. He had such a career ahead of him.

– Someone was speaking through him, Belinda, said Darius. He wanted you to know. He didn't just blurt it out. He needed to have it said. It's still inside him now. That's why we're here too: he wants to go and he doesn't want to go without us understanding.

– I asked him what he meant, Belinda continued, but then he was gone again, and he looked at me as though he didn't know who I was. He never said anything like that again. I didn't know what to do. I knew it had something to do with what happened here, what happened to Annabel. I tried to talk to you Francis, but I couldn't articulate it. I couldn't tell you what I feared might be the truth.

She looked up at Darius.

– So I came up with this, she said, shrugging her shoulders. She looked exhausted.

– I just thought that if I got us all back together here, something would happen. And it did.

Darius walked over to the plinth.

– This target, and the bow. That was you too?

Belinda nodded.

– I ran them down here when I knew you were all doing things earlier today. I bought them in Harrods last week.

She turned to look at Francis, who was still standing a little distance away.

– I don't think I ever loved you, Francis, she said. We've never been happy, really, have we? I married you because… because somehow it felt safe. It felt safe because we both knew about Annabel dying and I thought we both knew what had happened and it was still a mistake, it wasn't that Darius had meant to do it but it was just a horrible mistake that was the result of us all being really stupid. And all these years, when we tried to make a happy family – you know, sometimes I'd watch other families and try and work out how they did it, how they were happy. I've tried so hard. But it's no good.

She waved her arm around.

– This place, the house, the gardens: we can't even keep it up, we just let it all fall apart around us. It's all ugly. I thought it was because we were cursed by it. Sometimes I thought we could take the kids and disappear somewhere the other side of the world and start again and maybe we could escape it. But I knew we couldn't really.

– And now we know, she said. It was all a lie. The last twenty-five years have all been based on a lie.

Her voice was dulled, and her head sank down between her knees.

– It's what I told you yesterday, Darius, she said, her voice just audible now. It wasn't just you whose life was ruined. I know you went to prison and I can't imagine what that was like. But it wasn't just you.

She lifted her head and looked at Darius.

– We were all ruined by this, she said. Don't you see? When Annabel died, all our lives were ended. None of us had any choice after that. Why do you think I got back with Francis after all that time? I thought it was all I deserved.

She looked up at Darius again.

– I know it was worse for you, Darius. But can you at least see? Can you see how horrible this is now? Everything? How everything is ruined?

The clearing was silent again. Darius was still acutely aware of the natural world all around him, the lichen on the side of the plinth, the smell of the grass, the occasional quiet lapping of the water. How intense it all was, how supremely vivid. Then Francis began a slow, loud clap of his hands.

He walked slowly back towards the plinth, still clapping his hands, the red weal on his cheek now very visible. He came up to Belinda.

– Well done, my dear, he said. He reached his hand up and just touched her chin lightly. She flinched.

– Quite a performance, he continued. I'm so glad you've both enjoyed it. Nothing like a spot of amateur dramatics in an English country garden. And you were so sweet to get the props too. You've really pulled out all the stops, my darling.

His face was ugly now with a sneer.

– Well, I'm sorry to tell you folks, but the show's over. It's time to go home. There will be no encores, no repeat performances, no reviews. This was a once-in-a-lifetime presentation, brought to us by the inimitable Belinda Frome. Congratulations again, Belinda, what a show. You missed your vocation in life, that's for sure.

He turned and began to walk back towards the opening in the hedge where the path back up to the house began.

– Francis, Darius called out. His brother stopped, but didn't turn around. Darius walked slowly over to him, and stopped a couple of yards away.

– You're wrong, Francis, he said, gently. Like you're wrong about everything. It isn't over. The show, as you call it, it's just begun.

Darius turned around to look back at Belinda. He was smiling.

– And you're wrong too, Belinda, he said. We weren't all ruined and everything isn't ruined. It's going to be fine. You did an extraordinary thing. You did a really extraordinary thing.

Chapter Twenty Six

– I find it difficult to believe that we are still alive, said Felicity. I'm going to be eighty next month. What a ridiculous notion.

– You'll have to have a party, said Jenkins.

As was their habit, the two of them were strolling around the gardens at the Range. Her old publisher walked with a cane, and he stooped a little now. Felicity's arm was linked with his, and they walked slowly.

– Of course you had a party for your eightieth last year, she said.

– I invited you. You didn't come. It was very churlish of you.

– You know I can't stand that sort of thing, Nigel. Even for you. What was it like?

– Oh, you know. Sprinkling of girls. Mostly nurses, in my case.

She laughed.

– Richard said it was very smart. The Garrick, wasn't it?

– Yes. In fact, we were all so old I had the doorman count us all in and out, in case any of us pegged it during the party.

– How is your old firm doing?

– It exists in name only really, a scalp on the wall of Random House. I call in every so often and they all look rather sheepish. I think I might leave them in peace now.

– We're not of much use any more, are we?

– Not really. If I'm honest, I don't even fancy girls any more. Since my wife died, I can't really seem to summon the interest. What did that chap say about impotence? Like being unchained from a lunatic.

She laughed again.

– The debutantes of London will be bereft, Nigel.

– Do debutantes still exist? he asked. I wonder. Perhaps we should get Richard to commission a feature in the *Chronicle*: the Lost Tribe of Mayfair.

– He's working very hard, she said.

– He's a very good editor.

– He's such a serious man, she said. I just wish he and Violet would let their hair down every so often.

– Difficult in Richard's case.

– You know what I mean. Zachary was serious of course, but he had a twinkle in his eye. It never left him, that twinkle. It was like the Star of Bethlehem to me.

– What about the boys?

– Francis is very much cut from his father's cloth – he's studious, polite, very interested in politics already even though he's only eleven. Darius is very different. He's what you would call a tearaway. Won't read a book. But you know, Nigel, he has that twinkle. I've seen it. It makes my heart stop sometimes. It makes me fear for him too.

– He'll be all right. He's a Frome. And any grandson of Felicity Drummond is fine by me.

– I worry about him, though. His mother, Violet, is not necessarily the most – how can I put it? – sensitive of souls. I'm not sure she knows how to be with Darius.

– You've never been too fond of Violet, have you?

– That's not fair. She is an excellent wife to Richard, she keeps the Range in a wonderful state and she indulges me no end by letting me boss the gardeners around.

– All the same.

– All the same nothing. She and I are not necessarily cut from the same cloth, that is all. But we respect one another. It's just that, she is so trenchant in her view of life, and I think what poor Darius needs more than anything is some freedom to explore a little. He is a square peg in a round hole, I fear. If books are not for him, then he should be in-dulging what he loves, which is the country. If I had my way, I'd take him up to Yorkshire and have some of my relatives roam the moors with him. He would love that.

– I'd take him myself if my legs would carry me. Past it, I'm afraid.

They continued to walk in silence for a while. Then:

– Do you remember, Nigel, how you would come down here and badger me about writing another book for you?

– What rot, he snorted. Nobody could have stopped you from writing, Felicity. You were born to it.

– Oh, but when I married Zachary and his career took off and then Richard came…you know, Nigel, I was so impossibly happy that sometimes you did need to badger me. Without you, I would have become plump and contented like a porpoise and never written another thing. I'm just saying, I'm glad you did.

– We did all right, didn't we?

He squeezed her arm.

– Yes Nigel, she said. We did all right.

They sat down on a bench, looking out over the carefully clipped ornamental hedges and the early Spring roses in the enclosed garden they had chosen to walk in that day.

– Always loved these gardens, haven't you? he said.

– Yes, she sighed. It all seemed a bit daunting at first, when we were married. I'd never so much as deadheaded a rose before I came to the Range. I thought life was all about exotic hotels and witty conversation and disreputable publishers like you.

– Most unfair, he said.

– But then when I came here, it was as though I were gripped by something, like a fever, although really it was more like a lovely dream. I just became obsessed with these gardens. Not just for me: I had a strong sense that they had meaning too for Zachary, and I wanted him to experience complete happiness here at his Range. It did make him so happy, you know. I don't think he would have been able to do all that he did without this place. For him it represented some kind of innocence, of natural equilibrium; a return to nature, if you like. We were like two little children here really and I was so happy, playing with my enormous dolls' house and dolls' garden.

He chuckled.

– It was the talk of London, I remember. Felicity Drummond's gone native, she's abandoned us all for the allure of the rhododendrum.

– I suppose I did abandon you all, she said. It was as though a spell had been cast. I would lie for hours out here on the lawn, watching the clouds skim by. Or down beside the river, where Zachary and I had our secret place. Hours and hours, Nigel.

– A couple of incorrigible romantics, that was you and Zac. They don't make them like you any more, dear Felicity.

– Perhaps they don't, she said. Zachary did worry about that towards the end, about how the world was going. He was the most positive and optimistic of men, but towards the end, he worried more and more about a future that he knew he wouldn't see, but which seemed to fill him with dread. He worried about the world that Francis and Darius would face – "a world without dreams" he called it once.

They sat in silence again, watching a robin peck at the newly turned soil around the rose bushes. Felicity noticed Jenkins's eyes closing, and she let her old friend doze quietly. She looked down the line of one of the flagstone paths between the borders and for a moment imagined that she saw Zachary walking down towards her from the other end, his boyish gait and always slightly embarrassed smile giving him that incongruous look which so melted her heart. For a moment, she closed her eyes too and she imagined Zachary taking her hand and the two of them walking off out of the garden back onto the lawns.

She couldn't tell what he was saying but he was speaking with his familiar passion, gesticulating with one arm while the other held onto hers. They walked over the lawns towards the house and she felt filled with happiness as his voice rang out over the land and she clutched onto him for fear of missing a second at his side.

Jenkins stirred.

– What's that? he said. Did I drop off? So sorry.

Felicity opened her eyes and smiled at him.

– That's all right, Nigel, she said. It's what happens to us now: we live in our dreams.

Chapter Twenty Seven

Darius and Belinda stayed Down There after Francis had turned and left. They didn't talk at first. It seemed to Darius as though the clearing was absorbing all that had happened, transforming it and making the world anew. That's how it seemed to him. He lay on the grass looking up at the over-hanging branches, and the sun was filtering through creating sharp, bright patterns all over.

Remember the fire in the desert. He thought of his vision yesterday when he had sat beside his father, how he had come across his father and Francis in the desert. They had seemed somehow empty, totally lacking in strength. They had just sat there on the sand, looking impassively at him. There was no need for him to feel anger now. Whatever they had done to him all those years ago, the years he had spent in prison for no reason, had only brought him to this pow-erful feeling which he was experiencing now. It was joy. He sat up.

– I think I'd like to try something, Belinda, he said.

Belinda was sitting on top of the plinth with her eyes closed. She looked up.

– With Dad. I want to try a ritual that I learned back in Mexico. It's a ritual they use for the dying, to help them to shed the pains of this world before they leave for the next. Most cultures have had rituals like it. The ancient Greeks used to imagine that Hermes served as the escort for the dead into the afterlife, and part of his role was helping the soul to pass through unencumbered with the traumas of life on earth. I'd like to help Dad offload what he's been carry-ing inside of him for the last twenty-five years. I think it's why he spoke to you, I think the need was so great that his soul broke through the dementia, just for that moment. I think Dad needed you to know, I think he wanted you to be able to tell me the truth about what happened. It's been weighing on him all these years. He and Mum, they did a bad thing and he's always known it.

– Maybe, said Belinda. I was probably the only person he could tell by that stage. He couldn't really have rung you up.

– Exactly. Even if I had been around for him to tell me, he'd have been too scared to tell me. He'd have thought I'd have exploded. He'd kept his secret all these years and he just wouldn't have been able to tell me. He got through to you, and then once you'd heard it, you decided to send those cards, and it all came round to today. It's a closing of the circle, Belinda, and it's what he needs to find peace.

– You must do whatever you think is right, she said.

She looked down at her hands.

– I was scared too, she continued. When I thought about setting all this up. I didn't know what would happen. I didn't even know if what I suspected was what had actually happened, but if it did turn out to be true, then I was scared what would happen to you, Darius. How you'd take it.

– It's strange, said Darius. It's because it's happened here, I think. You've restored the balance, that's how it feels. It doesn't feel like something that could make me angry, it's the opposite: it's like a blessing. It's like restoring something that got lost a long time ago, setting it back in its proper place. Don't you feel that?

She nodded.

– Are you OK, Belinda? he asked.

– I think so, she said. When Francis said all those horrible things just now, I did think it was like the end of everything. But I think you may be right. This may be what had to happen. Now perhaps it might be possible to make sense of everything again.

– You were very brave.

– Was I? I don't think so. Well, maybe I was.

She sat up and smiled and looked at him.

– Actually, I do feel brave, she said. I used to feel brave when I was young. When we came here, before it happened, I felt I could do anything.

She looked at Darius. He smiled.

– You were, he said. I thought you could do anything you wanted then.

– I thought that too, she said. But then after, I couldn't do a thing. For what seemed like years. It took me ages to get my confidence back. I did eventually, that's how I ended up joining the Board of World Action. I finally realised I was pretty good at stuff. But then these last few years with Francis, it's all been so draining. Now that I've confronted it, confronted him, maybe now it's finally over.

– What will he do now? asked Darius.

– Francis? I don't know, said Belinda. He's lived with that secret for twenty-five years. He married me knowing that it was him who shot poor Annabel, not you. Maybe that was his final triumph, in his mind, getting the final say over his brother. I think he will just retreat into that mad world he inhabits, that horrible world where men with too much money spend all their time trying to work out ways of making more money. He'll carry on supporting the Labour party and one day whenever it's their turn to be back in power, he'll probably end up in the House of Lords. I don't really know who Francis is, and I don't really think he does either. There's lots to think about. I need to look after Alice and James. Perhaps I'll bring them to that festival of yours in Cornwall, that might be a good start.

Darius smiled.

– That's not a bad plan, he said. Bring them down to Level Ground and I'll teach them how to be real pirates.

Just as he finished speaking, they heard a scream. It was high-pitched, a girl's scream, and it came from the other side of the willows, from the river.

Belinda leaped off the plinth.

– That's Alice! she said. Then she shouted her daughter's

name: Alice! Alice!

She ran to the edge of the clearing and began to wade into the water, pushing the willow branches aside. Alice screamed again and then there was a big splash.

– Something's wrong! Belinda called. I can see the rowing boat, but there's only Alice on it.

She looked back at Darius, who was pulling off his jeans and his T-shirt. He raced over to the water, pushed past Belinda and began to swim. He could see the boat out in the middle of the river and he could see Tink in the water.

– Alice! Belinda called out, louder now. What's happened? Where's James?

– I don't know, the little girl screamed. He jumped in the water and I can't see him.

Darius kept swimming. As he came up close, he saw Tink's legs disappear into the water as she dived below the surface. He dived down too, keeping his eyes open but the water was so murky it was difficult to make anything out. When he came back to the surface, he saw Tink a few yards away.

– I can't find him! she screamed.

– Again! Darius yelled, and they both dived again. He kicked deeper down and soon felt the soft muddy floor of the river. He swam rapidly to and fro, feeling to left and right with his hands which brushed through thick reeds. Suddenly, he saw him: just a shape ahead, and it was wriggling. He lunged forwards and grabbed the boy's arm. He could feel some resistance and realised that James's leg had got caught in thick reeds. Darius pulled at him and felt the reeds give way and together they rose back up. As they broke the surface of the water, James heaved a massive gulp of air, then his high-pitched voice wailed across the surface of the water.

– It's OK, Darius said, keeping hold of him. It's OK, James, you're all right.

Tink swam over to them.

– Is he OK? she called out. Her face was wracked with fear.

– He's OK, said Darius.

– James! James!

Darius looked back to the bank and saw Belinda halfway up to her neck in the water, still wading.

– He's fine, Darius shouted. Stop and head back, I'll bring them all to the bank.

James was crying now and so was Alice, on the boat. Darius gathered the boy up and raised him to the side of the boat.

– Alice, help your brother back on board, he instructed. With him pushing and the girl holding his arms, they managed to get him back in the rowing boat and he began to swim with one arm, the other holding on to the prow. Tink went behind and pushed, kicking her legs. Slowly, the boat moved across the river and soon they came alongside Belinda, who was still standing in the water. She reached into the boat and placed her hands on her son's head.

– James, are you all right?

He nodded, still sobbing, and Darius gently guided Belinda back towards the banks of willows.

– Come on, he said, everyone back on dry land.

He pushed the boat through the hanging branches and drew it alongside the grass of the clearing. First he lifted Alice out and then James. Belinda clambered out of the water, her clothes completely covered in mud. Darius helped Tink to follow and she too was soaked through. Finally, he heaved himself out of the water and sat on the grass, the water dripping off his bare chest.

Belinda was clutching James and Alice. The children had stopped crying now and Belinda was gently rocking them, making quiet soothing sounds. Alice still had her life-jacket on and Darius looked over at the boat, where he saw two others. He looked over at Tink and pointed at them, questioningly. She sat beside him and whispered:

– He just took his off when my back was turned and he dived in.

Darius nodded.

. They all sat still for a while until James said very quietly:

247

– I didn't mean to, Mummy. I didn't mean to. I wanted to see if I could find a dreaming fish.

Belinda looked up at Darius, tears still in her eyes. He reached out and held her hand and then he said:

– James, here's a deal. If you promise me you'll never do that again, then I promise you one day I'll take you out to Madagascar and we'll go and find the dreamer fish. Is that a deal?

Chapter Twenty Eight

The next morning, Darius woke early and went to his father's room before anyone else in the house was awake. He entered the room quietly and saw that his father was still asleep. He sat on the chair beside the bed and placed his hand gently on the old man's head.

– Dad, he said. Dad. It's me. Darius.

The old man's head was twitching slightly on the pillow. His mouth was open slightly, saliva dripping down his chin. The veins on his bony, bald skull patterned the dry skin.

Darius leaned forwards.

– I'm going to help you, Dad, he said, his voice deep and strong. We're going to close the circle. We're going to let you leave all these things behind.

His father's body shook suddenly and a spindly arm shot out with surprising force from the sheets. The hand shook rapidly and Darius gently closed his around it, slowly lowering it back down.

Darius remained still until his father's breathing became more regular again, then he bent down and took out a small drum with a pale cream skin strung across the top of it from inside a canvas bag. He also took out an old leather notebook that was filled with papers. He leafed through the papers and found a handwritten sheet, then stood up.

– Dad, we're going to make this room a sacred space, he said, firmly but not so loud that his father might wake.

He got up and went over to the window. He turned around and faced the room and began to read quietly from the sheet.

– I call upon the energies of the quarters, he said.

He tapped the drum three times with his palm. For such

a small instrument, it created a full sound, a deep reverberation in the room.

– I call upon the spirit of the South. Great Serpent, let your light illuminate this room, let your power transform us and help us to shed the past. Arrive!

He hit the drum once. Then he turned to the right and faced the wall. He made three more beats.

– I call upon the spirit of the West. Golden Jaguar who shows us the warrior's way of courage, let your emerald eyes pierce all our fears and help us to see clearly the truth behind them. Arrive!

Another beat of the drum, then he turned again to look out of the window. Again, he hit three times.

– I call upon the spirit of the North. Wise and ancient Dragon, let your fire connect us to the knowledge of our ancestors. Arrive!

One more beat, then he turned once more to look at the other wall. He hit the drum three times.

– I call upon the spirit of the East. Great Eagle soaring in the heavens, let your sharp eyes illuminate our path and bring clarity to our thinking. Arrive!

After another beat, he looked down to his feet and lowered the drum, beating it three times.

– I call upon the great Mother of the earth upon whose fertile stomach we walk. Through your nurturing you show us grace. Arrive!

He hit it again, then lifted his face up towards the ceiling, holding the drum up and beating three times:

– Father, Great Spirit, watch over us and bring my own Father's Higher Spirit down upon him. Arrive!

A final drumbeat, and then Darius stood still, his eyes closed.

Richard's body twitched a little inside the bedclothes. His eyes were still closed.

Darius came back to the other side of the bed and laid his hand on his father's arm. He closed his eyes and began to speak:

– Renounce all attachment and yearning, Dad. Do you hear me? Renounce all attachment and yearning. I ask you to let go of the ties that hold you to this house, to me, to Francis, to Belinda. I ask you to give up what you know and leave it behind. Renounce all attachment and yearning. Cast aside what's done, Dad. It can be left behind now, it has no place within you any more. Leave it here.

Darius sat still for a moment with his eyes still closed, and his father breathed quietly now. The room was still. In the silence, a blackbird sang outside. Then Darius reached down and picked up the notebook again.

– Dad, he said, as he leafed through the book. I'm going to read something to you. It will help you to let go of the past. I want you to listen, and I want you to shake yourself free finally.

He found what he was looking for, and leaned forward to be closer to his father's head. He began to read.

– Obscured fool that I am, burdened by negative past acts, Propelled by the momentum of past actions, I have taken birth as the personification of rampant egohood within this world of desire. I regret having taken such birth, and am dismayed by my past acts. Yet, regardless of my regret and my dismay, past actions cannot be re-made. The momentum of past actions is as strong as a river's inexorable flow. So how can the mighty river of past actions be reversed in a mere moment? All that ripens is born from one's own past actions. And I am one who has been swept along by the violent whirlwind of my past actions, And accordingly have roamed over countless past aeons, Lost within the dark prisons of cyclic existence. O Lord of Loving Kindness, through the blessing of your compassion, Purify the ob-scurations caused by my past actions and dissonant mental states, And secure me in the presence of your mother-like loving kindness!

– When I am terrified by the utterly unbearable and vir-ulent power of past actions, And my hair stands on end, out of fear, I call out this lament, in heartfelt passion, And cry out to you in a voice of utter despair! O Lord of Loving Kindness, if you do not attend to me with compassion now, At the time of my death, when my mind and body separate, When I am cut off from the company of spiritual friends, and dragged away by Yama, at that time, when my relatives stay behind in the world, Yet I alone am led away by the power of past actions, At that time, I will be unprotected and without a refuge, So, do not on any account hesitate or delay now, But draw near to me at this very moment, And enact the wrathful rites of liberation.

There was silence in the room, the sound of his father's breathing just audible.

– Do you understand, Dad? said Darius softly. You are free. You have set yourself free.

His father breathed quietly, his eyes closed, his head as it lay on the pillow so light that it barely made an impression.

Darius put the book back down on the floor and closed his eyes once more. He soon saw the desert landscape and he felt himself walking across the sand under the hot sun. In the distance he saw a shape and as he walked closer, he saw his father sitting alone beside the fire. There was still smoke drifting up into the sky from the embers lying on the sand. He approached and sat down the other side of his father, whose head was lowered and whose face was hidden by the pale cloths wrapping him. They sat in silence, and Darius could feel the slight heat still coming from the embers. The space in which they both sat felt enormous, an unending sensation of light and space. Slowly, his father raised his head and then he looked directly at Darius, the cloths falling away from his face. He was smiling and his face was a young man's face, a young man with that familiar distinctive bald head, a slight figure whose smile lightened up his eyes. As he smiled, he began to speak but there was no sound, as though Darius were watching with the volume off. Darius smiled back. The old man reached out his hand and placed it on Darius's shoulder, then he stood up, turned away from the fire, and slowly walked off across the dunes.

Darius opened his eyes. His father lay sleeping in the bed, his chest rising and falling slowly.

– It's done, Darius said.

Chapter Twenty Nine

It was early afternoon a month later and Darius was walking back through hot Cornish sunshine towards Level Ground. He had spent the morning coppicing wood in the nearby forest to prepare the next batch of charcoal the following day. As he reached the top of the hill which overlooked his valley, he sat down on a bench beside the path. From up here, you could get a glimpse of the sea at Penzance several miles away and it showed now as a glimmering turquoise line in the summer haze.

The path split here by the bench: over to the left, it stayed up high and headed east through fields where daffodils had grown earlier in the season and where now the land had been turned over once more and late vegetables sown. To the right, the path began to drop down towards the valley where he lived; after another few hundred yards it would meet the untarmaced road which was the only vehicle access in and out of the valley.

He sat for a while, smelling the scent of gorse on the soft breeze and listening to birdsong. Only he and his friends in Level Ground and the local farmers tended to use this path so it was a quiet spot. In the distance he could hear the drone of a light aircraft, probably the daily flight back to Land's End from the Scillies. He closed his eyes for a while and felt the heat of the sun on his shoulders.

He was glad that Belinda had told him he didn't need to come to his father's funeral the previous week. He would have done to support her, but she had assured him that she had plenty of help from her sister and from friends in Marlow and that it would be a fairly formal affair which he probably wouldn't enjoy. So he had stayed away. The newspaper obituaries had been quite fulsome, particularly as Richard had been one of their own and they had noted that the new baronet was now Sir Francis Frome.

Belinda had told him on the telephone that Francis had mostly been in New York since the weekend at the Range. Perhaps his brother was back there now. He wondered whether he would ever see him again. Strangely, the thought didn't particularly move him either way. That sense of completion which had immediately enveloped him when Francis revealed the truth Down There had stayed with him and if anything was sustaining him more and more as each day passed. The sense of wholeness, of equilibrium in the world, had given him a new level of energy which was as invigorating as it was surprising. He felt himself wanting to explore this far more than the emotions connnected with the death of his father or the betrayal of his brother. It was a powerful connection to the natural world which filled him with an as yet unexplored sense of purpose.

Tink had been right: these deeper emotions were what mattered, not his own anxieties about the impact of the police raids on Level Ground. His two friends would be in court next week. After he and Tink had come back from the Range, he had tried to re-establish a sense of community with them, to let go of his own concerns. They hadn't exactly buried the hatchet, but they had all agreed to start again. If his friends got jail sentences for the cannabis farming, he had promised them that he would look after their properties in the valley and support them while they were away.

There would be some money from his father's estate too. Not a huge amount, the lawyer had indicated, because of the death duties on the Range and its poor state of repair. But there would be some and Darius had pledged to put whatever came his way into the co-operative of Level Ground. It could be a new start.

He got up and continued his walk back home, descending now on the rough path into the valley he shared. Soon the path joined the the single track road and he walked on it until he could see the roofs of the houses and barns laid out at the bottom of the valley. The sunshine was glinting off the surface of the pond down below and there was a flash here and there when the rays caught something like a metal woodburner chimney or a spade left outside one of the houses.

There were about twelve buildings in the valley, all of different shapes and sizes. One of the houses had scaffolding around it, where one of his friends was putting a new roof on. As he came down still lower, he began to pass the cultivated fields where they were growing vegetables. Two goats wandered over to greet him. Another field away, a woman who was digging out potatoes called out to him:

– Post office van delivered a big parcel to you Darius, she said. It's at your place.

He waved, and carried on towards his cottage. He opened the gate and walked down the path bordered by tumbling nasturtiums and wild flowers which Tink had planted earlier in the season. She was working in Penzance today and wouldn't be back till later. Inside the kitchen, he laid his bag down on a chair and inspected the writing on the large brown box sitting on the table.

It was from Belinda.

He took the bread knife and cut the parcel open. There was a cardboard box inside, and a letter from Belinda in an envelope taped to the box. He took the letter out first and began to read.

Dear Darius

I'm sending you this package for reasons I'll explain.

The funeral was all fine. We held it in Marlow Church and the place was packed. Quite a few people came down from London, even though there's going to be a memorial service for him as well up at St Bride's in Fleet Street. I don't know whether I'll go to that, it's probably going to be a Francis special filled with Labour bods and newspaper editors.

I wanted you to know that, whatever you did with Richard that last morning you were here, I know it helped him. His last ten days after you and Tink left were very peaceful and he didn't go on about being in Parliament or being late with the Sunday edition – all those things which seemed to be such a strange distraction for him during his dementia seemed to slip away. He didn't really talk but somehow he seemed to be, I don't know, he seemed somehow to be content, happy even. You helped him, Darius, I know that and I wanted you to know.

We didn't get much of a chance to talk about everything but I am sure that we will. James and Alice are beside themselves with excitement about staying in a teepee at your festival next month, so I'm afraid you will have to have lots more stories about dreaming fish prepared. I'm looking forward to it too – do tell Tink that I'm looking forward to seeing her again.

As for Francis, well he's gone back to New York again. We appear to be communicating mostly through email and it wouldn't surprise me if his emails weren't typed by his PA. We haven't discussed what happened in any way and strangely, I don't feel a great desire to. I suppose at some point I'll divorce him but I'd rather see how it is for James and Alice – maybe we can carry on like this while they're young. I don't know. I'm going to go ahead with the big World Action event here at the Range next year for the 65ᵗʰ anniversary. Will you come back soon and help me start getting the grounds back into shape? I want it to look beautiful like it did in Zachary's day when he and your Nana staged those conferences. And I'd like to spend time with you here, if you want.

I know what's happened must be a hundred times worse for you, because of everything you went through which you shouldn't have. But even though nothing will ever change what happened, and nothing will ever bring back poor Annabel, it does feel now for me at least that it's in the past. Do you feel that?

Which brings me to your parcel. I had to do quite a bit

of sorting out while I was getting Richard's things in order, and I found in his office a complete set of first editions of each of your grandfather's books and each of your Nana's books. I thought you should have them. I think with how everything has turned out, they would have wanted you to have them, not Francis. I don't think Francis will even notice they've gone, to be honest, he would never have read them anyway.

So here they are. One other thing. You'll find a letter inside the copy of Level Ground, the original manifesto which Zachary published before the Second World War. The letter is addressed to you.

Send my love to Tink and we will all see you next month.

Love, Belinda

Darius put the letter down on the kitchen table and cut the tape sealing the large cardboard box. Inside, the books were neatly stacked with tissue paper to protect them. He began to pull them out. Hefty hardback editions of his Nana's novels with dramatic colour illustrations on the front. As he turned one over, he was startled to see a full page photograph of her on the back, sitting on one of the benches in the gardens at the Range, her hair blonde and full and her bright red lipstick smiling. He could have imagined running up to her, an eager little boy wanting to share some new piece of information about what he'd found in the nearby forest. She looked impossibly beautiful and glamorous and happy.

He separated the books out into two piles as they came out, Nana's in one and his grandfather's in another. Zachary Frome's books had titles like *Forward To A New Future* and *The Common Inheritance.* Almost at the bottom of the box, when both piles were now quite high, he pulled out a slight hardback with a plain brown cover and red lettering on the front: *LEVEL GROUND.*

He opened the book and a folded letter of light blue paper lay inside. He opened it. The handwriting was spidery and he didn't recognise it. It was dated 1979 and it started out, *Dear Darius.* He scanned down to the bottom of the page, and it ended, *Your loving grandfather, Zachary Frome.*

He read the letter.

Dear Darius

Today you are three years old. Your grandmother and I came up to London to celebrate your birthday with your mother and father and your elder brother. You were in excellent form and you threw a cake at your brother which hit him square on the nose but as it was your birthday you were not reprimanded very severely. I congratulate you on the accuracy of the throw.

I do not intend for you to read this letter until you are older. I shall keep it in a safe place and hopefully you may come across it when the time is right. I am an old man now, my dear Darius, and I do not know how much more time I shall have amongst you all.

I want to tell you about a dream I had at the Range the other night. A long time ago, I tried to encourage some fundamental changes to the way in which our country was organised. These changes were part of a political and philosophical and religious framework which I developed mostly in a little place down near the river which your grandmother and I call Down There.

I was not successful in introducing these changes to our country. I fought very hard, I did my best, but ultimately, as I view it all now from my so very advanced years, I failed. It is not a happy realisation to know one has failed, but I have the consolation of having done my best, and along the way of having met and worked with some splendid and admirable people without whom I wouldn't even have had a chance of succeeding.

But fail we did, and I fear for the future of the world I shall soon be leaving. I fear for the world which you and your brother will inherit and I wish I were a young man again so that I could take up the struggle once more and try this time to win over my fellow man.

I shall not be that young man again, Darius, and let me now tell you about my dream the other night. I dreamed that I was a little boy and I was pottering about on my own on the river Thames in my rowing boat, doing what I did when I was a schoolboy back home from the holidays, exploring the riverbanks and looking out for otters and other wildlife. I pulled my little boat under the curtain of some willows whose branches were hanging down over the water and I found a clearing with a stone plinth standing in the centre. As I pulled my boat into the bank and stepped ashore, I saw you were sitting on the plinth. You were a grown man and you hopped off the plinth and came up to me.

I said:

– My name is Zachary Frome, and I am your grandfather. You said:

– My name is Darius Frome, and I am your grandson.

And then I pointed at my little boat and you clambered aboard. You were a bit big for it, but you settled in the back and then I got back on board and pushed us off the bank and we slid through the curtain of willows back out onto the river and I rowed us away.

That is when I woke up. The dream had the most powerful effect on me my dear Darius, which is why I have recorded it and kept it for you one day to discover. If I am right, you will understand its meaning and I may leave you with the hope that, one day, you may find a way to try and achieve what I failed to do.

Your loving grandfather,

Zachary Frome.

Afterword

In 1988, I travelled to Devon to interview Sir Richard Acland in his house which stood on the lands of the Killerton Estate which he himself had given to the National Trust in 1944. He was 82 at the time and graciously agreed to be interviewed by me on the subject of his latest book, *Hungry Sheep*, an attack on the individualistic political philosophy he identified in all contemporary parties. He was a truly remarkable man: in the 1940s, he led Commonwealth, the ultra-left wing political party which won byelections against both Conservative and Labour oppositions only to founder with the Labour landslide of 1945; in the 1950s, with Harold Wilson, he formed War On Want and subsequently championed Harrison Brown's seminal green document, *A Challenge for the Future*. In later years, in his own words, he believed that "good causes will founder and evil causes will prevail unless moral and religious forces are brought in on the side of the good."

I have thought about this decent, determined, kind and intelligent man for thirty years since that meeting, which is perhaps why he has served as the inspiration for the fictional character Sir Zachary Frome in this novel. The novel and the characters portrayed in it are entirely fictitious and the extended Frome family bear no relation to any people alive or dead, but I would simply like to express my thanks to Sir Richard Acland for indulging a curious young man all that time ago with such sincerity and humour.

I would also like to thank my friend Tim Maltin for hugely entertaining and stimulating discussions about Kenneth Grahame (*Wind in the Willows*) and Northern European romanticism, over kippers in central London;

my friend Milos Stankovic for illuminating insights into the shamanic tradition; my agent Leslie Gardner of Artellus for her boundless intelligence, perspicacity and generosity of spirit; the Clark Art Institute, Williamstown, Massachusetts, USA for permission to use *Bathers of the Borromean Isles* by Jean-Baptiste-Camille Corot on the cover (from the Museum's website www.clarkart.edu: "The Borromean Islands, on Lake Maggiore in Northern Italy, are famous for their isolation and natural beauty. In Corot's painting, nude bathers frolic in the water, the gray-green branches of tall trees shading their bodies from the warm, golden sunlight. The artist painted this scene more than twenty years after his last visit to Italy, presenting the traditional theme of the nude in a landscape as a nostalgic memory—more poetic fiction than realistic fact"); and most of all Tamsin, for everything.